The Unbroken Bond

Day Hardeman

ISBN: 979-8-9889136-0-3
Printed in the United States of America

Cover design by J'Lon Hardeman

Jeri Darby
Writing Coach & Author Services
989 402-4721

Content Guidance: Several chapters of this novel include detailed sexual encounters, consensual in nature.

DEDICATION

For My Bestie:
Your support, inspiration, proofreading, critical feedback, and bravery motivated me to do the unthinkable. You were instrumental in this journey and if you had not believed in my dream, it would not have come true. Thank you for not letting me give up. I love you dearly.

Table of Contents

Table of Contents (Continued)

Acknowledgments

Thank you, God, for the many blessings I have encountered in my life. This journey has not been easy for a newcomer while I'm learning this industry.

To my husband, thank you for letting me write in the late night hours, bringing me breakfast when I woke with the computer in my hand, and cooking dinner when I couldn't stop composing.

Thank you to my three sons: Darrence, for being my target to practice with and inspiring me. Quintavious, for ideas exchange and giving me insights. Keep pushing to your acting stardom where you are destined to be. J'Lon, for being creative and doing my book cover after I kept making changes, you will soon find your fame!

To my grandson, Braelyn, your uniqueness overfills my heart. A future of greatness is waiting for you to conquer.

To my goddaughter, Mashanna Pile (Jamicia), Thank you for sharing valuable business tips that have undoubtedly contributed to my growth. Your warmth, care, and love have made our bond strong, and a meaningful connection. Your dreams are waiting for you to seize.

To my grandfather, Eddie, thank you for showing me a hard work ethic and business sense of mind at an early age. Rest in heaven, I miss you dearly.

To my mother, Judy, and sister, Consuela, you two have been my cheerleaders, market partners, and were brutally honest when needed.

To my fathers, Lucious and Jerry; Thank you, it does

take a village to raise a child. Because of you two, I am full of love.

To my brother Tray, thank you for stepping in and being more than just a brother.

To my cousin, Jessica, thank you for being exactly where you needed to be. WE thank you!

To my cousin, Tezra, thank you so much for being my Beta Reader. Your critical feedback and promptness were outstanding!

To my other family: Grandma Lanie, Aunt Gloria, Aunt Lynn, Toni, Keisha (thank you for the helpful information), Daytwon, Peanut, and Cookie: The group texts played a role in my regrouping and getting back on track. I truly appreciate all of your help with book cover designs, feedback, ideas, family dinners, support, laughs, dinner, and more. My nieces, nephews, and little cousins, I love you all. F.O.E. - Family over everything!

To my best friends: Mico, Vanessa, Leah, and The Divine Ladies of 89: Thank you for your sisterhood, love, acceptance, inspiration, and laughter. Ladies, you are phenomenal! Mico – your worth surpasses any words. Your blessings are within reach, my sister!

To Jeri Darby, my writing coach: Thank you for sharing this experience with me as I grow. I look forward to more opportunities with you.

Last but not least, to all of you that has supported me in purchasing my book and sharing it with others, I'm forever grateful. I hope you all have learned something from the pages of life.

See you all in my next book!

Make Me

I'll never forget,
the first moment that we met.
The attraction flared;
and then you threw your net.

You reeled me in,
so charming and so sweet.
You snared my heart,
You didn't miss a beat.

I sigh in wonder,
because this relationship is for real,
I exhale with happiness,
reveling the love you make me feel.

A storm has passed,
the sunset blankets the sky.
connecting with the waters below,
I no longer cry.

We are now one,
together we respond,
As The Unbroken Bond.

Prologue

Jackson sits anxiously in the waiting room, his eyes fixed on Brave, who is happily playing with a miniature motorcycle toy. Thoughts swirl in Jackson's mind as he wonders what Jazzie wanted to discuss with him. A few days ago, she had not been feeling well, and he vividly recalls her symptoms leading up to this moment. Panic takes hold of him while reaching for his phone with trembling hands. He rushes to make an urgent call for emergency services. Desperation fuels his actions as he runs downstairs to open the front door and gate wide, ensuring a clear path for the paramedics to enter Jazzie's property.

Returning to the bedroom, Jackson begins performing CPR, trying to revive Jazzie. The sound of approaching sirens brings a mixture of relief and anxiety. Jackson directs the paramedics by yelling, "Hurry up! We're upstairs in the bedroom at the end of the hallway. She isn't breathing!" Their presence offers a glimmer of hope. During the chaos, the paramedics mistakenly rushed into the wrong room, leaving the door open. Jackson shouts, "We're at the end of the hall!" to redirect them to Jazzie's room. Jackson is pouring sweat and getting tired, though determined to continue CPR.

The paramedics burst into the room taking over the life-saving measures from where Jackson had been performing compressions with expert precision. Time felt like a blur as they worked tirelessly to revive her, using the defibrillator twice to restore a normal heartbeat. Once Jazzie stabilized, they wasted no time, carrying her with the highest care to the waiting ambulance. One of the paramedics made a swift call to the hospital, notifying them of their imminent arrival, and ensuring that a team would be prepared to receive Jazzie's critical condition.

While making their departure, the seriousness of the situation hit Jackson like a stun gun.

"Which hospital are you taking her to?" Jackson would soon follow after ensuring Jazzie's home was securely closed. With urgency, one of the paramedics exclaimed, "She's flatline again! Move! Move!" He shouted, urging everyone to move swiftly.

Fear gripped Jackson's heart, but another paramedic provided a glimpse of hope, "She's going to Gwinnett Medical." At that moment, Jackson clung to a tiny glisten of faith, while desperately praying for Jazzie. The siren blared, as the ambulance raced off to the hospital while Jackson's mind flooded with worry for Jazzie's well-being. He knew he needed to inform Vivian, Jazzie's sister, and Mrs. Williams, Jazzie's mother, about what had just happened.

Rushing back upstairs to retrieve his cell phone, he approached the open bedroom door that the paramedics had mistakenly left ajar, thinking it was Jazzie's room. The moonlight poured through the window, casting a soft glow on the room's interior. It was enough to provide a faint glimpse of the scene inside, and something caught Jackson's attention.

Curiosity and concern drew him further inside as if an unseen force compelled him to investigate. As he stepped into the room, he could hardly believe what he saw before him. His heart raced, emotions swirling inside him like a tumultuous storm. "This cannot be true, is it?" he questioned himself in disbelief.

CHAPTER 1

Magic Moment

ebruary 19, 2010, it was 45 degrees, and you could see clouds of your breath on this chilling night. The forecast has predicted the temperatures will plummet to freezing. Jazzie pranced in and out of her massive walk-in closet tossing outfits onto her chaise and king-size bed for the past three hours. "This is too old, this is too long, this makes me look bigger," she debated with herself while feeling undecided about what to wear for a girl's night out planned with her cousin Yvette.

Jazzie is thirty-seven and prefers staying home to perch on the sofa eating classic lays potato chips and making fruit smoothies while spending time with her two children watching a movie. Genesis, her daughter who is fourteen, and Brandon, her son who is ten, kept Jazzie on the run with school and activities. Jazzie missed them as she devoted much time working full time as a Paralegal and attending school at night to be a Criminal Attorney. Her busy schedule required long hours with some weekends and holidays. There was not much allowance for playtime therefore she really could use an outing with Yvette. Finally, holding a pair of black leggings and a matching blouse to her while peering at herself in the mirror modeling and thinking "I feel like being sexy tonight, this outfit is perfect!"

Sashaying to her chifforobe that housed her undergarments and skimmed for a lace black front closure bra and matching lace black low-waist panties. After closing the drawer, and standing in front of her bedroom mirror, she slides the bra on. Gathering her full large breasts, she firmly placed them securely inside and then snapped them closed. Gracefully stepping into her panties, a slight pull brought them up over her curves.

Sliding into a pair of black leggings that painted every aspect of her toned legs, shapely thighs, full-figured hips, and round butt. The matching fitted black blouse hugged her curves and rested at the top of her hips. Jazzie's eyes swept over the shoe selection in her closet and grabbed the black and dark green thigh-high boots that made her six inches taller. Her perfume danced in the air leaving a sweet lingering rose scent. The mirror confirmed that her eye shadow which gave her a slightly contoured smokey look was spot on. The long eyelashes framed her eyes perfectly, while her favorite Mac red lipstick made her look even sexier. Parting her hair on the right side amplified a more youthful appeal. After adding Curl Talk mousse to her black hair which swung to her lower, mid-back, it waved to fall slightly over her left eye.

"Yes, now I'm flawless!" she says feeling dazzled. Ring! Ring! Yvette's name flashed across the screen. Grabbing her cell phone she answered, "Hey girl, I'm leaving out my house right now and will be on the way!" Yanking her purse and car keys off the kitchen counter she paused to wave goodbye to Genesis and Brandon before jetting out the front door.

"Hey Cuz, I'm sorry I can't make it tonight, I have a date with a dick!" Yvette said excitedly. Jazzie stops in the middle of her driveway and placed her left hand on her hip and frowned.

"I could have stayed planted on the sofa and watched a movie with the kids. I got all dressed and looked sexy but now I have no place to go." Her mind was racing while recalling that she was the one to invent the code—Dicks before Divas! Breathing deeply, she said, "That's cool girl, I understand. Have fun!" She ended the call and continued walking toward her purple Cadillac Escalade. Flopping into the driver's seat she wondered, "Where should I go? I can go by Shoreline Sports Bar. Oh yes, it's closed for remodeling. I can go to my sister, Vivian's house. Wait, she is on a date again. I'll figure it out." Jazzie drove away feeling undecided about where to go.

Aiden, her husband, ventured out with his friends for a thrilling basketball game, leaving Jazzie to bask in a rare moment of freedom. Meanwhile, the kids were comfortably settled, enjoying dinner and engrossing themselves in a series of captivating movies. "I'll grab a bite to eat and head back home to spend time with the kids," she thought. Just up the street, a Taco Bell beckoned her, and she steered her car through the drive-thru. Jazzie placed her order for a number one, which includes two tacos supreme and one chicken burrito. With a craving for something more potent than soda, she tells the cashier no beverage. Jazzie is known for being a rather infrequent social drinker and found herself at a loss as to what to order from the local package store. Whatever she drinks, it usually made her frisky, therefore it was not often. Jazzie paid for her order and double-checked for accuracy when she received it. The tantalizing aroma filled the car as she placed it safely on the passenger seat. As she drove away, Jazzie phones her mother, relishing the simple pleasure of a night conversation and a suggestion as to what to drink.

"Hi Mom, how are you?"

"I'm lovely; your dad and I are having our date night," her mother says boasting.

"That's a sweet way that you guys keep the romance going after all these years. I have a quick question."

"Okay, what is it?"

"Yvette and I were going out tonight, but she had a plumbing issue at the last minute. Instead of going right home, I picked up some dinner for myself and wanted to get something stronger than a soda from the package store, any suggestions?" Her mother laughs because a few sips of Jack Daniels wine coolers or one glass of Stella Rosa wine would have her daughter quickly buzzed or fast asleep.

"You love the peach flavor, get a Southern Peach wine cooler or Stella Rosa Peach. You can also get drinks already mixed such as margaritas. Try Cayman Jack margarita, you'll love that!"

Smiling, she thought, "It doesn't matter how old you are, you'll always need your parents, I'm grateful I still have mine." The store was a few yards ahead and she said, "Thanks Mom, tell Daddy I said hi and I love you both, get back to your date."

Jazzie pulls into the parking lot of the store and notices several young-looking guys gathering outside the store near the side where someone was selling barbeque food. She hurriedly exits the SUV and sets the alarm. Once her purse is secure across her body hanging to the left side, she continues toward the front entrance. While walking past the guys, one shouted, "Hey momma, let me go with you!"

"Looking good tonight, let me take you out!" shouted another man.

"Damn, that's a fat ass!" the irritating cat calls continued.

She was not in the mood to read human ethics to a pack of dogs and ignored their remarks but her eyes like lasers sent them a foul look. Strolling into the Lovejoy Package Store, clueless that the store's name would become her fate. After pondering over what to drink, her eyes spotted the Cayman Jack Margarita in the refrigerator area. When opening the door while reaching for a four-pack, the fitted blouse slightly rose to share more curves. A remark from behind startled her.

"Damn! You almost made me drop my drink!" She turned abruptly while releasing the refrigerator door and locked eyes with a cocky man to who she gave a brief cold stare. Quickly walking past him to the checkout clerk, she was not paying him any attention.

"He needs to go outside and join the rest of his dog pack and leave me alone," she thought while exiting the store. Shortly afterward, the stranger did too. He walked behind her and enjoyed watching her curves swaying side to side.

He caught up with her and asked, "Excuse me, Miss, how are you doing tonight?"

Deciding to get this over with so she could be on her way, she offered a dry reply, "Fine," intentionally never looking at him. Opening the back door of the driver's side of the SUV, she bent to put her purchase inside on the floor. Standing up their eyes connected once more catching her off guard. The cocky man had the most attractive eyes. Like a fishing line, they reeled her in, and she lost herself in them. They were magical! She struggled to gather her thoughts swiftly before he noticed. Glancing toward the side of the store, the pack of dogs was gone.

"Hmmm…Maybe he was not with them after all." Getting directly to the point she asked, "Are you married?" Exploring his finger for a wedding band, it was bare, but this does not mean he isn't. Mr. Cocky hesitated to answer, then Jazzie thought, oh boy, here we go with the lies. Assuredly she states, "It's ok for you to answer the question, I'm married too, next month will make sixteen years so there is no need to lie."

He modestly answered "Yes," and smiled. "What a nice smile and beautiful white teeth," she thought.

"How long have you been married?"

"This year makes ten. Let me properly introduce myself, my name is Jackson Davenport."

"Hello Jackson, my name is Jasmine Collins, but my friends call me Jazzie. They spoke briefly because he had his young six-year-old twin daughters in the car sleeping.

"Can I call you sometime?" he asked before they departed. Jazzie thought for a moment and did something she rarely does. She pulls his cell phone from his jean pocket, types her name and number on it, then places it in his hand. He jokingly questioned, "Is this your real number?"

Seductively she walks closer to him, allowing her sweet scent of roses to engulf his nose as she responds, "It's only one way to find out! Good night." She smiled while stepping backward gazing into his captivating eyes. He stood to the side and held her door open for her. Once she fastens her seat belt, he closed her door and watches her drive away. Jazzie drives home in deep thought, "Damn he is sexy as hell and has gorgeous eyes! What just happened? It feels like a magic wave came over me."

CHAPTER 2

Pass or Play?

J ackson walked the twins inside the house and tucked them into bed. His wife, Tammy works nights as a 911 operator. Jackson usually stayed home with the girls until the weekend when Tammy was off. While pouring a glass of Crown Royal XO and chasing it with three ice cubes he was thinking about just one thing, meeting Jazzie. She was intriguing to him. He could still smell her scent dancing in his nose as he was standing inside his closet. He replayed images of her strutting out of the package store with those leggings fitting her thick thighs, and curvy hips clinging to accent her round behind. "Damn!" he says out loud. "I wonder if I have the right number?"

Once Jazzie got home, she gobbled up her dinner and then relaxed with a drink. Pulling a t-shirt over her head and getting more comfortable in bed, she thought, "Jackson is an attractive man! Mmm-mmm-mmm!" Instantly the cell phone rang, and she wondered, "Who would be calling her at 10:30 pm?" It was an unfamiliar number, but she answered anyway.

"Hello?"

"Hey, just checking to see if you gave me the right number." the sexy baritone voice utters.

Her eyes gleamed while sitting up in bed "Oh my goodness it's him!" She laid the phone down and smiled hard then quickly regains herself and replied, "If I was going to give you the wrong number, I wouldn't waste my time putting it in your phone."

"Are you still going to be cold to me?" he asked.

"It's a difference between being cold and being direct," she teased.

"What's a lady like you doing out alone at night anyway?"

"What type of lady would that be, you only know the name I gave you?"

"A classy lady. If you were mine, I wouldn't let you go nowhere alone."

Blushing and responding, "I was going out with my cousin, but her plans changed so I picked up some dinner for myself and something to drink then came back home."

"If I knew you wanted to go out, I would have taken

you," he said sincerely.

Jazzie was surprised to hear him say this because he barely knew her, and he was kind enough to say he would have taken her out.

"So, Jackson, tell me how old you are?"

"I'm old enough to do what I want," he stated with cockiness.

"Really?" laughing at his reply. "That can be any age, ask my children."

"Seriously how old are you?"

"I'm thirty, well over twenty-one."

"Thirty! I am thirty-seven, which is too old for you!"

"I'm a grown man and I know exactly what I want."

"My sister is closer to your age, twenty-eight. I can introduce you."

"It's not your sister I want to get to know. Would it be better if I were the older one?"

Jazzie thought about his question. Men always date younger women; this is just the reverse so women should be able to do the same. She concluded; that it should be fine; she was not planning on talking to him on an intimate level anyway. Jackson divulged details about his family life throughout their hours-long conversation that night on the phone. He has been in Georgia for four years, but he is originally from Dallas. Mia and Tia, his twin daughters, are six years old. He often has free time on the weekends while his wife is off work because she works nights, but he could hire a babysitter if he wanted to go out during the weekday.

Jazzie shared that she has been married for sixteen years and her children ages. Glancing at the clock, they did not realize it was 2:30 a.m. Jazzie was getting sleepy but was enjoying their riveting discussions and debates on current issues in the world. Aiden would be home soon, and she needed to bring their conversation to an end.

"I have to get ready for bed, it's getting late," she said while yawning and trying to fight the sleep coming over her.

"Time flies when you're having fun. When can I talk to you again?" He questioned.

"I'll call you."

"Okay, I'll be looking forward to it."

"Good night, Jackson, it was a pleasure."

"Likewise. Good night, Jazzie."

After making sure her phone was hung up, she reflected on their long conversation. It was educational, entertaining, and interesting, it had her curious. Debating herself, "He seems to be a nice guy, but he's seven years younger than me! He just wants to play in my sandbox; I don't have time for any drama. I think I will pass on this. Hmmmmm, I enjoyed our conversation, it's different, he was different. It doesn't have to be a fling; we could be friends, no harm in that." For several years, as a child, Jazzie observed her parent's emotionless marriage. Until a few years ago they re-dedicated their life to Christ and saved their marriage of forty-two years. Jazzie perceives it is easier to shield her heart from love instead of broken hopes.

While she was a student at the University of Georgia, Aiden entered her life. He was working part-time as a math tutor at the school and was just hired as a Project Coordinator after completing his internship with Apple. Jazzie made an appointment with Aiden after searching for a math tutor at the student resources office. After passing the Statistics class and no longer needing a tutor, Aiden asked her on a date. Even though they were eleven years apart in age, Aiden fell in love with her quickly and asked for her hand in marriage.

Jazzie adores Aiden and is aware of his dedication to being a provider, but something is still lacking. Being in love with someone is different than loving them. Never being in love with anyone before made her think she was incapable of doing so. Jazzie is a paralegal in a renowned law firm in the Buckhead neighborhood. She enrolls in a local university at night to pursue a job as a criminal attorney to advance her professional objectives and serve as a role model for her kids. Jazzie is an involved parent in the lives of Genesis and Brandon, who take part in a variety of activities. They all volunteer together on Saturdays once a month at the downtown Atlanta homeless shelter.

Aiden makes handyman repairs, Genesis and Brandon assist in serving meals, and Jazzie bakes cakes, pies, and other special treats. One day she hopes to own a bakery. Tucking away her happiness on a shelf while focusing on others has become a habit. As her graduation grows closer, she is seeking to do something for herself as a reward, this has been challenging. Jazzie always desired to learn how to ride a motorcycle. She was passionate about doing it as a hobby! But her family and friends viewed her as too much of a princess and a girly girl and they had doubts about her sincerity. They could not understand why she wanted to do such a male-dominated activity.

Aiden encouraged her to try something new and outside the box. A motorcycle would amplify her life's resume by making her feel strong, attractive, empowered, and free. Because there is more available leisure time now than ever before, it is the perfect moment to learn. Speaking to Jackson, she discovered that he rides motorcycles. "I can give you some training and safety tips for riding a motorcycle," he had offered. Jackson could be her link to launching this new hobby without being clueless. Jazzie has never been unfaithful to Aiden, the thought never crossed her mind…until now. Searching for a Maintenance Man is not her way of behaving, but Jackson is certainly worth the thought!

"Beep Beep! Beep Beep!" The front door alarm redirected her mind, alerting her that Aiden is home. Shaking her head side to side in an attempt to rid the thoughts of Jackson, she concluded, "I better not."

CHAPTER 3

The Bubbles Begin

Over the next couple of months, Jackson and Jazzie spoke often and laughed about any and everything. She was enjoying hearing from him. Jackson starts sending her texts, "Hey beautiful", "How is your day going?" "Can you talk?" This technology was useless to her—until now. He explained the simplicity of texting to her because she was unfamiliar with it. They practiced texting each other after he texted her some instructions. Jazzie began to pick up on it and frequently texted him. When Jazzie texted Genesis to remind her to walk the dog, Genesis was astonished Jazzie sent a text instead of yelling as usual. Her interest in him and his philosophical perspectives on life was increasing more and more.

Jackson made many requests to speak with her, but Jazzie was constantly preoccupied with her family, getting ready for graduation, baking for the shelter, or working on her career.

Jazzie did have the time available, but she chose to maintain a safe distance. "We're both married, I'm seven years older than him, and this is just not a smart idea, she reasoned." Nevertheless, the tempting thoughts persisted. "This would only end up being a fling." Jazzie is a woman who possesses a strong sexual desire, a zest for life, and a commitment to giving her all in everything she does. She is intelligent, enjoys embracing her sensuality, loves adventure, and enjoys playful experiences both inside and outside the bedroom. Doubt crept in, wondering if he could handle a woman like her, given her vibrant nature. Not just anyone was permitted to play in her universe because she was picky. Jazzie valued harmony and did not want any unnecessary controversies or distractions. She realized that engaging in a relationship with him would eventually lead to meaningless sex, which she deemed unfulfilling and purposeless.

Jazzie knew that she could not keep putting him off, he was not that type of man and was determined. Jackson eventually lost patience and insisted on seeing her. With a lot of aggression, he called and was not buying any of her "I'm too busy." justifications. "Rinnngg," "Rinnngg," and "Rinnngg!" Aiden and Jazzie were watching television when Jazzie heard her phone. Jackson was disguised as Deborah in her contacts when she looked down to see who it was. He typically texts her beforehand to see if she can chat before phoning, so this came as a surprise. "I must take this; it's a client from the office. I'll be right back," she informs Aiden. She closed the door to her office before answering the call.

"Hey, are you ok?" she asked Jackson.
"Not really. Do I have to make an appointment to see you?"

Jazzie laughed because Jackson got straight to the point. "Yes, you do," she said jokingly.

"This Friday at 7 p.m.," He firmly replied.

"I will check......."

Jackson interrupted her, "I wasn't asking."

"Okay, Friday it is!" She exclaims blushing.

She found it incredibly arousing when a man took charge, displayed a bit of aggression, and confidently led the way. Deep down, she secretly desired to experience his assertive side and was genuinely excited about the prospect. This marked the start of their intimate connection, creating a special and exciting beginning of their "bubble."

Friday, while at work, Jackson could not stop daydreaming about Jazzie. Knowing that they would be hanging out soon, he wanted to make sure everything was still on track. Since Jazzie was also at work, he decided to text her to confirm their plans, hoping that she would not cancel on him.

"Hey."

"Hi, Jackson…I was just thinking about you."

"What were you thinking?"

"You never told me where we were going so; I don't know how I should dress?"

"I figure we go for dinner and drinks and whatever we feel like doing."

"Okay, that's great. Does the restaurant have a dress code?"

"It depends on whichever you choose."

"You want me to choose?"

"Yup, I want to take you where you want to go."

"I'm simple; we can go to Finley's Tavern, that way you can be close to home if the girls need you."

"Thanks, but they will be with a sitter, I want uninterrupted time with Ms. Jazzie."

"You have me blushing. Finley's Tavern is a safe zone, with many options on the menu to choose from."

"That will work; I can pick you up someplace?"

"No, I rather drive but thank you."

"Okay, see you at 7:00 pm."

"Okay, it's a date!" Jazzie said excitedly.

"Yes, it is."

Since their initial meeting, Jackson had not seen Jazzie, but they had been exchanging pictures via text. Some of the pictures she sent had his mind racing, and he could not help but think about how sexy she looked. Jackson was eagerly anticipating seeing her again. Even though he was at work, the clock seemed to move incredibly slowly. However, being the owner of Crown

Performance Centers, the most popular chain of auto shops in Atlanta with four locations, had its perks. Jackson was currently working on a new site that included motorcycle services.

Finally, when it reached 4 p.m., he wasted no time and swiftly shut down his computer. He informed Corey, his front office manager, "I'm taking off now, I'll see you Monday!" With that, he hurriedly dashed out the front door. On his way, he made a quick stop at the barber shop to get a fresh haircut and shave, preparing to see Jazzie.

When Jackson arrived home, he reminds Tammy, "Don't forget that you need to drop the twins off at Miller's house on your way to work tonight. The fellows are doing a birthday party for one of our buddies, and I'm going to stop by." He used a little white lie. Before getting ready to go out, Jackson took a shower. Then, he searched through his wardrobe to find the right outfit. He settled on a pair of duck boots, loose-fitting black Levis 501 pants, and a black golf shirt. To smell good for the occasion, he spritzed some Versace cologne on his face and behind his earlobes. He then selected a set of traditional diamond stud earrings from his jewelry collection on the dresser, nodding in approval as he put them on. Finally, Jackson fastened his Bulova watch, signifying that he was ready to head out.

CHAPTER 4

Liquid Courage

F or Jazzie, Friday could not have arrived soon enough. She tried on almost every dress in her closet. She wanted to appear sexy and classic rather than desperate and thirsty. Sliding on a red pair of satin and lace butterfly panties with a matching sheer lace uplift bra, she decided to wear something simple. Searching the dresses once more, Jazzie chooses a green wrap-around dress that is tied at her waist and toyed with her full hips and divulges a peek-a-boo cleavage enclosure. Parading in the closet mirror, she ensures that it looked great on her.

Looking at the shoe rack, she picks a pair of open-toed six inches green heels. Her gold elongated teardrop earrings dangled from ear lobes and underneath her loosely long curled hair. A delicate touch of makeup just enough for a natural appearance was applied. One of her favorite scents, Marc Jacobs Daisy, was lightly sprayed on. When ready to go, she texted him, "I'm on my way."

Butterflies began to form in her tummy as she made the turn into Finley's Tavern parking lot. "Why do I feel so nervous?" Jazzie gathered her nerves and questioned. "I have this; it's just dinner and drinks!" Jazzie walks with a distinct style that is obvious. Her full hips wiggle as she takes small seductive steps with her feet turned slightly outward. Nearly a vicious, "come get me" walk. Jazzie enters the tavern and looks about for Jackson, capturing the attention of a few patrons. Spotting him across the room, they exchanged glances. "Wow!" Uttering to herself, "He is incredibly attractive!" Jackson stood from his table and embraced her.

She felt marvelous as his arms wrapped around her and squeezed. Feeling his touch made her entire body tingle with electricity, leaving her weak at the knees. His neck oozed an alluring aroma tempting her hands to wander but Jazzie collected herself, grinned, and sat. They placed a dinner and drink order. She asked for a sweet tea, and he ordered a Crown Royal and Sprite. Noticing her drink was non-alcoholic, he asked "You're going to let me drink by myself?"

"I know we met at a liquor store but I don't drink much."

"Just have one drink, with me." He innocently convinced her.

Jazzie is only familiar with the names of a few drinks but tries to act as if she knows more and says to the waitress, "I will have a Long Island Iced Tea."

"May I see both of your IDs please?" the waitress asks.

"Here you are," Jackson says.

"I'm sorry, here is mine," finally Jazzie finds hers hidden in her purse.

The waitress checks their licenses before returning, but Jackson takes both and examines Jazzie's.

"May I ask what are you looking for?"

"I can't believe you were thirty-seven."

"Already you are doubting me?"

"No, but you appear younger, what's your secret?"

"I make an effort to follow The Serenity Prayer," she answers "When my mom was troubled, she would say that prayer," he remembers.

After returning her license, they continued the evening conversing. Jackson and Jazzie joked, laughed, and relished their time together over dinner. She found herself entangled in their conversation. Jackson was attentively listening as she spoke, it was noticed. He made remarks on simple things, such as her pointed nose, long designer nails, matching toe designs, and sweet-smelling perfume. He is an observant man, and she appreciated it.

At one point, Jackson brushed her hair away from her face, gazing into her eyes. Jazzie could not help but feel something special in that moment, though it was not just butterflies this time. Sensations ran through her body, and she felt her nipples becoming more sensitive. She discreetly tried to adjust herself, but it did not quite work. Feeling the need to gather herself, she stood up and said,

"Excuse me, I have to go to the ladies' room."

"Would you like another drink?" he questioned.

"I really shouldn't but thank you. I will have an ice-cold glass of water."

"Come on, it's early, one more drink, please?"

"Okay, okay one more Long Island! Order for me and I'll be right back," giving in to his pleading.

Jazzie was taken in by his charisma and was not quite ready for the night to be over. When she goes to the ladies' room, she is startled by what she discovers. "Oh my goodness! My panties are wet!" Jackson was intensely turning her on and her click was throbbing, drenching her panties with ecstasy. "What are you doing, pull yourself together? You're strong, it's only dinner," she chatted out loud. After freshening up, she was able to regain control and not feel weak. She took confident strides back to their table. While sipping their drinks, she admires his lips and nicely black-trimmed mustache. "Mmmmmmm, those eyes!" He was her ideal of a perfect, handsome, and smart man. She was ready to go before doing or saying something that could not be taken back.

While Jackson walked her to the car, Jazzie's curiosity was growing. While he spoke, she was pondering whether he had good bedroom skills. Thinking back on her second drink, she should have passed on it. "Oh my, look at his eyes, his lips, nicely trimmed haircut. Will he kiss me?"

She battles with her conscience, but her kitty is purring, and she craves to sample his lips.

"Good night, Jackson, I had a pleasant time with you."

"I enjoyed you as much, and I hope to see you again soon. Good night," he walks away after she is safely in her car.

Jazzie was hoping he would try to kiss her, but when he did not attempt, she was disappointed. While Jackson follows her out of the parking lot, she phones him.

"Hi, it's me, Jazzie. Do you have a few minutes left before you have to be home?"

"I know who this is, how can I forget a sexy voice like yours? I have plenty of time, what's up?" he beams.

"Follow me, I have something to show you."

Jackson followed her to a neighboring park, but because it was closed and dark, he was not sure what they were doing there. He followed her lead, they parked next to each other and got out of their cars. Jazzie stood leaning against the driver's side of her automobile as Jackson approached. Uncertain of the situation and what to do, Jackson stood in front of her. Suddenly Jazzie barges into his personal space, tilts forward, presses her full breast into his chest, and says, "I want to taste your lips."

He looks down at her because she shrunk three inches without heels on and says "Okay." He was given the forewarning that she was taking it. Jazzie gives him a tender, passionate kiss while sensing something growing in his jeans. She lowered one of her hands and rubbed him through his jeans, but preferred to feel it without the barrier. She pulls out his manhood after unzipping his pants and massages until he enlarges. The more Jackson observed her getting hotter and hotter, the more his desire intensified to fully experience her. Jazzie slid her panties off and tossed them inside her car through the opened window.

She seized his hand and laid it on her kitty underneath her dress. It was wet, juicy, and ready! Jazzie guided his finger inside of her, the sensation was out of this world. Both she and he kissed each other eagerly. She needs to feel him because she cannot handle it any longer. A surprised look covered Jackson's face, he was perplexed by what was happening. All he knew was she felt wonderful, and he wanted more. Lowering his jeans and underwear, he spreads her legs wide.

With his firm erection in hand, he guides himself inside her playground. "Mmmmmmm, he feels so damn good!" Was all she could think. Jackson gives it to her with each thrust going deeper and harder as they stand gasping along the side of her car. He is ready, she is ready, and together they explode until evidence of their climax is visibly spilled from her, dripping onto the ground below.

They exchange glances, knowing that they both want more but this is not the right setting. Suddenly, Jackson notices a police car driving into the park and they hastily get dressed. The police officer approaches their car, shining a light on them, and questions, "Is everything okay, we had a report of noises here?" Jazzie quickly came up with a cover story, explaining, "My car was running hot and had a leak. He has fixed it now."

The police officer grinned at them and requested their identification, he knew it was a lie. The police officer goes to his car to verify. When he returns to Jackson and Jazzie, he lets them off with a warning, "The park is closed after dark," the police officer declares as he hands them their identifications. "Next time, I suggest you both find a better place to plug your leaks. I can escort both of you out of the park now." After that, sex was amazing, adventurous, and spontaneous…MAGICAL.

The next morning, Jackson initially believed the events of the previous night were just a dream until he went to the bathroom and noticed evidence of dried climax on his pelvis. The reality of the encounter hit him, and he could not shake Jazzie's intoxicating scent that still lingered on his neck and fingers. He could not help but reminisce about how incredible Jazzie had made him feel especially her assertive and passionate approach. The memory of how Jazzie had entered the restaurant with her alluring presence, and how he had been captivated by her full breasts, played in his mind, arousing his desires even more.

As Jackson stood in the shower, he could not escape the vivid mental images of their intimate moments, with her lips and bouncing breasts teasing his senses. He recalled the feeling of her thighs wrapped around him and how soft and round her buttocks were. The intense sensations overwhelmed him, and he couldn't help but let out a sigh of satisfaction as he released his pent-up desires in the shower, "Aaaaahhhhhh!" he sighed in relief.

"Jackson, we need to go to the grocery store!" Tammy's yelling from the bedroom greeted him while getting out of the shower.

"Okay!" He yells back. Then he grabbed his phone to text Jazzie and noticed that she had already texted him.

"Good morning, Jackson."

"Hey! I was getting ready to text you. I had a nice time last night."

"I did too, thank you for dinner and dessert."

"You are something else!"

"No sir, I am just me."

"That would be a special lady."

"You think I'm special because I made a move on you first?"

"Not just that, it was the way you did it. You are confident and know what you want. You are so beautiful, and our conversation was real."

"Thank you, Jackson, I have to admit you have certainly impressed me with many of your views on life, being seven years younger than me. And your manhood last night was impressive, very impressive!"

"I'm blushing! Do I have to book another appointment

to see you again?"

"Lol…no you don't."

"Let me know when you are free again."

"I'm free today or if this is short notice, we can try next week?"

"No! Today is fine with me, anytime."

"Let's meet about 2 pm, I want to show you more of who I am," Jazzie smirked.

"Okay, but this time, No police!"

Jackson had forgotten he told Tammy he would go to the grocery store with her and the twins. "I'm sorry, I can't go to the store. One of the shop managers had an emergency and had to leave. I need to cover for him." Tammy has little knowledge about his shops and employees. Though disappointed, she accepted his excuse.

"We can wait for you to finish," she suggested.

"No," you and the girls go ahead," he insisted. "I may have to do some inventory and that could take a while." Jackson was looking forward to seeing Jazzie and by any means, he was going to.

CHAPTER 5

The Bridge

Jazzie had prepared a homemade picnic basket with a tote bag attached for two people. Unsure of what Jackson likes, she figured on having a few things that almost everyone eats. She made gourmet sub-sandwiches, with the fixings on the side, fried drumettes with a moon dust dry rub, Carolina wings, southern red potato salad, summer fruit salad, a variety of potato chips, peanut butter chocolate chip cookies, and Arnold Palmer to drink. A scented Yankee Candle, "Picnic in the Park," a frisbee, small pillows, a speaker, and a sizable blanket were all included in the tote bag. It is the first day of Spring. The weather was accommodating to her plans because there was no chance of rain, it was sunny, and eighty-three degrees. Jazzie's long, fitted, white summer dress with golden spaghetti straps made her appear to be angelic. Near their home, Jackson parked his truck at the

Marta Train Station and waited. When he sees Jazzie's car pulling into the parking lot he exits his truck. After parking next to him, she gets out of her car and walks to the passenger side to make room in the front seat for him to ride with her. When Jackson saw her, he was mesmerized by her serene look. "Do I get a hug?" he inquired.

Smiling, she answered, "Of course!" Turning toward him she leans into his arms. Jazzie felt his shorts expanding as she pressed against him. She kisses him passionately while perched on her tiptoes and strokes his face. They had to pry themselves apart after forgetting for a brief second that they were in a public parking lot.

"Mmmmmm, we better stop before someone calls the police on us," she said jokingly. Jackson smiled and agreed.

"You can park your car here."

"No sir, you are riding with me. Lock your truck and hop in," she instructs him.

"Where are we going?" he asked.

"You have to wait and see Mr. Nosey!"

"I'm curious but not nosey. Cool, I can just go along with it. You on the other hand need to write everything into your planner before you can do it. I bet you schedule when to breathe in there! Can we stop by the package store?" he chuckles.

"I'm going to show you that I can be spontaneous, and unplug from my planner, Mr. Nosey! Smarty Pants! Now…let me know if you see a package store you want to stop at. Ready to go?"

"Let's do this!" Jackson said while sliding his seat back to allow more leg room, putting on his shades, and pressing his remote to lock and arm his truck. Cruising down Hwy 78, Jazzie notices how Jackson is looking at her.

"You are aware that I can feel you staring at me. Is something wrong?"

"There's nothing wrong; you look lovely in white. Last night seemed like a dream."

"Thank you! I did what we both contemplated after I consumed some liquid courage," she blushes.

"I never had a woman to take me like that and in a park," he acknowledges.

"For the record, I have never done anything like that before, but it is something unique about you."

"Is it something good?"

She giggles, "So far, it's good, but the verdict's still out."

Gripping onto the grab handle bar in the car, he jokingly remarks, "You're a speed demon! Is there a specific time we need to reach our destination?" She steals a glance at him and notices his tense expression.

"Nope, I just don't like slow drivers in my way while I am trying to get somewhere," she replied while reducing her speed. Jackson directs her to turn off the freeway after spotting a package store billboard. She does so abruptly and pulls up to the business. He screams out in relief,

"Damn we made it!" as he leaps out of the car while clutching his chest.

"I don't drive that badly!"

"Of course not, but I'll take the wheel next," he teased.

"You are unaware of our destination."

"I can turn when you tell me to."

He asks, "What would you like to drink?"

Jazzie confessed, "I don't know much about alcohol."

Jackson spent twenty minutes explaining brandy, cognac, vodka, rum, gin, whiskey, and moonshine to her. "You'll eventually try them all," he continues, "but today we'll start with a whisky." They proceed to the checkout counter after selecting a pint of Jack Daniels and a bottle of Coke. Jazzie is a sociable individual who engages with everyone. While standing at the checkout counter, the female cashier was so taken with Jazzie's outfit that she inquired where could she find anything similar.

Jackson had to yank her from the store because the line had grown long from Jazzie and the cashier's conversation. He approaches the vehicle and courteously opens the passenger side for her. Jazzie enters nicely and lets him take the wheel. After traveling on the highway, they arrived in the vicinity of downtown Atlanta. "Take Exit 245 and turn left," she instructs him.

"Can you tell me where we are headed?"

"I will tell you when we get there."

"I see you are a comedian too," he smiles.

"I am a woman of many talents."

"I will be the judge of that, the verdict's still out," he jokes.

"Using my words against me. I like that. This is it! Turn onto the street on the right up here and we can park along the curb."

"Who are we visiting?"

"We are visiting nature."

Jackson was perplexed when he observed people passing him while jogging, roller skating, and walking their pets. They parked in a residential area close to the curb. He could make out a black metal gate that appeared to be the entrance to a park a few yards away. "Can I help with anything?" he asks Jazzie as she pulls out a wagon from her truck.

"Yes, thank you. Could you take that tote bag and basket and put them inside the wagon?"

Jackson loaded the basket, tote bag, ice bag, insect spray, and a few other things into the wagon. They strolled over to the gate and opened it after setting the car alarm. The words "Welcome to Piedmont Park" were displayed on a sign on the left.

"I've heard of this park. This is where gay people go, right?"

"Are you frightened of homosexuals?"

"Of course not, however, some native Georgians told me that this park is gay-friendly."

"Those individuals are idiots. There are no gay, black, white, or other racial parks here. It is a public park open to everyone."

"I firmly concur!"

They kept going until they came across a pleasant

spot not far from the lake, where they laid out the blanket. She said, "Okay, this will be fine," after setting up a few things. "We can take a little stroll while keeping an eye on our belongings right here."

They walked leisurely towards the lakeside, and at the entrance of the walking trail, they came across a vendor selling fish food. Jazzie's excitement was evident as she exclaimed, "I love feeding the fish!" She bought a bag of fish food so they could enjoy observing the fish swimming around while feeding them. As they continued along the trail, they encountered several bird feeders where a few birds were happily enjoying their meals. Jackson could not help but marvel at the picturesque view of the lake. The tranquility of the surroundings helped him feel more at ease, and he began to take slow, deep breaths, savoring the moment. It was a unique experience for him, and he cherished every bit of it. With Jazzie by his side, he saw things in a new light, gaining a fresh perspective on the beauty of nature. He admired how the lake and its surroundings remained untouched, preserving their natural state of pristine beauty.

After a few hours of touring the area, Jackson was getting hungry. "I worked up an appetite," he claims. They returned to the blanket and Jazzie set up the mini buffet. "Where did you get the food?" She burst into laughter and said, "I have children and a husband, so I cook often."

"Do you need help with something?"

"Can you grab the candle out of the tote bag with the holder and light it?" Jackson was impressed when she thought of this and placed the candle on top of a basket and made their drinks for the wine glasses. He does not typically eat anyone's food, but the spread Jazzie prepared made his stomach growl loudly.

"Okay, we may eat."

"Yes! This looks delicious Jazzie," Jackson says just as he is about to grab a plate. "Thank you, let's say grace first," signaling to him. This was a tradition he did as a child but as an adult, he has forgotten it. After Jazzie said grace, he dived into the food as if he had been on a twenty-four-hour fast. They stuffed themselves and Jackson felt drowsy afterward and thought, "I could use a nap." Then his eyes connected with Jazzie's and sleeping became the farthest thing from his mind.

"Damn, you can cook! Those cookies are the best I have eaten!"

"Thanks, I love baking more than cooking. Come on, let's burn some of these calories off!" Jazzie says while grabbing the frisbee and moving toward more open space.

"I don't want to hurt your feelings, but I will win so do you want to do anything else?" he brags.

"Sounds like someone is afraid of losing," she teases him.

"All right, I tried warning you. Disconnect your phone from the speaker and let me get us some gaming music on." While waiting for him to get the music playing, Jazzie puts her hair up in a ponytail. When she heard Dj Khaled's song "All I Do Is Win" blaring from the speakers they both started laughing hysterically. Three lost games later, she had enough of being defeated by him and retreated onto the blanket and pillows pouting.

While beside each other, holding hands and engrossed in conversation, Jackson fails to notice the encroaching darkness. Jazzie gestures towards the horizon, inviting him to witness the breathtaking view. As Jackson looks, he is taken aback by the downtown Atlanta skyline adorned with stunning pink and purple tones. The tall buildings' lights cast a warm orange glow, and as the night deepens, the sky becomes sprinkled with stars.

Despite having driven through the city countless times before, Jackson had never seen this side of it. Overwhelmed by the beauty of the moment and the feelings between them, Jackson cannot contain his passion and begins kissing Jazzie with fervor, and she responds in kind. Desire intensifies as they both give in to their emotions. Jackson, now eager to explore further, lifts her dress and is surprised to find she is not wearing any panties.

He can feel her arousal, and it only adds to his longing for her. However, their intimate moment is interrupted when a jogger approaches them, prompting Jazzie to exclaim, "Not here!" Realizing the situation, they compose themselves, acknowledging that such a public setting is not appropriate for their intimacy. They exchange a knowing glance, silently agreeing to find a more suitable place for their passion to unfold.

"Where can we go?" He eagerly questions.

"When we came into the park we crossed a bridge, it was secluded and now it is dark. Let's go there."

They scramble to gather their things and hurl them back into the wagon. Briskly walking toward the bridge that leads to a neighborhood, it was facing the skyline. Stars were dancing around the white, loomed large glow in the sky. After checking their surroundings, Jackson parks the wagon and grabs her hand, kissing it. The gleam covers them giving just enough light to illuminate them.

Jackson turns her around, facing the skyline with her back to him. Glancing once more around, he bends her over the handrail of the bridge, unzipping his shorts. It felt heavenly as he pulled Jazzie's dress up and parted her legs to enter her world. From behind her, he grabs her breast and savors it until they both lose control and experience ecstasy simultaneously. Anyone may have seen them as he swiftly yanked her dress down, and they could not believe what they had just done. They speedily grab their things before running away laughing like two senseless teenagers evading the police.

After loading the car up, Jazzie was about to climb into the driver's seat, when he grabs her by the waist, "Thank you for an unforgettable time," and kisses her. Feeling her nipples responding, Jackson wanted more of her, right there. When she observed that his shorts were beginning to protrude, Jazzie stated, "We better stop before the neighbors call the police on us!" After giving him a friendly grin and getting in the car, they drove back to his truck.

As Jackson lay in bed that night, he reflected on how sheer Jazzie's view is of the world. She shared his qualities of kindness and patience. They are remarkably similar. Unable to stop thinking about her and visualizing her in that white summer dress, he tossed and turned in bed. He exclaims aloud, "She didn't have on any panties!" Pondering, he wants to know how it would be to spend time together without interruptions. Eventually, he drifts off to sleep with visions of Jazzie replaying in his dreams.

CHAPTER 6

Colorful Meanings

꧁ ♥ ꧂

The next morning, Jazzie woke up with a burst of enthusiasm. It being a Sunday, the family usually took care of their own breakfast, but today, she was in the mood to prepare a lavish morning meal. She got to work, frying bacon, sausage, and tilapia. Alongside that, she made some homemade biscuits, creamy Gouda grits, scrambled western eggs, and crispy hash browns. To complete the feast, she freshly squeezed some orange juice, adding to the delightful aroma that wafted upstairs to their bedroom. The enticing smell of the delicious spread roused Aiden from his sleep. Hearing Jazzie's joyful singing in the kitchen, Genesis and Brandon quickly made their way downstairs, drawn by the alluring scent. They knew they were in for a treat and could not wait to dig into the mouthwatering breakfast Jazzie had prepared. "Mom, are you all right?" Brandon inquires out of worry.

"Yes, everything is perfect!" already twirling around, taking his hand and saying, "Come dance with me!"

"Is everything okay? Do you have anything to share with us?" With a rumbling stomach, Aiden asked as he entered the kitchen.

She smiled answering, "Everything is amazing!" Genesis hurried to the cabinet to get a plate and asked, "Can I fix my plate before you ask us to do whatever it is you are setting us up to do?" Jazzie chuckled and maintained that everything was fine. Leaving the kids to do the clean-up, she went to shower.

She considers Jackson while taking a shower and how much fun yesterday was. Still, in disbelief, Jazzie recalls the outrageous bridge incident. She grinned and thought about how lovely it would be if they had a place to hang out without worrying about someone seeing them. Wanting some ample time, she was intrigued with getting more acquainted with Jackson and avoiding a quickie. Looking at her phone after getting dressed and out of the shower, Jazzie was ecstatic to discover that he texted.

"Good morning, Beautiful."

"Good morning Sexy. I was just thinking about you."

"I hope it was good," he replied.

"So far, I was thinking about, what if we had a safe place to relax with each other?"

"What do you have in mind?"

"Well.....we need a more relaxed environment to enjoy each other. Some place where I can see if Choir Boy has some skills?

"Choir Boy? So, you think I'm a Boy Scout?"

"Nope, just innocent and sweet," she says teasingly.

"Lol, don't be fooled Ms. Jazzie, I'm far from that. Be careful what you ask for."

"Hmmmmmm. I'm asking for it," she says sarcastically.

"You think I'm scared?"

"Are you?"

"I can show you better than I can tell you?"

"Show me!"

"Let's meet at a hotel," Jazzie suggested.

"Okay but not by our neighborhood."

"Okay, when?"

"Next Saturday, I have to go into the shop for a moment first."

On Saturday morning, a sizable cargo of motorcycles was being brought to Jackson's primary auto shop. His business would benefit from this new initiative, and his family will now be away for the weekend. Tammy will be visiting her hometown of Dallas for a birthday celebration with the twins. Work is a fantastic excuse for him to not join them. Jackson will get his close friend to oversee this project while he spends time with Jazzie. She was also free this weekend, so this was excellent. Due to a work trip, Aiden would not get home until Sunday afternoon.

Brandon was heading to a friend's house for a weekend overnighter while Genesis was visiting Jazzie's cousin Yvette and her daughters. They decided to get together in a hotel off Highway 124 not far from Jimmy Carter Boulevard.

Jackson visits the auto shop to make sure that his close friend Corey is aware of how to move the motorcycle sales along for the purchasers. If Corey can do this task successfully, he will be given further work and a substantial profit share. Jackson offers him one final directive after a quick training session: "Only call me in an emergency on my burner cell. I'll say it again, only call me in an emergency."

"I've got this, man! I'll text you when I'm finished later." Inquisitively, Corey says, "If I didn't know any better, I would suppose you had a date."

Jackson replies, "All right man, I'm out," ignoring him. Jackson could not wait to see Jazzie. He pictured himself smelling and tasting her as he left the shop, jumped into his truck, and drove off.

He recalls that Jazzie loved flowers and was a romantic while he was driving. She had resumed her workouts at the gym, and a massage would help with the soreness. Jackson enters a flower shop after pulling up to it. He didn't know what to buy because Tammy likes cash to flowers, besides he is not the romantic sort. Jazzie was unique—a rare individual who liked the smell of flowers. Jackson asked the salesperson's opinion as to what was appropriate. The salesperson displays a variety of warm roses and floral arrangements. None of these fit what he was intending to do, so he avoided them. Jackson notices bags of rose petals in various tones as he passes the section with the chilled single roses. In agreement with the salesperson, "This is great; I'll take a bag of these."

"What does the color of the roses mean?"

"My dear friend, picking the appropriate meaning for your message to go along with the appropriate hue is a masterpiece. A card with the colors' respective meanings is provided here," she gives him a small card.

"Can you blend colors for a meaning?"

"Definitely, but think carefully about what you want to convey to the recipient."

"Let me get six orange and six white roses."

"Is this a new love interest?"

"I believe so," he says, flushing.

"Orange connotes yearning, a potential new love interest, or an intriguing person. The white rose is a classic wedding flower because it symbolizes innocence, purity, and fresh starts. Additionally, it connotes youth, truth, innocence, reverence, and that you are thinking of someone."

"Then this will say all I need to. I appreciate you helping me and the card."

"Will this be all for you Sir?"

"Yes, for now."

Jackson ordered one of her favorite meals—seafood with the sides, an Arnold Palmer, and key lime pie—on the drive to the hotel. He speedily checks into the hotel after picking up their meal so that he may prepare the atmosphere for the room before she arrives. He began by scattering rose petals on the floor starting at the doorway of the room leading to the bathroom. He also placed some in and around the bathtub but refrained from filling it with water. Then he scatters rose petals and Hershey kisses on the bed. On the table where they were going to have dinner, Jackson strews the last of the rose petals. He spreads unlit fragrant candles throughout the room, on the dining table, in the vicinity of the bathroom, in the room's entrance, and on the dresser. After finishing, he texted Jazzie.

"Hello beautiful, I just checked into the hotel."

"All right, I'm on my way; what's the room number?"

"I'll text you the information before you arrive." He anticipates that once Jazzie arrives and has not gotten the room number, she will call, allowing him to light the candles and turn on jazz. For now, his rap music blares through the speakers as he sets the dinner table and waits for her.

CHAPTER 7

Seductive Surprises

❦

Jazzie and Genesis had a girls' excursion to the nail salon the day before. They both frequently receive a deluxe pedicure, but Jazzie chose to have a Cucumber Melon pedicure. It is more expensive for this service but it ensures her feet are baby-soft with gel polish to match her freshly manicured fingernails. Her hair was to match her freshly manicured fingernails. Her hair was loosely curled and parted in the middle by Genesis. Jazzie wore a solid front-zip, yellow spandex romper. She had a butterfly tattoo on the left side of her upper thigh, which the romper left half exposed. She grew concerned after seeing on the GPS that the hotel was nearby; the butterflies in her stomach were having a field day. Upon pulling into the Wyndham Inn & Suites, she discovered that Jackson had not sent the room number and phoned him.

"Hi Jackson, you never sent the room number, and I'm already at the hotel."

"I know, it was a reason," he says seductively. "Room 305."

She intriguingly answered, "Okay, I'll be up." Jazzie wondered why he did not send the room number in the first place then brushed it off. She was busy trying to calm her butterflies down. Rubbing her stomach, she takes one last look over in the mirror before stepping out of the car. After entering the hotel, she walks over to the elevator and presses the up button. She hesitated to step on when the doors opened but then did so after telling herself, "No turning back now." Jazzie got off onto the third floor, searched the room numbers on the wall, and went to the right. She lets out one last uneasy breath of air, then knocks on the door.

Jackson hears that sweet sound, her knocking at the door, and opens it. When she sees how handsome he is, her nipples immediately spring to greet him. He saw them through her romper, blushing, he stood aside to let her in, then closed the door. Jazzie is taken aback by the room's appearance, and the different colors of rose petals spread about. The perfumed candles provide a delicate, soothing fragrance. The room is not overpowered by the jazz music dancing in the air; rather, it enhances the atmosphere and soothes her.

Upon turning to face him, Jazzie asked, "Oh my goodness, this is lovely! Did you do all of this for me?"

"Of course, I did, only for you. These are for you." He gives her the dozen of roses he picked up. "They are so beautiful, thank you! Is this the reason why you didn't send me the room number?"

"Yes, I wanted to have the candles lit and the music playing when he came in," he says as he indulges her in a kiss. Her body was responding in ways she had no control over.

She stutters, "I don't know what to say." He hands her a glass of Grey Goose Vodka mixed with cranberry juice with a splash of Sprite and she swiftly downs it.

"Hold on, take your time with that, I want you to eat something, so you won't get sick," he says while laughing. The drink was calming and delicious, but he was right, she needed to eat something.

"Are you ready to eat?"

"I didn't have time to eat much today, so I'm starving. Where are we going?"

"We're dining here. Wash your hands at the kitchenette and have a seat. I'll reheat our food."

"You have us something to eat?"

"Yeah, I was up early today cooking for us."

"I wasn't aware you can cook. You are full of surprises!"

"Placing and picking up a food order is difficult and requires skills," they both roared with laughter.

"Chef Davenport at your service, everything is ready."

Jackson selected the Audubon Place Seafood Platter for them both, which includes fried tilapia, stuffed crab and shrimp, fried shrimp, crab legs, dirty rice, green beans, side salads with ranch dressing, and garlic bread. She was speechless; no one had ever shown her such kindness. He got the same meal, but instead of tilapia and green beans, he had catfish and gumbo.

"I have you an Arnold Palmer, do you want it now?"

"May I have another glass of the drink you gave me when I arrived?"

"Sure, I will make you another one."

They said grace and enjoyed their meals. To see if she would like it, he feeds her samples of his catfish and gumbo, and she does. The vodka drinks had her more at ease.

"Do you want your key lime pie now that I've got for dessert?"

"I'm full and still have a lot more food left. I can eat it later with my food. For dessert, I rather have you."

She starts flirting with him. The protrusion in his black Dickies pants proves that he likes it. Jackson puts their remaining food in the refrigerator before going into the bathroom to start the bath. "I know he is not about to take a bath right now," Jazzie thinks to herself.

He calls out to her, "Jazzie, come here!"

Entering the bathroom, she gasped at the sight of rose petals floating in the bathwater. She breathes in the soothing aromas and asks, "What's this?"

"It's called the water and a bathtub," he responds sarcastically yet humorously.

"I know that smarty pants!" she exclaims while laughing." Are you about to take a bath?"

"No, you are, take off your clothes," Jackson commanded.

"Me?"

"Yes, you, please remove your clothes now."

Jazzie hesitated but followed his instructions as he watched her get dressed. She appears to be the most exquisite woman in the world to Jackson. He used a string from the rose petal bag to pull her hair into a ponytail when she was naked in front of him.

"You're also a beautician?"

"Having two daughters taught me a few things."

Guiding her into the jacuzzi bathtub, he submerges her into the rose petals. While she sits soaking, he changes the music to "Miguel – All I Want Is You, featuring J. Cole" and gives her another drink. Jazzi was utterly calm; there were no butterflies or guards around her – just trust in him, for now.

"Come join me, it feels so relaxing," she declares.

"This moment is about you, let me take care of you."

Those words sound foreign, Jazzie has never heard them in connection with her. Jackson sits at the end of the tub to bathe her. As he admires her natural beauty, his urge intensifies.

Jackson washes and dries her off before bringing her back into the bedroom. She is positioned on her stomach in the bed. Jazzie hears him rubbing his palms together and notices a strong tropical scent tickling her nostrils. His oiled hands begin lightly caressing her back. This is a pleasant relief for her body, which has been sore after recent spinning classes at the gym. She mutters to herself as she enjoys feeling him caress her body and mind, noticing how smooth and gentle his hands are considering he owns numerous mechanic shops. She discovers a sizable package within his pants when he flips her over. He was in charge of this situation, not her, thus she wanted to open the package and play with her gift.

She wants to rip his clothing off as he keeps massaging her arms and then moves to her breast. Jazzie was expecting him to undress, but when he did not, she took hold of his belt to assist him. Jackson teases her by starving and forbidding her from touching him. He begins massaging her inner thighs after gently spreading her legs apart. He then positioned himself so that his head was between her legs while she froze.

He tells her to "Relax."

"Okay," she says softly.

Jackson continues softly kissing her inner thighs. He advances to her clitoris, which resembles a pea-shaped bulb that protrudes above the vaginal opening. He uses his finger to rub this region. "Oh my goodness," she yells. Her body reacts as he hits her sweet spot. His fingertips follow the contours of her body. She was getting more and more turned on. Her kitty was feeling different, "She's ready!" Jackson says to himself. His thumb and index finger were placed on either side of her clit to keep it spread wide as he wrapped one of his arms over her thigh. She felt a euphoria that was out of character when he pushed his wet tongue within her.

Jackson got closer and licked her entire universe. He inserts a finger inside of her while licking and fines her G-Spot.

"Awwwwwww, what are you doing?" Jazzie groans.

"Damn, baby! This is some good-tasting pussy!"

Jazzie seizes the bed linens, pillows, and his head because he is driving her crazy. Jazzie informs him that she has the urge to climax. Jackson responds, "Show me," despite his lack of fear. She loses all restraint and explodes in his mouth.

"What happened? What did you do to me?" Jazzie asks in confusion. Finally, he strips off his clothing and spreads her legs wide. Jackson looks into Jazzie's eyes and wants her desperately and intrudes into her world firmly. In response to her groans, Jackson groans and satisfies her needs, cravings, and desires. When he hears and feels her juices splashing against his balls, he vigorously and profoundly thumps more. Once Jackson feels how warm she is inside, he loses himself and releases his soldiers to claim his throne. He was blissfully frozen, his toes curled before he regained his mind and sighed in relief.

Jazzie mistakenly believed he finished, but he was not. "Come here and turn that ass up," he ordered while jumping off of her and flipping her over onto her knees. Before returning to her reality, Jackson spanks and strokes her butt. As he sees her butt bouncing on him with each stroke, she was turning him on. She accepts all of his blows, but she quickly loses the battle. Her leg quakes from within her sweet spot. Jackson grabs her hair and says into her ear, "I'm going to make this MY pussy."

To stop her from running, he clutched hold of her full, luscious hips, a specific portion he worships. Jazzie is abruptly fed as he gets hold of her and accelerates as quickly as he can. Jackson catches his breath and murmurs, "You okay?" before collapsing next to her. Jazzie marvels at his incredible abilities; she has never had such an intense sexual experience. As they lay in bed hugging one other and silently enjoying music, Jazzie whispers, "I'm wonderful." Abruptly, Jazzie tries to stand up, but Jackson clutches her while he rises again.

"Do you have to go to the restroom?"

He implores, "No, I need more of you."

She looks shocked and says, "Are you serious?"

"Let me show you."

After going another round, they worked up an appetite and needed a break. The rest of their meal was consumed as they conversed, drank, and laughed together. Jazzie urged him to slow dance once she heard a catchy track on Pandora. Normally, Jackson dislikes dancing, but with her, he would do practically anything.

They return to lying down after the song is through, with her head resting on his chest. Jazzie became engrossed with the moment as the seductive cologne on him filled her senses. His nude body pressing against hers was waking her sweet spot, and she reacted by getting wet once more. Jackson was experiencing the same thing since his manhood was prodding her stomach. Jazzie discovers he has a special talent that few guys possess— he can climax back-to-back! Unknowingly to her, Jazzie is the uniqueness, his aphrodisiac. They had nowhere else to be but right there with each other tonight, so they were free to lose themselves in one another. If this is what a young maintenance man is all about, in Jazzie's opinion, I need to tell my girlfriends that they should get one!

Deciding to herself, she will play with him for a short time before letting him go, ending this fling.

CHAPTER 8

The Meet & Greet

ackson and Jazzie got to know one another more as time went on. In their bubble, their universe, anything they had was shared. Even if you're married, loneliness is possible. They both were lonely souls looking to embrace life. It turns out that they needed each other in more ways than one. When they were together, they were energetic, full of adventure, not just alive but living. For him, Jazzie is more than enough. Jackson has a free attitude and moves with the flow. He makes plans as he goes through life and doesn't have an agenda book. In many ways, she makes him feel unique, sexy, and special, he does the same for her. They elevated as a team.

Both of them experienced emotions they had no idea they could. Jazzie finds herself dreaming, wanting, and seeing him in everything she does. Every time she texted Jackson, even with a simple hello, he grinned. Both were having fun together. Frequently, Jazzie reminds herself that it is a brief fling, the best sex ever, and nothing more. She was excellent at keeping her heart protected and not succumbing to feelings. With Jackson, it was different because he was bringing her to levels she had no idea existed. He inspired her to take on more, reach farther, and express her creativity without fear of criticism. On a spring day, he is a breath of fresh air. Despite having feelings for him, she concluded that it was probably only lust. Jazzie attempted to ignore the emotion, but she knew deep inside that it was more and it was getting stronger every day.

Jackson finds himself thinking of her throughout the day and night. She is considerably dissimilar to the type of people he often deals with. He wanted to be in her line of sight as he learned more and more about her. He wonders if she would still want to see him if she knew fully what he did for a living. Thinking about the woman Jazzie is, he knows she would never be in the world that he has created for himself, but he wants her.

Jackson receives an invitation from Jazzie to attend her friend's club-hosted Christmas party. She has talked about him a lot to her girlfriends, so now would be an excellent time for them to meet. Jackson was delighted that she wanted him to meet her friends and was looking forward to seeing her. "Get in good with the girls than I am in her good grace," he thinks. He informed Jazzie he would meet her there and that he was bringing one of his friends since he had another shipment coming into the shop. Jackson brought his clothing to work with him and planned to change there after the transaction. His lookout partner, Corey would be going with him to the party and had already put his clothes in the dressing room of the store.

"Hey man, the trailer just pulled up to the gate," Jackson says.

"Cool, it's early, we can get out of here and go party," Corey said as he left the building.

Corey asked the driver for his password to verify the buyer. Once he verified it was legit, he instructed the driver to pull to the back of the shop at Bay Door Four. Jackson and Corey unloaded a 1994 Honda Accord, 1995 Honda Civic, 1991 Toyota Camry, 1997 Ford F-150 pickup, 2004 Dodge Ram, 1999 Ford Taurus, and a 2002 Ford Explorer into the garage. Once they viewed the cars and made sure they were stripped of any tracking devices and vehicle identification numbers, they gave the driver a backpack with cash in it.

Once they secured the stolen vehicles, they went to get dressed in Jackson's office. Corey pulls his shirt off revealing a large tattoo across his back, "8/14/1953." Jackson was amazing with the artwork of the artist. "Who did your tac man?" Corey quickly puts on his dress shirt and replies, "A family friend, hurry up, I gotta get to the ladies!" They both were ready to celebrate the Christmas package they just pulled into the inventory.

When Jackson and Corey arrive at the club, they finish drinking a bottle of Crown Royal and Coke in the car before going inside. He observed Jazzie on the dance floor swaying to an oldie, "Wobble," performed by

Atlanta radio personality Frank Ski, as they moved to the bar to get drinks. He was flabbergasted at how stunning and seductive Jazzie appeared in a tight satin red dress with cleavage that spilled out and curls that cascaded down her back. Near the dance floor, she had attracted the attention of observers. When he saw a random dude join her and encroach on Jackson's space, the song abruptly changed. He watches them dance while continuing to sip on his beverage; he is spellbound by her but envious of a random dude dancing on her.

Jazzie is eager to introduce Jackson to her close friends. He is so fantastic in bed that she finds it unfathomable that she would joke about sharing him with the girls, this is her keepsake. She scans the club for Jackson while dancing with a familiar man. As soon as she notices Jackson back in the throng, staring at her, she swiftly leaves the man alone on the dance floor. She greets Jackson with a big embrace and kiss.

"Hi, How long have you been here?"

"Long enough to see you dancing up on that lame-ass dude," he responds gravely.

She downplays his reaction and asks, "Can I sip your drink?" Surrendering his drink, he introduces his friend, "This is Corey."

"Hi, I'm Jazzie, it's nice to meet you," she adds while extending her hand.

"We don't shake hands, we hug," Corey replies as he extends his arm to embrace her.

Jazzie walked them to where she and her friends were seated in the VIP Section. "Ladies, this is Jackson and

Corey, they will be joining us. Let me give you a quick introduction, these are The Ladies of 404, my social club."

Jazzie continues as Corey settles down close to his first victim of the evening. She introduces them all, quickly pointing to each one, saying, "This is LaToya (Lil Bit), Betty our Travel Princess, Erica and we call her Boss, Madeleine, the Baker, Willow, the Gentle Giant, Maggie is the Jack of all Trades, Thema is Queen, Damica which we call Free Spirited, Raven we call No Bull Shit, Kendra we call Baby Doll, my cousin Yvette, we call her Dimples, my sister Vivian which we call the Wild Child and my best friend, Haley we call Doc."

"Girl, look at that fine-ass body next to her! She is clinging on like a Christmas tree ornament!" They all started laughing at once.

Jazzie says, "Jackson is mine," modestly.

Betty and Yvette order two Heinekens and begin to dance to a loud rap tune.

"There is plenty of food and drink. It's great to finally meet you," Vivian tells Jackson while reaching to shake his hand.

"It's nice to meet everyone, but please forgive me if I don't recall all of your names." While sitting close to Jazzie, he says.

Jackson orders a pitcher of Blue Moon and a bottle of Hennessy for the table. After numerous cocktails and hot wings with fries, an hour later, Jackson and Corey felt quite at home among everyone. Corey made all of the women the objects of his flirtation, and while he chose to make them all laugh, he felt a particular affinity with Haley. She and Corey squabble about how men are more beneficial to relationships. Haley and the other women disagreed with him and debated back and forth. After a while, the waitresses and a few bystanders joined the discussion.

Jackson is just focused on Jazzie and how much he wants her. When a song began to play, she invites Jackson to dance and began to rock her hips side-to-side. They marched towards the dance floor, and despite the fact, he did not want to but could tell she was genuinely eager to dance. Even though the dance floor is crowded, Jackson can only see her. They danced to a couple of quick songs before Avant's "My First Love," a slow tune, started playing. He drew her in by the waist.

They had forgotten their location and were absorbed in one another. Jackson felt her nipples responding to him while she lay on his chest slow dancing. He is squeezing her tighter and closer despite her attempts to put some space between them. Gazing downward into her eyes, making her weak, he kisses her as if they were the only ones present. When the song ended, they realized she had felt him expanding inside his pants.

"I didn't see a mistletoe," Jazzie smiled and said.

He responds, "I don't need an excuse to kiss you."

She suggested that they return to the VIP Area as her sweet spot jumped with delight and led him off the dance floor. The ladies were enjoying gaining up on Corey. Jackson fit right in with her friends and they all felt as if they had known him forever. After a few too many drinks, Jazzie had to take her high heels off. She had a pair of flat shoes in her car that Jackson was so thoughtful to get for her. Jackson showed his comic behavior and had them all in tears from laughing. As it started to get late the party was thinning out.

"Who is taking Jazzie home?" asks Maggie.

Jackson offers, "I'm taking her."

"You're just going to take her to the front door of the house?" Raven wants further information.

"Trust me, I got her."

"This is my only sister, she has had too much to drink," adds Vivian as she stands up to hand Jackson the car keys.

"I promise and I can text you once I make sure she is home."

"Okay, here is my phone number."

Lately, he has been doing nothing short of taking care of her, and tonight is no different. Everyone said good night while leaving the club. Jackson tells Corey to follow them in his truck after getting her into the automobile, and he drives Jazzie's vehicle. Jackson was troubled because he needed to say something, but Jazzie kept bringing up Aiden's name. Hearing about her marriage was starting to irritate him. Jackson finally says, "I don't care anything about Tony, Melvin, Anthony, Charles! You should be with him if you're going to keep talking about him."

"Who is that?" She was confused.

"That dude you call your husband," he bluntly spoke getting his point across.

"His name is Aiden," she says cordially.

"Whatever his name is, I don't care about him. I need you to understand something about me. I don't like sharing and I don't like my girl dancing up on no dudes!"

Jazzie recognized his perspective and was moved by his ability to approach her and express his thoughts. Aiden was too busy with his work to comment on anything she did, which was to be expected. Aiden simply cared that she got home safely. She can relate to Jackson's feelings because sharing…HIM was something she loathed doing.

"I understand and I'm sorry if I made you uncomfortable," she said.

"Don't be sorry, be careful. You don't understand, do you?"

Jackson realized she was confused and confessed, "I'm falling in love with you." Assuming she was the only one who had these feelings, Jazzie was shocked. When she rubs her stomach, he realizes why.

She shrieks, "I think I'm going to get sick."

"Let me stop."

She rushes out of the car as soon as he pulls over to the side of the road and tries to puke but is unable. By placing his fingers in her mouth, Jackson approaches her and successfully makes her vomit. He held her hair back as she continued till a halting point was reached. She slumped back into the passenger seat and passed out. Jackson looked for paper towels on her dashboard to wipe her up and let her relax. He woke her after Corey silently parked her car in the driveway when they arrived at the destination marked "Home" on her GPS. Before they departed without Aiden spotting them, he made sure she walked inside the house.

"I will have to teach her how to handle alcoholic drinks better," Jackson thinks to himself as he drives Corey back to his car.

CHAPTER 9

I Love You

Before starting a conversation, Corey waited until they were far enough away from Jazzie's house to be secure.

"Man, I see why you have been M.I.A. these days. She's bad as hell and a phat ass!"

Proudly he responds, "Yeah man!" he said, "She's cool and easy to hang with," while ignoring his remark about her butt.

"I see. How long are you planning on keeping her around?"

"We kickin' it for now, but man, she's different from anyone else I have known."

"All right man don't get caught up out here. You're supposed to smash and not cuff. We don't need shit interfering with this money. Lately, you have been missing pickups which means we don't get paid. Does she know about the side hustle?"

"Hell no! She is too classic to know about that life and I intend to keep it that way, Bro." The reality is he wanted to tell Jazzie everything but was fearful that she would reject him. To keep it from her is bothering him.

"Hold on! Why are you screwing up our money, over this girl? Come on, man! Clear your head and let her go. Our cash flow is being disrupted by her, and your stupid ass is thinking with the wrong damn head!"

"She is not involved in this at all! Do your part, and I'll take care of the rest." Jackson replies defensively.

"Shiiiiii, she is fine as hell tho! I'm trying to get with her cousin man and best friend!"

"Hell, you were trying to get with them all!"

"For sure, no need to be selfish.......spread the love man!"

They joked while riding, but he worries about what Jazzie's reaction would be should she discover the details of his side hustle. Jackson was already caught up in Jazzie, but Corey was unaware of this.

The next day Jazzie awakened sensing the sunlight dancing on her face and the sound of chirping birds and she jumped up. Aiden's oversized t-shirt snuggling her reminded her that she was home. Without being able to remember getting there, she was petrified with fear over the prospect that she might have been negligent and had left a trail of evidence showing that she was out with

Jackson. Aiden believed that she was working late with a client for an upcoming college recruitment fair. He would go insane if he were to learn the truth.

The aroma of food being prepared dispersed in the air and entered her nostrils. Her stomach grumbles. Jazzie crept downstairs to see whether she needed to do any damage control and found Genesis grilling hamburgers and fries. Genesis approaches Jazzie, who is looking pale saying, "Hey Mom, are you feeling ok? You look horrible!"

"Why are you making burgers so early?" Jazzie inquires ignoring her question while wondering where Aiden was.

"Where's your dad?"

"I've just gotten home from work, and it's time for lunch," Genesis stated with a bewildered look on her face. "Dad needed tires on his truck and took Brandon with him." Glancing at the kitchen clock, Jazzie was surprised to see that it was 2:30 in the afternoon. Genesis continues chatting, "Mom, I was leaving for work and found you asleep on the sofa in the den at 3 a.m. You gave off the impression that you were not well. I put you to bed in your room after changing you into one of Dad's t-shirts from the laundry room. Your purse and car keys are in your office on the desk."

Jazzie starts to remember fragments and responds, "Thank you, sweetie, I wasn't feeling well. I believe there was a problem with the food last night." She probes for more information by asking, "Did your dad say anything about me not feeling well?"

"He didn't know because he was knocked out after taking some Melatonin for his sinuses. His sinus problems were irritating him, I knew he needed the sleep."

"After a long shower, I'll feel better," Jazzie said and climbed the stairs to her bedroom suffering from a pounding headache. Her cell phone started to chirp while she was searching for it. It was located on a table near the bedside secured to the charger. Genesis must have placed it there. Jazzie grabbed and swiped her phone and read the text from Jackson.

It read, "Good morning, how are you?" According to the timestamp. It was sent this morning at about 10:30 during the time she was passed out.

She replies, "Good Afternoon Jackson, Sorry for the delay but I'm just waking up."

"Headache?"

"Oh, my gosh, a large one!" she rubs her head and text.

"Take a Goody Powder, it helps with hangovers," he advises.

"I have some Advil, I will try that."

"Can you get away for a little bit today if you feel up to it?"

Even though Jazzie felt exhausted, she wanted to see whether she had dreamt about something from last night or if was it real. Besides, she was already missing him.

"Sure, what time and when?"

"Are you hungry?"

"I'm starving, but NO ALCOHOL!"

"Lol…. Okay! Pick a location."

"I don't care where we go; I'm just starving. They can serve peanut butter and jelly sandwiches!"

"I think I can afford to get you a real meal. Meet me at the spot in an hour."

"An hour?"

"Okay, thirty minutes?"

"Make it twenty minutes, lol!"

"Okay, see you soon!" Jazzie groans as she discovers the empty Advil bottle in the trash after searching around the bathroom for a pain reliever. She took swift steps to the shower and removed any remnants of the previous evening. Until she could acquire more medication, the steam started to relieve her headache. Following washing her hair she steps out of the shower. pats her hair dry, applies mousse, and then snaps a headband on while it air dries instead of blow-drying it. Jazzie chose some gorgeous medium gold loop earrings, a comfortable pair of tennis shoes, and jogging attire. After a few squirts of perfume, she walks downstairs to the front entrance. "Genesis, I'll be back in a few hours," she leaves.

The "Spot" is a public plaza close to Jackson and Jazzie's residence. The plaza houses more than a few eateries, stores, a gym, and a brand-new dinner theater. It is an excellent location for them to park and go undetected because several of the parking decks offer valet, self, and private parking alternatives. Jazzie was hoping Jackson had not yet arrived so she could run into CVS to get some headache medicine.

When Jazzie pulled into the parking lot in the area where they usually meet, Jackson was already waiting in his truck. Her headache seems to be getting worse and she moans again. While parking next to him, Jackson signals for her to get in with him. She gladly accepts because her energy level has gone to the grave. Once seated inside the truck, she kisses him and says, "Hi."

"Did you take anything for the headache?" Jackson enquired.

"No, can we please go over to CVS?" It was on the opposite side of the plaza. Jackson had already packed some Goody Powder for her to take because he anticipated that she would need something.

"Just in case you were still hungover, I brought you some."

"I never tried this before, how is it done?" She asked while flipping the packet to find the directions.

Jackson gave her instructions while handing her a bottle of cold water. Jazzie frowns when the mixed concoction enters her mouth. It was bitter, so she drank more water to wash it down before settling into the passenger seat. "He's thoughtful," she smiled. This thought made her feel happy because she needed relief from the hangover. Jackson noticed she was more comfortable and picked a place for them to eat that was fast in service, Oz Eatery.

By the time they arrived, she was feeling a little better and made a mental note to grab some Goody Powders for her first aid cabinet. The waitress scribbled their orders and returned with two glasses of chilled water. Jazzie rapidly downed hers, indicating that she was dehydrated. Their side salads arrived and shortly afterward their large pizza did as well. After consuming food and water, Jazzie felt much better. "I feel like a human again!" she declared. With her physical balance restored, memories of their last night's conversation resurfaced in fragments. "Did Jackson say that he was falling in love with me?"

Jazzie states, "I know I look like a bomb, but I'm better now," as she stares into his eyes. "Thank you for making sure I arrived home safely. I hope you won't think I'm crazy, but I remember pieces of the ending of last night. Can you tell me what happened?" she asks.

"You look beautiful to me." Jazzie starts blushing and turning red as Jackson continues. "I know you better not be dancing up on no dudes no more. Then your Buddy looked at me like I was stepping on his playground. I had to back his ass up, not this one player!" Jackson says with authority.

"I was only dancing. When he got close, I backed up." she knew it was a rather sexy dance, actually *too* sexy.

"Find another dance to do and not one that has your ass up on some other dude. Better yet, you only need to dance for me. I don't want my girl up on some other dude. And you can't handle alcohol at all. I have to teach you what your limit is." he says while laughing at her. He recapped their entire conversation from last night and how he and Corey got her home without being seen by her family.

Then she asked for clarity "I'm your girl?" He confirms saying, "Yeah…MY girl." Jazzie smiles again but then she starts feeling confused and looking puzzled.

"Wow, I must have been seriously drunk if I thought he had said something else." This is what she was thinking while trying to play off her disappointment. "Did you have a good time?"

"Yes, I did. It was cool meeting your girls. Corey was feeling your cousin and best friend." Jackson knows why she is digging and he boldly adds, "Oh yeah, I did say one more thing." Jazzie was looking out the window as he said, "I love you."

Jazzie jerked her head around to face him and their eyes locked as she struggled to contain herself. "You do?" Her voice broke as she spoke.

"Yes, I do?" he says smiling.

Jazzie was elated! She wanted to jump over the table and embrace him with every inch of her body. An excited smile formed on her face and pierced her heart.

"I love you too Jackson!" she admitted filled with pride. She was on a cloud that was close to heaven, and Jazzie felt like a schoolgirl. Then she thought about it. "Did we have our first argument?" she asked.

Jackson smiles and says, "It was a disagreement."

"It was an argument."

"Are we going to argue about a disagreement?" he laughs.

She laughed "Nope, you could just kiss me!" When they rose to leave the restaurant, Jackson kissed her passionately while playfully tapping her butt. "Don't have my ass up on nobody but me!"

She teases him and rubs her butt onto his manhood as they were leaving and said, "Let's go practice!" Jackson starts walking in a sprint to the car so they can get some practice time in.

CHAPTER 10

Rules of the Fest

Jazzie was a radiant presence, her happiness shining through with every smile. She has been spending less and less time with her girlfriends lately and is beginning to miss them. The "Ladies of 404" are known for their compassionate hearts, always lending a helping hand at various kid-focused events throughout the year. With unwavering enthusiasm, Jazzie eagerly looked forward to the upcoming charity event, "Toys for the Cause, Abused Children." Even though summer is almost here, it is never too early to start making a difference in the lives of vulnerable children. Working alongside her fellow ladies to bring joy and support to those in need brought her immense fulfillment.

Today, the sun bathed the city in its warm embrace. Jazzie, along with the other Ladies of 404, was determined to make this event a grand success. They had tirelessly gathered toys, books, and other thoughtful gifts to present to the children, knowing that even the smallest gesture could make a profound impact. After an arduous five hours of meticulously categorizing toys by gender and age, the women's stomachs began to growl with hunger. They decided to treat themselves to a well-deserved lunch at a local sports-themed café, exuding the delightful charm of Louisiana. The ambiance was vibrant, adorned with sports memorabilia and a taste of the Southern spirit.

As they settled into their seats, ready to indulge in some much-needed food, they placed orders for food and drinks. The waitress returned first with their drink orders. LaToya raised her glass, a Hennessy Margarita gleaming in her hand. With a captivating smile, she proposed a toast, her words filled with enthusiasm and a touch of mischief. "Here's to adding flavor to your life!" she exclaimed, the sentiment echoing in the hearts of her friends.

The women joined in, raising their glasses in unison, toasting to the joy of life, the joy of friendship, and the delightful moments that awaited them. Their laughter resonated through the air like a joyous melody, mingling with the clinking of glasses, creating a symphony of their bond. Maggie's eyes brimming with warmth, raised her glass, and declared, "To helping others!"

"To sisterhood!" Betty chimed in, her voice harmonizing with Maggie's enthusiasm.

Erica, with a smile on her face, prepared to take a sip from her drink and lifted her glass high, declaring, "Cheers!"

"What have you been up to lately Jazzie?" Willow questions.

"Besides my responsibilities as a wife and mother, I've been dedicating a significant amount of time to a project lately," replies Jazzie

Raven playfully interjected, "Oh, come on, we all know your 'project' is called Jackson. His young ass has been blowing your back out!. That's why she dumped us."

Blushing, Jazzie neither confirmed nor denied Raven's teasing remark, and the group shared another round of laughter. After several drinks and enjoying seafood rolls, wings, catfish, and fried broccoli, they were turned up.

"I need a young dude who can handle me and just leave afterward. No cuddling, no sleepovers," Maggie declared while rolling a special blend of cigarettes. "And if he can blow my back out, I'd dump all you bitches too. Dicks before Divas!" The group of friends exchanged high-five gestures, erupting into fits of laughter, thoroughly enjoying each other's company and their unapologetic fellowship.

Thema, nodding in agreement, added, "Apart from my sons, I love the companionship of an adult man. Men will act how you permit them to, therefore you have to set the boundaries."

Jazzie, seeking advice, asked, "What should I do if my man isn't open to trying new things, in the bedroom?"

Yvettee, with a nonchalant sip of her Heineken, boldly suggested a straightforward solution, "Dump his ass girl! If he won't explore new experiences, another one surely would."

LaToya, with a playful glint in her eye, advised, "Try spicing things up," Maggie, true to her spirited nature, dismissed the idea, "Hell, that's too much work, swap his ass in for an upgraded version." They all chuckle.

The conversation then took a daring turn as Jazzie reveals, "I've always wanted to have a "Fuck Fest," but Aiden said we're already married so why bother?

"Girllllll, all this time you haven't had an "Fuck Fest" yet?" Haley asked in a surprised manner.

"Not even close," replies Jazzie.

"Me either! What is it, a toy? I need some new toys," says Yvette.

"Sweetie, have one with yourself. It's safer and you don't have to worry about a stalker," Kendra charms in.

"Does it have to be Aiden?" Betty playfully inquired.

"Bitch, yes! Remember she's married," adds Thema.

With a sly grin, Erica leaned back in her seat, her eyes shining with delight, and shared, "My girl knows how to keep things spicy in the bedroom. I need to text her now so she can be ready when I get home. Cheers to that!" With a confident flair, she downed a shot of Hennessy, drawing laughter from her friends.

LaToya explained, "That's because she is spicy and on some other shit."

Damica's words carried a sense of wisdom and experience as she chimed in on the conversation, "I agree, adding some spice can work wonders. It's essential to find moments of contentment in a relationship, even if they come occasionally. And you know what? Sometimes, you just have to keep doing the same things that won the person over in the first place to keep that connection strong. If a "Fuck Fest" isn't his thing, don't worry. Just try something else on his level, something that excites him. It's about finding common ground and discovering what ignites the passion of both partners. My man loves it when I do this trick with my skillful hands. It always drives him wild." The ladies erupted in laughter as they recognized the truth in her statements while also praising her openness and ability to keep the flame alive in her relationship.

Madeleine, with a mischievous smile, playfully recommended, "Give him an edible, I'll guarantee he would be down for just about anything by then!"

"You're at the prime of your sexual life. Men do so by the age of twenty. Women reach it by the time they turn thirty. Jackson appears to be the one who can contain your flame at your best age. He's younger and has a lot of stimulants. Enjoy your time but don't forget it's temporary, Play and Pass." Raven utters.

Vivian, strong-willed and independent, declared, "I'm not seeking a husband right now; I'll enjoy myself with whomever I choose. I keep it real and let them know upfront."

"I'm enjoying Jackson and doing something different and exciting," confirms Jazzie.

However, Haley takes on the role of a concerned confidante. Her words carried a tone of concern and protective wisdom as she addressed Jazzie with heartfelt advice. "Jazzie, please use caution around this man. This situation goes beyond just you; it involves your family and his as well. I know Jackson seems cool, but remember, he's a married man. Married men can say anything to someone they're not committed to, and it might sound genuine, but actions speak louder than words."

Haley paused for a moment, letting her words sink in, before continuing, "You're not his wife, so his words may not hold the same weight as they would within a committed relationship. Be mindful that he could be using charm and sweet talk without true intentions. I care about you, and I don't want to see anyone getting hurt, especially in a situation that can be dangerous. Aiden has been like a brother to me, and he has always been there for you. Ask Aiden again about the "Fuck Fest" and explain your reasons behind it.

Communication, and understanding each other's desires and boundaries are crucial in any relationship. It's important to let go of whatever feelings you may have for Jackson and concentrate on your marriage. Nurture your bond with Aiden, strengthen your connection, and ensure that you're both on the same page." Haley's words were a testament to the depth of their friendship, reflecting her care and affection for Jazzie's well-being.

"I'm married to both myself and my career. I'm free to do as I wish with whomever I choose. Let's drink to…" Betty was saying before Willow interrupted and said, "Anything…Cheers!" They all burst into laughter.

With glasses raised once more, the group embraced the spirit of togetherness among the friends, their bond strengthened by a night of candid conversation and the affirmation of true sisterhood. As the night continued, Jazzie's heart felt lighter, knowing that she had friends by her side, who would always look out for her and prioritize her happiness and safety above all else.

When Jazzie got home from the café, no one else was home. After showering she got comfortable and fixed a glass of vodka and cranberry juice. Replaying what Haley said did not resonate in her mind. Aiden would turn her down again, therefore it was a waste of time. Letting Jackson experience her further is where her mind is, but she is apprehensive. He would appreciate her creativity; however, this Feast is a very intimate session of sex and rules. The chirping sound of a text on her cell phone pulled her out of deep thought.

"Hey beautiful, I am thinking about you."

Blushing, she responds, "I'm thinking about you too. Call me if you are alone." A few seconds later, he phones her.

"Hey Babe, how did your day go volunteering with the girls?"

"It went well. How is your day going?"

"It's cool. The twins are playing in their room, I'm on babysitting duty while Tammy cooks dinner."

"I'm home alone, and no babysitting for me."

"Show off! You better enjoy the quiet time."

"Indeed I am. Ever heard of a Fuck Fest?"

"Nope, I have never heard of it. Is it some pills?"

"No. It is a term for a session of creative sex with an alternate ego twist," Jazzie explains. "The goal is to screw your partner so senseless that he or she will need a few days to recover but there are some rules."

"Hmmm, what kind of rules?" he asked as he got deeper into the thought of the Fest. Jazzie goes over the rules with him: _Fuck Fest Rules_

1. Both parties must be in good shape and health. Required prep time is at least two weeks for someone in good/great health and one month for someone in fair health.

2. Both parties must have proper rest (at least seven to eight hours) the night before the Fest. The morning of the fest you must have a well-balanced breakfast and be hydrated.

3. Both parties must agree to remain inside a room for a set number of hours without any clothes on. Once you enter the room, you cannot leave for NOTHING unless it's an emergency. You must get all your food, drinks, and anything else you will need. You can order delivery, but you must stay inside the room.

4. Both parties cannot have any type of sexual contact for two weeks before the agreed date of the Fest. You may tease each other, which is strongly encouraged.

5. Both parties must decide on the limits of sexual desires and a safe word (e.g., any use of sexual toys, anal contact, bondage, role play, spanking, or choking). This is a creative time; therefore think outside the box and explore your inner self.

6. All forms of communication must be turned off until an agreed-on scheduled break time (e.g., 5 minutes, 10 minutes, or 20 minutes) but you cannot

exceed 30 minutes. This time can be used to call home to check in on the children, spouse, dog, work, parent, or whomever but you only get two breaks during the fest.

"Sounds like something you would be interested in doing?" she asks. Jackson never backs down from a challenge and frankly, is quite competitive. This Fest had him curious and he was always willing to try something, especially with Jazzie but he was firm on one issue.

"Okay, let's do it but one thing, no playing around my anal area, at all!" Once Jazzie stops laughing she says, "Okay, let's go over our personalized rules and set a date…in three weeks."

Jackson has been subjected to Jazzie's taunting for the previous two and a half weeks to gauge his degree of control. He felt on edge throughout their quick meetings because she wore beautiful, smug-fitting outfits. After observing her butt bouncing in her yoga pants while they jogged, he decides they should jog separately, until after the Fest. While glancing at his dark blue sweatpants which displayed his talents, due to her loss of focus, Jazzie consented. Jackson loves weightlifting and is in excellent form, but decides to abstain from drinking alcohol until their challenge. He wants to be at the top of his game with Jazzie.

"Only four days before the Fest," Jackson thinks as he finishes his evening jog. He enters the house sweating, and Tammy informs him that dinner is prepared. He takes a shower, puts on clean comfortable clothes, then picks up his phone. Jazzie had sent him a photo of herself in the shower, dripping wet with her finger inside her pink flower. Although he missed seeing her, he grinned despite knowing what she was doing to him. It had only been a few weeks since he last felt her, but it seemed like months.

Jackson enlarges her breast by touching the image of her on his phone. He decides to send her a picture after feeling himself rising. Once he was safely inside the bathroom, he applied lotion on his bulge and sent Jazzie the image.

"No fair, you know I want it and you sent a hot pic," she instantly replies.

"You initiated that."

"You are mine in four more days!"

Jackson laughs because he got her back and texts, "These are your rules and besides, you sent a pic first, all sexy, wet, and ready! Why can't we just do this today and stop torturing ourselves?" Four more days seemed an eternity since he needed her right away.

"Trust me, it will be worth it," Jazzie replies.

"I will be back later, gotta go."

"Jackson, we can eat now," Tammy called alerting him that their food was on the table. She and the twins were waiting for him. Tammy has obviously abandoned her diet, Jackson observes as he sits down to eat. She had started to exercise while also keeping an eye on her food intake with him. But a week later, she had resumed her previous eating patterns. For tonight's dinner, she made fried pork chop, spaghetti, salad, and hot rolls. Jackson ate a salad without any bread and a small piece of pork chop. He was almost finished eating when his cell phone rang.

It was Corey, which was alarming because he usually texts and very seldom calls. Jackson figures it must be important and leaves the dinner table and walks into his home office to answer. "Hey what's up man, everything alright?"

"The package won't move until they speak to you," Corey said in frustration.

"I don't do business with nobody man, you know this!" Jackson says forcefully.

"I told them, but they refuse to buy the package without you, and we need this money so we can pick up the next shipment of bikes since it's peak time to sell them," Corey pleaded.

"Damn man! I don't need you if you can't handle this on your own. Give me thirty minutes!" Jackson says angrily before hanging up. When he returns to the dining room, Tammy notices him frowning and assumes there is a problem with the shop. Tammy is aware of his hustle because it furnishes her fine quality of living.

"I have to run to the shop for a moment. Girls, we will watch the movie when I get back, don't start without me." He kisses the girls and waves bye to Tammy before rushing out the door. When he arrives at the shop, Jackson begins to feel uneasy. He cast a glance across the parking lot and found the eighteen-wheeler positioned next to the bay door rather than backed up. After he hears noises coming from within the shop area, he stops himself from opening the roller-up door as he approaches the eighteen-wheeler.

"Where is Corey," he wondered, he sensed that something was not right. He quickly entered the store and made his way to the loading/unloading area, where he found Corey. Three other men were present; one was carrying a briefcase, and Corey and the other two were sitting on the hoods of a few parked vehicles within the shop. Corey stood when he noticed Jackson come in. "Hey, this is Jackson," Corey said, turning to face the three men. The men offered their hands in a handshake, but Jackson took one look at them and declined. Just then he hears his cell phone, and notices a text from Jazzie asking, "Can you talk? If so call me."

Jackson looks at Corey and says "Man, let me holla at you for a moment in the office."

Corey brushes him off and responds, "Later man."
Jackson walked away to call Jazzie while feeling his rage intensify. When his bogus name displays on her caller ID, she responds, "Hi, you!"

"Hey Babe, are you okay?" he questioned because she rarely calls him at this time of the night.

"Yes, I wanted to hear your voice and tell you that I love you."

Jackson tells her, "I love you too, more than you know," feeling incredibly fortunate to have her.

Then Jackson heard a commotion and yelling all of a sudden saying, "Police! Police! Get down now!"

"Let me call you back, I have to go!" he hangs up.
After spending three hours in his store's office, the police conducted a raid and seized inventory of five luxury cars

and nine stolen high-end motorcycles. Jackson was being questioned about his shop's business matters by a detective, while Corey was in the rear of a police cruiser. Jackson was getting agitated and told them, "If I'm not being charged with anything, then I'm leaving. If I am, then you can speak to my attorney!"

Until they could gather further information from the undercover cop on this case, the detectives decided to put Jackson in the back of another police car. Jackson makes a call to Jazzie while waiting in the backseat. Whispering he utters, "Baby, I won't be able to make our Fest, I will explain when I contact you again. I am so sorry, and I love you. I have to go for now, but I will call you in a few days." As the detectives were walking back to the police car, Jackson hung up.

Later that night he was booked into Fulton County jail. Jackson ponders how he will tell Jazzie what else he does for a living as he sits in his cell. Would she abandon him? Jazzie had grown to be a significant aspect of his life, and the thought made him cringe. Confined within the grimy cell he was already feeling lost without her. His mind raced as he replayed the previous incidents of the evening, "I knew something wasn't right! Corey screwed up big time! Or did he?" Unable to calm himself, Jackson punched the wall with his fist and screams, "Damn!"

CHAPTER 11

Keeping Plans

Jazzie has an unpleasant feeling. Her recent phone conversations with Jackson were strange, and she overheard someone in the background yelling they were the police. He hasn't responded to her texts for the past two days nor called, and she cannot help but wonder what is going on. Today is Friday and she took off work to buy a few toys and other items for their Fest, but she has no idea where he is right now. Speculating, that perhaps his wife discovered something about their relationship, but it does not change the fact that she overheard voices in the background screaming that they were the police. When her phone rings, she immediately responds, "Hello," coming out of her reverie.

"Good morning Mrs. Collins, My name is Mr. Morgan, attorney for Jackson Davenport. He requested that I call you to let you know he is okay and should be released sometime today. The plans you two have for tomorrow will continue as planned and he will see you soon."

"Out of where? What is happening?" Jazzie questioned in disbelief.

"Mr. Davenport will go through everything with you in detail; my only task is to call you and deliver this message. Enjoy your day, ma'am."

"Yeah, you too," she says sarcastically. Jazzie was perplexed, but she followed Jackson's instructions until he could explain everything to her.

Later that night she and Aiden were watching television when her phone chimes. Retrieving it from the nightstand, she gets excited to see a text from Jackson and opens it right away. "Hello, Babe. I'll do my best to address all of your questions, which I know you have a lot of. Can I still see you tomorrow?"

"Hi, I do have many questions. Sure you can see me tomorrow. Are we still meeting as we planned?" she asked unsure of what to do.

"I would love that!" he exclaims in a hurry.

"All right, so tomorrow it is."

"Good night, Babe, and I love you very much."

Jazzie replies, "I love you too, and good night," but she is miffed that he had to leave.

Aiden is informed by Jazzie that she will be at the Homeless Shelter the following day for an entire workday. Aiden was happy since he did not want any distractions while he was working on his new building for his architectural firm. Since Jazzie is aware that something is going on with Jackson, she packs her bag of tricks lightly but is unsure of what to expect. She went to bed to have a good night's rest after making sure everything was tucked in her car.

This morning, Jackson gets up early in anticipation of seeing Jazzie. He made up a tale at the last minute to tell Tammy. Telling her that he would be gone all day to take care of some business did not make her happy. For the past few days, she has had to dash about with the twins while attempting to get Jackson out of jail and needed a break. Jackson was adamant about seeing Jazzie TODAY! He chose not to eat jail food because he could not tell what it was. To make up for missed calories, he went to the closest IHOP after recalling one of Jazzie's rules: "The morning of the feast you must have a well-balanced breakfast and be hydrated." While waiting for his meal, he texts Jazzie to arrange plans.

"Good morning, Beautiful."

"Good morning!" she responds promptly.

"We still on for today?" he asks hoping for the desired response.

"ABSOLUTELY!"

"Okay! See you soon and I will send the room number," he texted back excitedly.

"Okay."

CHAPTER 12

The Elephant

✦✦✦✦✦ ♥ ✦✦✦✦✦

Jazzie finished her balanced breakfast and hurried out of the house. In addition to wanting to know what was going on, she was eager to see Jackson. "He is too good to be true," she thinks while reflecting on their progression into becoming best friends, lovers, and falling in love. Jazzie visited the store to buy lunch and snacks for later. As she was heading to the hotel, Jackson texted the room number, giving her butterflies. Jazzie's mind was racing when she pulls into the parking lot. Anxious to discover what's been going on, she parks and dashes for the room.

Jackson was so struck by her beauty when he opened the door and embraced her passionately. Jazzie trembles with delight at his touch. After Jackson released her, he stepped aside to allow her to enter the room and get comfortable. Although Jazzie was glad to see him, she noticed that he seemed anxious. The unspoken questions hung between them like a thick fog, causing Jackson to feel uneasy.

"What is it Jackson, what's going on?" she questioned anxiously.

He takes her hands while saying, "I haven't been totally honest with you about what I do for a living."

"What do you mean; you have numerous auto shops and stores around Atlanta and what else?" she asked bewilderedly.

"I do, but it's also a chop shop cover. I've been doing this with Corey for years, and it has been quite profitable. You were upset because the homeless shelter where you volunteer needed money to stay open. I was the donor who paid the bill and left the additional money because I know those people and their welfare are important to you."

"What!" she says while releasing his hand, standing and penetrating him with her eyes. "What other lies are you hiding? I thought we were better than this Jackson?" Disappointment echoed in her voice.

"You inspire me to be and do better. I wanted to tell you everything but I was already in too deep. I couldn't stand to keep this secret from you any longer. I want to share everything with you, even the parts you won't be happy with."

"That night when we were on the phone, I overheard shouts claiming to be the police. What happened, please don't lie to me?"

"The DEA raided my main shop," with his face covered with shame, he continues. "In recent months, Corey has become increasingly greedy, and he made a deal with someone I don't know. I don't operate like that and immediately sensed a problem as I pulled into the parking lot. If you hadn't texted me to call you, they would have come after me for more. Because Corey made the deal and exchanged money with them, he is still being held. I walked into my office to speak with you, and shortly afterward, the police burst in. Since I was on the phone there is still no evidence of connecting me. I am aware that there is a lot here to process, a life you would never belong to. I will understand if you want to pull back. For the record Jazzie, I never lied about my feelings for you, I love you." Jackson was in a broken state because he did not want to lose her.

"Thank you for trusting me enough to finally tell me everything. It hurts because I thought we were at this place of trust already. Jackson, I'm not perfect, and I don't expect anyone else to be. I am not sure of your religion, but mine taught me something. It's in the Bible, do not judge, or you too will be judged. For in the same way you judge others, you will be judged, and with the measure you use, it will be measured to you. I am not a hypocrite, but I do choose what I include in my inner circle and it's not that lifestyle. We will find a way to get you out of this mess without something more serious happening. I have a friend that can help us but only if you want the help?"

"Us? We?" he asks for clarity.

"Yes… Us and We. I got your back, but you have to promise me something."

"Sure, what is it?"

"Do not lie or withhold information from me ever again! Our relationship is built on trust and I need to be able to do that. As far as the money you paid for the Homeless Shelter, it is tax deductible. Thank you for helping them but your life means more to me than your money. For the record, I love you too."

"Jazzie, you are one remarkable person! I'll never lie to you about anything again, baby, I swear." He hugged her while realizing that she was not with him for money or what he could provide, she genuinely wanted him, and he was not alone. Pulling back from the embrace, he asks, "So do we get to do the Fuck Fest?"

Chuckling she replies, "That depends on what's in that bottle?" Jackson had another type of alcohol to help her to gauge her limit. They refrigerated the food she picked up for them and the snacks were spread on the table.

"Make your phone calls now since you won't be able to use it for a while," she instructs him.

"I don't need to call anyone; I have all I need right here."

Jazzie makes a little dance as she says, "Flirting will get you a treat."

She turned off their phones, hung the *Do Not Disturb* sign on the outside of the door, and locked it. They relished food, beverages, and lively conversation. Then she invited him to follow her as she strolled into the bathroom to undress. Jackson leaped from the chair as if he had a Superman cape on.

"Are we good Jazzie?"

"Yes, we are." He looks into her eyes and says "Let me love you Jazzie. Trust me with your heart." He was asking a lot of her. She was ready to trust him, it was something about him that made her feel safe, but she did not know how.

"I don't know how to trust you with my heart. I don't want to get hurt and with what we are doing right now someone will get hurt."

"Baby, I never want to hurt you and I don't want anyone else to hurt you. Give us a chance. I was in love with you, from the moment we met. Trust what you are feeling, let me love you."

They kissed while the water covered them both in the shower. Jazzie is ready to show him she loves him. She turns the water off and they both dry off and walk back into the bedroom.

CHAPTER 13

Rock-a-bye Jackson

❦

Jazzie activated Pandora on the Bluetooth while Jackson mixed their drinks. She takes a sip, places her drink on the nightstand, and motions for him to get on the bed. Jackson followed her instructions and put his drink on the nightstand next to hers. Jazzie straddles on top of him, takes some of his drink into her mouth, places her mouth on his, and gives him a shot. This method of sharing shots was enjoyable and new to him. After giving him a few more shots, she gets up and grabs the silk red bag of treats.

It contained handcuffs, a mouth gag, fluorescent edible paint, warming lubricate, a tongue vibrator, a blindfold, climax beads, and a cock ring. These objects were arranged on top of a satin scarf on the nearby table. Jackson scanned the materials and wondered, "What have I agreed to!" Whatever it was, he decided, he was prepared. Jazzie takes the handcuffs and is about to restrain him to the railing of the headboard when Jackson blurts out, "Wait! Do you have the keys for those?"

"Quiet!" she commands while shoving the gag ball inside his mouth. "You always have to be in control… not tonight! Nod your head if you understand," she adds.

Jackson nods in agreement, so Jazzie continues. "We have safe words, and they work like a traffic light: Green means keep going because it feels amazing, Yellow signifies almost too much but I can handle it, move forward with caution. Red signals stop immediately. I'll take out the mouth gag ball now, but if you ask me a question again, it will go back in, and you will have to speak with your eyes."

Jazzie gives him another drink from her mouth, followed by her nipples. Observing his pleasure growing as he sucks her breast, she pulls away. Jazzie makes a sensual dance while perched on the side of the bed. When she bends over and makes her butt cheeks clap to the music, Jazzie swings her hips and backs her round, voluptuous butt near enough for him to see her finger within her flower.

Jackson cries out, "Baby let me touch you, uncuff me," to satisfy his hunger. She does not say anything before grabbing the edible fluorescent paint and turning him into her canvas. Jazzie took care to avoid touching his manhood because she had other plans for it. Jackson is deteriorating as she caresses him with her hands, lips, and tongue. Her talent as a painter is shown by the fluorescent light bulb, on his six-pack covered with a silhouette of her face.

Jackson gave her the freedom to try new things, and because they were the same, he supported her sense of adventure. After feeding him another shot, she then queries, "What's your safe word status?"

He exhales heavily, ready for the next level, and exclaims, "Green, it's green!" They haven't felt each other's touches in a few weeks. Jazzie is aware that she needs to feel him, and he wants to feel her, however, the handcuffs prevent it. As she releases the restraints, he grabs and kisses her hungrily. She had never intended to try fellatio, not even with Aiden. Jazzie explains to Aiden, who ultimately stopped asking,

"My grandma always warned us growing up, never eat something that would get up and walk and talk to you." That comment alone turned Aiden off. On the other hand, Jackson turns her on to a different degree, motivating her to try it. He is pushed back onto the bed, and she makes him comfortable by adding pillows behind his head so he can see her. Jazzie softly touches his inner thighs, manhood, scrotum, and balls with her hands to observe his reactions and discover his weak spots. With one finger, she moves it up and down the shaft. Jazzie then uses her tongue to gently, gradually, but systematically rub his manhood. She recalls reading the literature on the subject and using a lot of saliva to give him the feeling that her pink flower was naturally lubricating him. As Jackson develops, she desires him more and more.

Jazzie moves her lips to the tip of his manhood again but this time applies pressure and slowly slides down his shaft. Jackson turns his head towards the ceiling and moans, confirming he likes it. Jackson continues by flattening her tongue to give a nice wide, wet stroke and pulls upward stopping before the glans. Along with a light squeeze from her hand, Jazzie strokes the tip of her tongue across the glans, going around in a circle, back across, and off his manhood. Jackson's body was responding with joy, his toes were curling, and his eyes were soaring. The sloppy, juicy wet sounds she makes while slurping aroused him further.

Jackson continues to moan and begins to thrust. Jazzie briefly removes her lips to tease him, leaving his manhood wet. Her mouth returns but this time she adds a jaw squeeze, palms slide and twist over the glans. He thrusts once more, prompting her to move faster and him to expand. Even though Jackson is getting weak, she continues to use her skills while holding his hands on the bed, forcing him to enjoy the pleasure.

She asks, "What's your safe word status?"
"GREEN!" Jackson muffles incoherently. She hears him but does not stop: "I'm about to cum baby!" Jazzie desires to taste him completely. Feeling her kitty getting wet, Jazzie takes a finger and shoves it inside of herself to gather some kitty secretions, then sticks her finger in his mouth while she still gorging on him. Jackson is on the verge of releasing himself but tries not to yet since she is driving him crazy, he is powerless.

"Babe, stop, I am about to cum," he warned her again but she does not stop. Suddenly Jackson screams, "SHHHHHHIIIITTTTTT!!!!!" he releases into her world. Jazzie gives him a small smirk and puts his hand around her throat so he can feel her stifle his flow. Jackson lost all senses when she did that. All of a sudden, Jazzie hears snoring, he is asleep.

"What the hell!"

Jazzie and Jackson were merging into one. They feigned to be free with one another anywhere in the world. Jackson would construct their very own home, they discussed. Because they both cherished the bounds of one another amid the untainted splendor of the world, they would have a balcony that opens off the bedroom. Entertaining is a favorite of theirs, therefore having a sizable patio with a tropical design. For the football season and other events, they would have an 80-inch flat-screen television that hangs on the wall, a surround sound system, a tiki bar, and other amenities.

Jackson wanted to create a unique shoe case for her because she owned a vast collection of footwear. The natural beauty of God's creations, including the birds, flowers, trees, and butterflies, has always been appealing to her. He planned to build a gazebo in their backyard with a fish-filled pond and a close-by connecting waterfall. To enjoy hanging out with the guys and hosting game nights, he wants a mancave with a kitchen, bar, a large pool table, and extra bedrooms for passed-out guests. With numerous hookahs and cigars, it would be a location where his boys could unwind.

One day, they would have the luxury of laying in bed

with each other and not having to move unless Jackson became agitated by hunger. Jazzie picks up on this quality he has quite fast. Jackson becomes grumpy when overly hungry, therefore she kept snacks handy.

They were so passionate and fiery in their lovemaking. Every opportunity they had, they explored each other anywhere they could. She was skilled in ways to touch him and satisfy his craving and desires. Jazzie was made thirsty by his touch, and he was happy to feed her. He was claiming her as his own.

Their connection is intense, and Jazzie's tongue explorations elicit a profound response in him, stirring his soul. Whenever she gazes into his eyes, her passion ignites, and he has a unique ability to mesmerize her with his tongue. The mere thought of Jackson makes her heart race and arouses her deeply. Their lovemaking is unrestrained, and she embraces his manhood as her own, craving his touch and attention. Jazzie yearns for his skilled tongue, which knows precisely how to bring her to a state of euphoric ecstasy. His touch on her breasts and nipples sends shivers of pleasure through her body. His gaze has a magnetic pull, making her long for him intensely. Jackson's deliberate touch inside her brings her a joyous sensation as if he were playing a harmonious tune that makes her dance to his every movement. This experience with him is entirely new and heavenly, taking her to a place of unparalleled bliss.

Jazzie always wanted to learn how to ride a motorcycle and asked him to teach her. Jackson admonishes her to take a beginner's motorcycle class for the fundamentals and safety's sake. Jackson presented her with a yellow and black Suzuki GSXR 1000 that had her name painted on the fairing when the ten days of training were completed. Her favorite color is yellow, and the bike contrasts with his all-black ride, his and her motorcycle set. Jackson put in a speed regulator so she could increase the bike's engine performance. They put into practice what she had learned in class as well as aspects that were not covered. Jackson performed all necessary repairs on her bike in his shop in addition to his. He protected Jazzie and rode closely behind her, making sure she was all right.

Jazzie always smiled as he rode since he loved bikes so much, which made her kitty smile as well. He was seductive on his bike and despite all his skill as a rider, Jazzie still worried occasionally. "I would never leave you by way of a motorcycle accident, don't worry about that," Jackson assured her.

"I trust your word, but I bought you a better guardian angel to ride with you, similar to the one you bought me," Jazzie tells him.

Sometimes while riding together, they would become disoriented and ride for hours until the moon finally led them home. They communicated on a level that only they could understand. He was pleased with the way other motorists would pass them and be shocked to see a woman riding a bike with such strength. They frequently made laudatory hand motions while glancing. She is his girl, so he is elated.

CHAPTER 14

Let's Ride!

⊰⊰⊰⊰ ♥ ⊱⊱⊱⊱

Jackson and Jazzie have been hanging out a lot lately, neglecting their other responsibilities, like their homes. To make up for it, they decided to spend the weekend doing something at home with their families. The kids had left the house to hang out with their friends while Jazzie was trying to spend some quality time with them having an outing. She believes that now is a fantastic opportunity for her and Aiden to spend time together and build a stronger relationship.

"Are you up for seeing a movie, Aiden?

He utters while watching television, "Nope, not really."

"Let's eat lunch somewhere and roller skate in the park. It would be wonderful, we used to do it a lot."

"Have you gone insane? Unless you intend on taking me to the hospital after breaking my legs, I'm not getting on any skates. We are too old for that," he declares gravely.

"It's only a short journey to see your parents, can we

go, it could be a day trip?" Jazzie rolled her eyes then took a slow deep breath and released her exasperation.

"It costs money every time we move those cars. Monday through Friday I commute to work through gridlock, today I don't feel like it." She continues to bother him, so he offers a suggestion "Go ride your motorcycle; you'd have fun doing that." Aiden wanted to watch some movies in peace and silence by himself.

Jazzie slumped her shoulders, scowled, and dragged herself away feeling defeated. She was trying to do more family things at home but truthfully, she would rather be with Jackson. Her kids had their things going on and Aiden was getting used to her being gone and preferring the quietness of an empty house. He rather watch television or work on new projects for work. The weather is nice and sunny outside, about seventy-eight degrees on a new spring day. Jazzie knew Jackson was busy, but she sent him a text of affection.

"Hey Jackson, I'm thinking of you."

"I was doing the same thing, thinking of you," Jackson immediately replies.

"Thank you, Babe, text me later when you've done visiting with your family."

"We aren't doing anything, I'm so bored."

"Neither are we. I am bored too." She wanted to see him, but she did not want to impose on his family time.

"Can you get away for an hour?" he asked.

"YESSSSSS!"

"Lol, cool, meet me at the spot in your car and bring your riding gear."

"Don't ride my bike?" she questioned, perplexed.

"No Babe, come in your car but have your riding gear."

"All right, when?"

"I'm ready now; I need to get out of this house!" He yearned for her.

She smiles and says, "I'll get ready now and be there in thirty minutes."

"Put some jeans on, no leggings!" He dislikes it when she wears leggings because you can see all her curves through them. Besides, jeans add more protection when riding a motorcycle.

"Mannnnnn OK…" she chuckles.

Jazzie arrives at the designated location forty minutes later, and Jackson is there waiting. After exiting the vehicle she melts in his arms as soon as he embraces and kisses her lips. They are noticed by nearby shoppers in the plaza, who grin.

"Are you ready?" he queries.

"I'm unsure because I'm not familiar with your plans."

"You trust me, right?"

"Of course, but I'm curious as to what we are preparing to do."

"Where is your riding gear?"

"It's in my trunk."

Using her vehicle keys, Jackson opens the trunk, removes her belongings, and then closes it. He places her helmet on her head and fastens it securely. Then he takes her compact wallet, which contains her car keys, lipstick, Identification, and phone, and he places it inside the compartment of his motorcycle, Suzie. As she slips on her gloves, he zips up her motorcycle jacket, and they are now ready. He fastens his gear and instructs her to climb onto the back of Suzie. Jazzie did not bother asking where they were going because it did not matter at this point; she just wanted to ride with him.

Once she was seated comfortably on the back, a few other motorcyclists pulled into the parking lot that Jackson knows.

"The Stillwater Boys, what's up with you fellows?" Jackson says giving them dap.

"What's up, man! We haven't seen you out on the set in a while," says Preston.

"I been busy with work and hanging out with my girl." Jackson signals for her to take the helmet off. "Babe, these are The Stillwater Boys, the tall dude is Preston, the one with the mobile bar is Dean, his backup is Josh and the laid-back dude is Scott.

"Hi everyone," Jazzie says waving at them.

"Want a drink?" Dean asked them all.

"Yeah, what do you have?" Jackson questions. Dean opens his saddlebag and it looks like a full bar on two wheels. "Damn man, you have everything in here!" Jackson exclaims.

"Where are you guys headed to?" Preston asked.

"Wherever this bike takes us," Jackson responds.

"Mind if we roll too?" Preston questions while burning his special blend of herbal smoke.

"Hell naw, It would be like old times." Jackson excitedly responds.

"Man, don't be riding crazy while we're with you,"

Dean cautions Jackson while passing out Reservoir shooters.

"Give me two shooters since we are rolling with Jackson," expresses Josh.

"Let's go then, it's hot as hell sitting here in this gear," Scott spoke.

"Dean said his customary toast, "Up to it, down to it, fuck those that don't do it. We do it because we are used to it."

After downing the shooters and tossing the bottles, they geared up to ride. Jackson gets onto his bike and Jazzie signals with a hand gesture that she is on and secure. Jackson performed his safety check to make sure she was prepared. People nearby turned to observe the display of motorcycles and then revved the engines. Once Jackson blasted off, the others followed. When Preston catches up to him, Jackson shifts into second gear and accelerates aggressively through the gridlock. He enters third gear and leaps onto Interstate 85, passing everyone. As if left over from a storm, Jazzie sees the cars flying past her eyes.

She thought they were on an aircraft by the time he put Suzie into sixth gear. While navigating Interstate 285's curves in the direction of Atlanta Airport, they lean together. The group of motorcycles maneuvered swiftly through the backed-up traffic to reach the Camp Creek exit. They travel quickly on back streets two hours from their house to South Georgia's countryside. Jazzie was able to take in the sights of people canoeing on the lake and blooming flowers because Jackson led the group along a scenic path.

When they come across a windmill blowing in the breeze and a cascading waterfall, he stops and allows her to take pictures. While Jazzie takes the picture, the guys are looking for a food stop that serves pitchers of cold beer and downs more shooters. Jackson smiles at her because she is beautiful and happy, and he is happy too.

They all pause at a sports bar for food and drinks after working up an appetite. The trip was only meant to take an hour but ended up lasting more than five hours. Jackson chose a faster path, on their return home, giving a clear view of the moon circling the treetops. Suzie's music blared as he drew her closer and her tight grip united them. Jackson likes having Jazzie nearby and sharing his territory. Taking her right hand, he placed it over his heart and held it there. Jazzie wished they were returning home together as she sprawled on his back and watched the moon follow them.

After several hours of riding, the group reached a familiar exit to home. Before Jackson and Jazzie branched off from them, they waved goodbye to the guys. Jackson locates a park near their home and drives into it, and parks near a picnic table. They removed the riding gear and he asked, "You good?"

"The guys are awesome! My goodness, I wish I could ride like that but that took many years of practice!"

"They are a great group of fellows. To ride like that you have to pay attention to other drivers, not the bike."

"You look sexy riding," she wanted to be with him anywhere because of the way he rides his motorcycle.

"I want you Babe, right now, here," he confesses.

Enveloped by the starry sky, they kissed. Jackson

unzips her jeans out of the inability to restrain his wants. Jazzie kicks off one of her motorcycle boots, and he assists her in taking her panties and pants off one leg. If someone else comes, it is simpler and quicker to replace one leg. She was taken aback when he bent her over onto his motorcycle and took her there, in the park. This was their bike lifestyle.

They would spend the day enjoying each other's company, which is what they do best. On occasion, he would ride her motorcycle and she would ride his. More and more motorcycle rides took them to hotels, and they became less and less visible to their fellow motorcycle riders. After Jackson's legal issues were resolved, they scheduled a motorcycle journey to Tallahassee, Florida.

CHAPTER 15

Defense Strategy

❧ ♥ ☙

Jazzie discussed Jackson's predicament with her best friend Haley, a criminal defense attorney. Haley offers to assist and assigns the case to her top investigator. The investigator discovered that Corey had indeed become avaricious. He was snooping around for the cops to gather information on Jackson. In exchange, the brother of Corey who had been imprisoned for armed robbery would be released. In the process, Corey believed he could close some side deals and steal some of Jackson's best customers. Jackson, he reasoned, was going to prison for an extended time, leaving Corey to oversee the business.

Corey was unaware that a second undercover agent was working on the case with the authorities. The agent paid Corey while acting as the client. Haley devised a defense strategy, but it required that all of Jackson's assets and records be moved to a person in whose hands he has complete faith, allowing his financial records to be untarnished and clean.

Jazzie is aware that they will need to inform Jackson about Corey. It would be difficult for him given how close they are and how for more than ten years they were like siblings. "There's more Jazzie," Haley says as she turns to face Jazzie with a worried expression. "I was given access to a recording of Corey speaking with the uncover agent by a source I have in the police department."

Jazzie massages her forehead and asks, "Did he incriminate Jackson?"

Haley returns to her computer, pulls up the video, and clicks the play button. She says, "Listen for yourself."

"Before we conduct business, Corey, I must meet the top man. Surprises and ghosts are two things that I dislike." The undercover agent adds, "I want to make sure he's cool."

Corey responds, "Man, Jackson is losing his game. I hate when brothers have good fortune and don't know it. He got a wife at home that handles shit, and he got a side piece of ass, greedy motherfucker! When he started smashing her, he lost focus on this money and our purpose. He's heat, a liability, and needs to be put out. His side piece is only ass for him, but she is causing us to lose some cash flow. I can't risk him being distracted and making mistakes. His full attention on business is required and he doesn't have it. That's good for me because I'm going to take his shops, his contacts, his life, and show him how to smash his side piece and ditch her ass. I'm the head man; you deal with me!"

"All right, Bro, let's do business. The agent enquired, "I want to know when the next cargo is due?"

"I can have one for you in a few days," Corey responds.

The undercover agent replies, "Okay, we can settle then."

"That's what's up, it's an agreement!" Corey exclaims. "I'll contact you a few days from now with more information."

"Jazzie, you are endangering yourself and your family for this man," Haley said as she halted the video. "Jackson's jerk-of-a-friend said that you are just some random ass. As soon as I met Corey, I could tell I didn't like him. You might be trapped in the crossfire because Corey is determined to bring Jackson down!"

Jazzie paces the floor while standing up, shaking her head in disbelief because she knows Jackson doesn't feel this way. "Corey is not a creditable person and clearly has a green eye when it comes to Jackson," she sighs and claims. "I'm aware of Jackson's motives and heart concerning us. He would never treat me like that or allow anything bad to happen to me. I'll be alright Haley, just help him, please."

"We need to get started on this immediately, when can he meet with me?" Haley asked.

When Jackson responded to Jazzie's text asking when he could meet them, he had just finished working at his primary store. Haley had already secured some favors and had his businesses freed from the seizure so that he could fix the vehicles he had waiting for customers and pay his staff.

Jackson visits Haley's home an hour later, and Jazzie opens the door "Hey, Babe," he says kissing her.

"Hi Babe, come in. We're sitting in the den," Jazzie says as she gives him an embrace.

"Hi Jackson, good to see you again, please have a seat," Haley says as she stands to shake his hand. "We have a lot to cover this evening, but before we get started, would you like something to drink or eat?" She motions for him to settle down. Jackson declines, though he is eager to get going and see what she might be able to do to save him. In addition to playing the police audio, Haley and Jazzie discussed Corey. Jackson, who treated Corey like family, was wounded, enraged, and in shock. Jackson had no idea that he had been envious of his existence all this time, and it hurts, even more, to hear Corey treating Jazzie with contempt.

Haley's strategy was to transfer all of his assets into the name of a trustworthy third party until the accusations against him were dropped. Haley demanded that he address all of Corey's criticisms of him. He did, but he didn't address Corey's comments about Jazzie. Jackson decides to place Tammy's name on everything. Jazzie was upset by this because she knew Tammy was aware of his unlawful activities and encouraged him to engage in them so that she could maintain her opulent lifestyle.

Jazzie frowns as she rests in her chair, becoming angrier at Corey's comments, Tammy receiving benefits without working for them, and Jackson for allowing it to happen. They heard her grabbing her keys as she jumped out of the chair and stormed out of Haley's den. They both followed, asking what was wrong. As a woman, Haley already knows, but a man can be clueless about some things and Jackson is no exception to the rules.

"You guys keep working on this, and I'm heading home to make dinner for my family," Jazzie replied quickly to them both.

"Hayley, I'll give you a call later. Jackson, please contact me later or tomorrow after speaking with your cherished wife." Blocking the front doorway, Haley advises her, "He can't read your thoughts, Jazzie, so you need to tell him how you truly feel," Haley tells her as she blocks the front doorway. I'm heading upstairs to change for a date. When you leave, lock the door using your key. Jackson, I will be in touch soon, good night you two." She hugged Jazzie, waved bye to Jackson, and went upstairs.

"Are you going to tell me what's wrong?" Jackson inquired as he waited for her to begin speaking. "I'm sorry; I realize this is a lot for you to manage."

Jackson wipes her eyes when he notices tears streaming down her cheeks. He implores her, "Talk to me baby." She gives him a startlingly sad expression; one he has never before seen on her face.

"Am I just another sidepiece for you?" she asks. Jackson regrets being the cause of her negative emotions; when she suffers, he suffers.

"Baby, what Corey said was just his opinion. You inspire me to make good decisions and to do better. I've never thought of you as anything but my girl."

Jazzie can tell he is hurt by this when she peers into his eyes. "I know that Corey doesn't care about me, and it doesn't matter. It stings when you don't speak up for me. I'm aware that we are having an affair, but it appears that you and Corey have painted your wife on a pedestal. I'm mindful that you're married, and even though she is reaping the rewards, I don't see her fighting for your innocence. Corey doesn't appeal to me at all, and I don't care for Tammy, she is selfish. I just need some time to process this, she says, adding, "It's okay, I'll be fine."

Jackson beckons her in, saying, "You are all I want—only you. I'm carrying this out for us. Please give me some time; I'll make it better."

Jazzie is conscious of his sincerity but recently becomes aware of how resentful she is becoming of his wife. She makes an effort to alter her perspective because she is not this kind of woman.

She says half-heartedly, "I understand it will be a process, and I'm ok with it." Her safety is assured as he gives her an embrace. They silently departed Haley's home after locking everything up.

CHAPTER 16

Unveiling Shadows

⊱⊰ ♥ ⊱⊰

Jackson was found not guilty of all charges after several months and numerous judicial appearances. The day the court plays the tapes for the jury, revealing his infidelity, Haley advises Jackson that Tammy should not be present in court. The evidence that sealed Corey's fate was the tape in which he acknowledged being the "Head Man" and taking the cash from the undercover agent. Corey kept insisting that Jackson was the main one behind the operation but could not offer any evidence to support it. Jackson let Corey assume the blame for all charges because Corey was trying to discredit him.

"This shit ain't over bro!" Corey shouts to Jackson in court after being given a twenty-year sentence for his third strike. "Your time will come!" Corey is pushed out in shackles by the bailiff. Jackson is grabbed by Haley, who tells him to remain composed because the court is still observing. Jazzie was sitting in the rear of the court, watching Tammy, Jackson, and an unknown man speaking to Haley without Tammy's knowledge.

Despite not having met him, Jazzie thinks it is Elijah because she is aware of Elijah's status as Jackson's other close friend. Elijah, Tammy, and Jackson expressed their gratitude to Haley for a job well done. Jackson caught Jazzie's gaze as she turned to leave while they were talking.

Tammy noticed the direction he was looking and asked, "You ok?"

"Yeah, I'm fine," he answered but did not look away from Jazzie until she turned to leave the courtroom. "I love you so much, baby," Jackson texts Jazzie as soon as he can.

"I love you more," she replies with a smile. Jazzie returns home, resuming her roles as a wife and mother.

It has been a month since Jackson's situation stabilized. He wished to express his gratitude to Jazzie, Haley, and Elijah for their encouragement and support throughout his legal proceedings. They decided to go out to dinner and have fun instead of Jackson paying them. Jackson and Elijah ride together to Haley's house to pick up the ladies. The women looked beautiful in their black cocktail dresses. Since meeting Haley in the courtroom on business, and this meeting planned for pleasure, Elijah was surprised by how different Haley appeared.

Jackson spins Jazzie so he can see how her fitted dress looks from every aspect of her curvy body. She melts in his arms as he enfolds her for an embrace and kiss. Although she was unsure if Elijah knew who she was, she realized he did after witnessing their smooch. They were off to a wonderful evening.

Elijah and Haley got along great and shared several common interests. Knowing that Elijah had heard so much about her impressed Jazzie. She appreciated him as a person and could see why he and Jackson were such good friends as opposed to Corey. They all headed to a rooftop bar in downtown Atlanta after dinner for beverages and jazz music. All night long, they joked around and giggled.

"Do you guys want to take a carriage ride around downtown?" Haley asked.

"That sounds like fun, sure," responds Elijah.

"Jackson and I had other plans," Jazzie says as Jackson grabs her hand.

"Man go handle your business, I can get an Uber for me and Haley back to her house," Elijah confirms.

"Yes, we will be Gucci!," validates Haley.

Jackson and Jazzie desired some private time for themselves. "All right, Jazzie and I will roll out, thanks guys!" Following good night wishes, everyone departed for their locations. To make up for missed time, Jackson and Jazzie experienced what he calls a "Happy Ending," another phase he uses for saying making love.

CHAPTER 17

Romeo & Juliet

❧❧❧❧ ♥ ❀❀❀❀

They made arrangements for a motorcycle trip that was postponed until Jackson's legal issues were resolved. Because Jazzie had never taken a long bike ride and this would be excellent practice, Jackson wanted to go far enough but not too far. They wished to escape society and enter their bubble. In each other's arms, they awakened, liberated to love one another. They did not need to keep their relationship a secret or act as if they were strangers. To spend the weekend, they traveled to Jacksonville, Florida.

Even though neither of them could swim, they still liked to explore the shore and create sandcastles. Jazzie quickly picks up the game after he instructs her how to play dominoes. She kept savagely beating him, and Jackson wished to play something else. The drinking game they were playing was easily won by him. After eating dinner by the river, they strolled and discovered an arts festival.

"Babe, wanna try these cigars?" Jackson looks over at a booth of cigars and asks her.

"At a certain age, making a bucket list is no longer necessary; instead, we should be living our bucket list. We need some drinks to go with it also. Let's do it!"

A Groovy Blue vanilla cigar for her and a Cognac cigar for him were two delectable cigars that Jackson purchased from the vendor. *Wet Your Whistle,* a frozen daiquiri bar was situated alongside the route. He laughed when Jazzie asked for the strongest drink because he knew she could not handle it. They spotted a vendor selling jewelry and diamonds in unique forms as they persisted in their festival exploration.

"What's your ring size?"

"I'm not sure, I haven't bought a ring for myself in years."

"Beyonce's song says, "If you like it put a ring on it." I love it!" He chuckles as he spanks Jazzie on her butt while calling the salesperson's attention to himself.

"Are you serious?" Jazzie inquires in shock, but she already suspected it when he started talking to the salesperson. As they browsed the diamond assortment, Jackson asked the salesperson to measure both of their fingers. Finally, Jackson settles on buying Jazzie, an 18k rose and white gold band with two diamonds in the center, size two carts, and an identical men's ring for him.

"May we have them engraved and ready before we leave here in a few days?" Jackson grills the salesperson.

"Yes sir, but it depends on what you want, I can have it ready in an hour. I'll let you decide, and return in a few minutes," the salesperson tells them.

"Baby, think of something safe for us to wear at home," he instructs Jazzie.

"Our anniversary is on February 19, 2010, and while my name is Jasmine Collins, you refer to me as Mrs. Davenport and yours is Jackson Davenport," she says after giving it some consideration. "I got it!"

It would be about an hour before the rings were ready so Jackson left his cell number for the salesperson to call. Scrolling the festival, Jackson found a spot where they could chill, sip their beverages, and smoke their cigars while watching a tugboat navigate the river. Leaning on the rails in front of the river, Jazzie began to experience dizziness from the up-and-down movement. Momentarily, Jazzie thought her limit with the drink and cigar had been reached.

She calls to Jackson, "Ummmmmm something is wrong. Something is moving us!"

"What the hell are you talking about?" Jackson turns to face her.

"We're moving up-and-down! Why? Jazzie says incoherently, "I think I've had too much to drink, or this cigar is too potent."

"Babe, we are on a dock, the ocean is moving underneath us!" Jackson was laughing so hard that he had to sit on a rock that doubled as a seat. By the time they were done smoking and drinking, the salesperson called to let them know the rings were ready. Struggling to walk because she was buzzed, Jackson assisted Jazzie back to the vendor. They examined the rings and were ecstatic with the results. She assumed he was giving it to her there, but the salesperson secretly suggests Jackson make the occasion memorable.

"Not now." He said when Jazzie reached for her ring. "I want to save it and present it to you on a special occasion."

"Come on Jackson! This is a special occasion!"

"It is; however, I want you to be fully sober."

"You have a valid point!"

They carried on enjoying the evening after Jackson put the rings in his pockets for safekeeping. Later that evening, she felt exhausted and ready to return to the hotel so she could rest her feet. After showering, they both made themselves at home on the bed and searched for a movie on television.

As he strokes Jazzie's legs, he commands, "Slide to the end of the bed." Jackson got on one knee and says, "I love you." He is a kind man, and she adores him wholeheartedly, she smiles and responds, "I love you too baby."

"You have opened my heart and eyes to many new things, all of which I'm happy to experience with you," he adds while taking a small jewelry box from behind his back. He takes her left hand and places the ring on her middle finger but does not put it on all the way. "You were the driving force behind me reclaiming my life. Never once did you ask for anything besides my love. You have my unwavering love, and I'll always protect you." Jackson proceeds to slide the ring all the way onto her finger and declares, "I'm proud and fortunate to have you for my lady. You have my heart. This represents my love for you and the special relationship we have."

Jazzie motions for Jackson to join her on the bed as she gets the other jewelry box off the dresser. "When you asked me to put my faith in you and allow you to love me, I wasn't sure," she says as she takes the ring out of the box and stares into his eyes. "You are my best friend, my universe, and you make me whole. I'm blessed and grateful our paths crossed." She puts the ring on his finger and says while placing one hand over his heart, "I love you more than any actions, any distances, and any words." Jackson and Jazzie inscribed the rings: 2/19/2010 JD Loves JD. It was a symbol of their affection.

On this particular night, unlike the others, they made love to each other's body, spirit, and mind. Jazzie lay on her favored spot, his chest, where she could hear his heartbeat, as he held her close. In their bubble, their world, they nod off to slumber. She was the woman in his life, and he became the man in hers. They were inseparable; when you see him, you see her. They were images of love, vitality, passion, support, and essence.

They were Romeo and Juliet.

CHAPTER 18

White Carnation

❧ 🖤 ☙

The White Carnation's graceful blooms invite us to accept the unpredictable journey that lies ahead by representing growth and endless possibilities. Like this blooming flower, their affair blossomed into a relationship.

Jackson and Jazzie have overcome some obstacles, which strengthened their bond. Jackson created enemies despite ignoring his old routines and acquaintances from the streets. Corey vows to get back at Jackson and sends a threatening letter. It was not until Jackson's shops started to struggle financially that he realized his accountant was stealing money. He then filed criminal charges. Since he needed qualified personnel, Jazzie's desire to help him succeed became her objective. She starts reorganizing his company after getting approval for a personal leave of absence from the law firm.

Jazzie dove in with a vengeance! She began qualifying both existing and new employees by screening, testing, interviewing, and hiring them. The new IT specialist upgraded the equipment and created a new website to make it possible to provide high-quality and efficient vehicle service, among other services. The marketing team she recruits is working on social media pages and advertising. With her business sense, the company not only got back on track but improved. Working together proved convenient.

"Jazzie, I have to go get some equipment. I'll grab us some lunch while I'm out. Anything you might like?"

"We should eat salads because we had a large breakfast. I'm still stuffed after my seafood omelet, grits, biscuit, and juice, and it went to my hips."

"I'll keep an eye on your hips and that ass!" Jackson comments as he enfolds her in an embrace.

"Stop it, Mr. Nasty! The employees can see us and we have work to do!"

"Come into my office, then shut the door."

"When the work is done, maybe I'll sleep with the boss!"

"Okay, Mrs. Davenport, how about later?"

"Absolutely!" Jazzie giggles.

Every day they shared breakfast and lunch. On some days, he would pick up breakfast for them while she prepared lunch the previous evening at home using new recipes for him to try. Their new set of friends was acquainted with them and aware of their close relationship. Although Tammy never visits any of the shops, she knows that Jackson has a new female manager working with him. The business is doing well which is the focus for Tammy so she can enjoy her lavish lifestyle. Aiden neglected to ask about Jazzie's job, whereabouts, or projects since he was too busy traveling from state to state on business. He is unaware that she is working with Jackson in his shops.

On the day of filming the second commercial, Jazzie prepared lunch for her and Jackson to eat in his office before things got hectic. The previous night she tried a recipe to get his opinion, chicken mushroom sage casserole, Asian purple cabbage slaw, homemade dinner rolls with butter and herbs, and homemade cherry limeade. For dessert, a serving of Jazzie. While they conversed about converting from sport motorcycles to cruisers, Pandora was playing Paul Hardcastle. Jackson ignores the ring on his phone and assumes Tammy is calling. When his phone rings a second time, Jazzie becomes irate and sarcastically exclaims, "Answer it so she will stop interrupting my time!"

Jackson answers and says, "It's your sister, smart ass," before handing her his phone.

"Hi Vivian, what's going on?"

"I called your number multiple times, but you never picked up. I called Jackson because I assumed you were with him. Have you heard from Daddy today?"

"He normally calls me in the mornings, but I believed he was out in the yard today, so not yet." To check her missed calls, Jazzie asked Jackson to get her cell phone from her office on the desk.

"He hasn't texted or called me, Vivian. Mom is with her church group at a Swap Meet. That's odd. Maybe he left the phone in the house." Every day, Jazzie and Vivian called their parents to talk. Jazzie served as the main point of contact for Jackson, and the camera crew was on its way to set up to film in a little while. Jackson decided to leave it in her hands because she was more knowledgeable about commercials.

"Babe, would you like for me to go by your parents' house to perform a wellness check?" Jackson volunteers.

"Can you please? He may be outside planting."

"You know I don't mind. When I get there, I will call you."

"Here, take the house keys just in case he doesn't come to the door."

Jackson was friendly with her parents. He has made a few repairs around the house, maintained their vehicles, and taken her father to sporting events and fishing trips. Jackson kisses Jazzie and exits the store while hoping all is well. He calls Tammy while on the road.

"Hey, you have to pick up the twins from practice today."

"Jackson, what's the issue now? It's your turn."

"My office manager had to leave for an emergency. I must stay onsite until she gets back, or the crew is done filming the commercial."

"Sure, she does! I'll pick them up but thanks anyway. Should I save you dinner or will you be eating elsewhere again?"

"No, someone from the film crew will bring us dinner. I'll text you later."

Jackson observes the dogs sitting in the extensive driveway as he approaches the home. The pets are never left unattended by Mr. Williams. Then Jackson spotted Mr. Williams on the ground, he was unconscious and lying near his riding lawnmower. Jackson rushes over from his truck and dials 911 while flipping Mr. William over. Jackson started CPR and continued it until the ambulance arrived a short while later. After the paramedics took over, he called Jazzie at work to inform her and secured the dogs.

"Which hospital are they taking him to?" Jazzie asks frantically.

"You have to calm down, they are taking him to Gwinnett Medical Hospital but I'll be there to pick you up so you won't have to drive, you're hysterical!"

"No Jackson, please go with him so he won't be alone and find out what is going on. I promise to calm down."

While driving to the hospital she phones Aiden but he is still in meetings out of town, so she leaves a message for him to call. Jazzie pulls into the first "Physician Parking Only" space that is open parks and dashes into the emergency department. The lobby was cold as if it was the North Pole and sick patients waiting to be called for the golden ticket. Together with her mother and Vivian, Jazzie spots Jackson and rushes toward them. Dr. Lester announces, "Williams Family?" as he enters the waiting room. Jackson, Vivian, and Jazzie stood right away, but her mother remained seated while preparing for what the doctor may say.

"We're the Williams. How is our father doing?" Jazzie questioned with quivering words.

"Your father had a heart attack. I'm not sure who performed CPR before the paramedics arrived, but they undoubtedly saved his life! He'll spend a few days in the ICU. We'll monitor him carefully and run additional tests. Once he's released, he'll require extensive rehabilitation. With a lot of effort and self-care, he will recover well."

Jazzie collapsed into Jackson's arms in relief and expressed her gratitude to him for saving their father. "Brother-in-law, I owe you a sizable steak dinner and drinks," Vivian teased. "Will you lend me some money so I can treat you?" Everyone chuckled.

Jazzie's life was crowded with nonstop activities over the next several months. She continued working at Jackson's stores while taking care of her family, managing her father's financial affairs during his stay in rehab, and volunteering at the Homeless Shelter. She was busy and worn out. Jackson knew she needed a vacation. "Jazzie, can you get away next weekend?" Jazzie debated whether she wanted to go away. She was concerned that circumstances could get worse with her father. "We will be close by in case anything goes wrong. Jazzie, right now Mr. Williams is doing better than you."

The following weekend, Tammy and the twins were supposed to fly back to Dallas to attend a relative's wedding. Jazzie needed to drop off some of their father's belongings to Vivian, so Jackson picked her up from there. He informs her the plan is for them to spend the weekend at his house in the guest room to keep her close by in case she is needed. "If this is too weird or uncomfortable being here, we can check into a hotel room." Jazzie agreed to try it.

She was loved, cared for, and given a life hook. Jackson cooked dinners for them and even showed off his BBQ skills followed by him running a bubble bath and bathing her. He stroked her hair while she dozed off on his lap. Jackson offered to take her out to dinner, but she chose to stay in his company, resting in his arms and watching television. Instead of being so tough, she could let it all out and she did. Her body trembled as she wept and Jackson gently wiped her tears. His comfort infused her with the courage and strength needed to process her current experiences.

Jackson's fortitude came from Jazzie. A couple of months later, while at work, he discovered that his urine contained blood. "Look at this Babe!" Jackson says while handing her a water bottle filled with a pink liquid.

"Oh yes, let me try it, you made an alcohol drink last night?"

"Don't drink that! It's my urine."

"What? Baby that's blood! Are you in pain?" she was horrified.

"No pain." Jazzie gathers her things without saying a word to Jackson which leaves him confused.

"You leaving?"

"No, we are leaving. I will call a doctor while we are driving."

Jazzie immediately found a doctor who saw him right away. It turned out that Jackson had bladder stones. If Jazzie had not insisted on him seeking medical attention right away, he would have gotten worse and would have been in pain. They talked about having their own "Love Nest" and looked at locations that were nearby but sufficiently apart from their homes. Jackson's business was doing well in Atlanta, and he opened two more locations in Georgia's Roswell and Savannah areas. Since things were better for him, Jazzie returned to work and found a few locations for their "Love Nest."

"Jackson, did you get a chance to review the places I saw for us?"

"I didn't because Tammy wants us to build a new house."

"Let me guess, we won't have our place and I don't get my shoe case either. Congratulations, you let her have her way again."

Jackson located some land near Jazzie so he could remain close to her and built Tammy's dream home. Jazzie was dissatisfied because her vision of their hide-away would now have to wait, if at all, but she dealt with it. When his mother passed away, she was encouraging and prayed for him and his family. Jackson now becomes his father's caretaker and moves him in. Ultimately his father returned to Dallas to live with his brother because of being homesick.

Jackson observed Jazzie's kids growing up over the past six years. After several tutors, Genesis gets accepted into college. Brandon learns how to drive and will receive a car on his sixteenth birthday. "Brandon's birthday is soon, and I want to get him a car but a used one since he is a new driver. What cars do you have at the shop to fit what I need?"

"I have the perfect car; it would be a project because it's not upgraded."

"About how much with the upgrades and other things cost?"

"Nothing if his mother repays in other ways," Jackson says flirting with her.

"Sounds like a wonderful deal, let's shake on it."

"Okay, turn around and shake for me!"

Jackson completed every upgrade in the shop. The most recent technology including a Bluetooth radio and hands-free phone service was installed by him. Brandon's preferred color, green, was chosen for the vehicle by Jackson's friend at the body shop. He also tinted the windows and added chrome wheels. Jackson is known to Genesis and Brandon as their mother's college buddy, but Brandon has grown closer to him. Despite attending the same university as her, Aiden did not get to know all of her acquaintances. Jackson was proud of his other family; he saw how joyful he had made Jazzie and Brandon with the car.

Jazzie observes Jackson's young twin daughters as they mature, they are almost thirteen years old. The twins had a full schedule and participated in every activity that helped them gain societal recognition. The twins and Tammy were aware of Jazzie as someone who works for Jackson. In just six years, they were able to weather the raging storm of life, but storms come and go.

Jackson and Jazzie began engaging in more marital-style behavior. Jazzie enjoys baking and cooking and has a goal of opening a bakery someday. Jackson encourages her to sell baked goods in his shops. Together they attend numerous activities. Visiting New Orleans was on her list.

CHAPTER 19

International Waters

❦

Jazzie has always wanted to visit New Orleans for five reasons: culture, food, libations, fun, and Big Freedia. Visiting this city is like stepping into another country. The people are happy, and welcoming to all. They embrace their diversity and celebrate it regularly, always ready to party! If you're lucky, you might catch a glimpse of a second line, which is a parade typically held to honor a marriage or a funeral. Food is so important to New Orleans's culture, it shows history, soul, and love. Some of the choices include red beans and rice, gumbo, beignets, alligators, oysters, and more. Deciding on which restaurant to try is the most difficult.

One of the few cities where alcohol is offered continuously is New Orleans, which is renowned for its vibrant bar scene. Drinking on the street is allowed granted the drink is in a plastic to-go cup. A few favorites on Jazzie's list to try is the hurricane and hand grenade.

You will find fun everywhere, from the jazz-filled nightlife to the kid-friendly activities, girls' or guys' weekends, and getaways with your significant other. The performer Big Freedia is well-known for her work in the hip-hop style known as bounce music from New Orleans.

Big Freedia was an inspiration to Jazzie since she never cared what other people thought of her and always acted fiercely. Jackson and Jazzie checked into the hotel following their arrival in the city and then went exploring. After five hours of sightseeing, bar-hopping, shopping, and looking for Big Freedia, Jackson was exhausted.

"Jazzie, we have walked this entire city and no sighting of Big Freedia. My feet are hurting and worn out."

"Okay, let's get some Popeye's Chicken to take back to the room and I will massage your feet."

"I'm not a fashion guy but why do you have on two different shoes?" Jazzie's only pair of walking tennis shoes were different from one another, but she was so enthused about the trip that she did not notice. On the way back to their hotel, Jazzie admired a body necklace she saw on display at the jewelry shop on Canal Street. Jackson spotted it as well and sneaked out to get it for her while she was in the shower.

After getting out of the shower, he instructs her to turn around and pulls her hair up. Because Jazzie believed he was going to apply moisturizer to her back, she did. When he put the necklace on her, she was rendered silent. Before she could ask anything, he says, "We are one baby. I feel your heart and thoughts, you don't have to say a word." They made out so noisily that night that when they left the room the next day, they noticed gawks from guests in the neighboring rooms.

They had such a great time in New Orleans that they returned a second time with their best friends, Elijah and Haley, who were now dating. They attended a football game, explored the nightlife, and attended a dinner cruise, and an art festival, still no sighting of Big Freedia, maybe next time they told Jazzie. They rode motorcycles on excursions to different Florida cities, Tennessee, Daytona Bike Week, and other Georgia cities. Jackson organized a bike trip to St. Peter's Island knowing how much she loves the ocean and the outdoors. The Gulf of Mexico surrounds this stunning, tranquil sanctuary that is located close to Tallahassee, Florida.

Jackson and Jazzie had fun interacting with one another and learning about the island's inhabitants. She took him to Ruby Falls over the weekend for his birthday. They spent the weekend in St. Augustine celebrating another one of Jackson's birthdays, touring the alligator farm and dining at the renowned Harry's Seafood Restaurant. They continued traveling even though Jazzie fractured her leg when a motorcycle collapsed on her.

Jackson loaded her up on the back of his cruiser with the crutches, and they rode to Savannah. In addition to numerous other activities, they held picnics by the lake, events at the Civic Center, and performances in the park. On the beach in Barbados, one of their friends was getting married. Jazzie wished to attend with Jackson, but Tammy would find it difficult to understand where he was going. After work, they went out for tacos, and Jackson noticed she seemed preoccupied.

"You doing okay, Babe?"

"Yes, I'm all right."

"I know when something is weighing on your thoughts and bothering you. What is it?"

"Richard and LaToya are getting married and I wanted us to attend," she says after letting down her guard.

"Okay, let me know when so I can make time to come."

"It's in Barbados, not here in Atlanta, we will need a passport."

"Are you sure you want to go?"

Yes, Jazzie admitted, "I really do."

Jackson, who takes pleasure in seeing her smile, said, "Okay, let's do it, we can go. Arrange it and let me know the cost. We need to make an appointment for our passports."

Jazzie was so ecstatic that she leaped up from her seat, raced over to his side of the booth, and gave him a passionate kiss and embrace. Jackson wished to go, but he was unsure of how he would manage Tammy. Nevertheless, he managed.

Jackson and Jazzie were thrilled because this was their first time traveling abroad and flying together. Jackson wished to cover the cost of their trip on his own, but Jazzie insisted they both pay. After receiving their passports, they went shopping to purchase shoes and coordinated bridal attire for the wedding. The journey began inside the airport with a sit-down breakfast and alcoholic beverages at one of the eateries. It was confirmed when they got on the aircraft that they were adding another memory to their collection. Once the plane touched down, they went through customs to get permission to enter the country. A wave of heat struck their faces as they made their way outside to get a taxi. In Barbados, it was scorching hot, and there were lots of peddlers attempting to sell all kinds of things. It was freedom to be Mr. and Mrs. Davenport and they donned their rings as wedding bands.

When they arrived at the resort, the staff welcomed them and provided mimosa and refreshing cold face cloths to cool off. An escort led them to their room after checking in. An inviting floral fragrance greeted them as they walked inside. Jackson handed the bellhop who assisted them with their luggage a tip while Jazzie surveyed the marvelous view from the sitting area. The king-size bed is heart-shaped with plush pillows. When booking the room, a pillow type had to be specified along with a preferred time for evening turn-down service.

Rose petals and puppy-fashioned bath towels were positioned on the bed. As soon as Jazzie enters the restroom, she notices the two-person bathtub with the waterfall and candle-like lighting in the background. A sizable flat-screen Television and Bluetooth speakers are mounted on the wall. White marble is used to construct the Jack and Jill basin, walls, and floor. A massive white marble shower with two separate shower heads and a long white marble bench is visible when she opens a stained glass. When she unlocks a different door, it leads to a white marble-themed room with a mountain view, a phone mounted on the wall, and a flat-screen television facing the toilet with a button to wash between your legs after using it.

Jackson follows her around the room, and when they step onto the balcony, they're both in awe of the vista. A view of the mountains and a blue sky with swirling white clouds could be seen on the corner's left side. They had a glimpse of the ocean in front of them and a private infinity pool to their right. The lounge bed, two plush seats, and a table are separated from the pool by a gate. They had a regal atmosphere. Impatient to try the amenities, they stripped and descended the steps into the pool. The water was a cool treat in the intense heat, and the wind was pleasant. After horseplaying in the water, Jackson was feeling adventurous.

"How long do you think I can hold my breath underneath the water?"

"You can't swim, so not long!"

"I could hold it long enough to make you have an orgasm."

"What? Now you are just being silly." Jackson inhaled deeply before diving beneath the surface and spreading her legs out so his tongue could raid her pink castle. Jazzie was initially worried because he could not swim, but Jackson insisted on going until he achieved his goal. They made love in the pool and on the balcony before they saw anything else on the resort. Pre-selected beer, soda, tea, wine, and premium liquor were all present in the refrigerator. Jackson advises Jazzie to take it easy on the alcohol since it is limitless. Jackson does initially, but by that evening, he has forgotten himself.

Following dinner, Jackson and Jazzie joined their friends at the resort's nightclub for dancing and drinks. He assures Jazzie he will return after getting some much-needed fresh air following several shots too many. A few hours later, everyone leaves the club because it is closing time and proceeds to their rooms. Jazzie waits for Jackson to return, but is getting drowsy and weary. Since he had their room key, she phoned for help to enter the room. She was concerned because he would never leave her alone in this situation and it had been four hours.

Jazzie still had not heard from him and only received his voicemail when she called. To inquire about any incidents, she dials the security office and provides Jackson's description.

"Mrs. Davenport, I'm confident he's okay. We frequently observe this in visitors who have consumed too many intoxicating beverages."

"There is a problem! He wouldn't ever leave me alone or remain silent. He hasn't contacted me, and his phone goes directly to voicemail. You are wasting time!" she pleads to the officer on patrol.

"Remain in your room in case he returns, and if we come across anyone who fits Mr. Davenport's description, we will contact you." By this point, Jazzie was agitated and her thoughts were bombarded with negative potential outcomes. She went looking for him herself rather than waiting as the officer had instructed. Frantically she circled the sizable resort three times as night fell, but Jackson had not appeared. Replaying the night's events searching for hints; feeling defeated, she dragged herself back to their room.

Puzzled by how he vanished without a trace, she paced. Another hour passed when she heard the door open and Jackson entered. Relieved, she rushes to examine him for injuries. Jackson explained he overindulged in alcohol and passed out inside one of the beachside cabanas when feeling the ocean air comforting him. Jazzie felt a mixture of joy, fury, and gratitude. She let the Security Office know that he returned safely. Jackson was never a concern for them, but he was for her. After hanging up, she sobbed and Jackson felt awful.

"I'm so sorry baby!" he says embracing and kissing her.

"I looked all over for you. I thought something terrible happened, maybe the Gorillas had taken you!"

"Look at me baby, I'm okay. Please don't cry!"

Jackson comforts her by holding her close while wiping her tears. Before they traveled to Barbados, he taunted her regarding rumors that the Gorilla Gang abducted Americans and subjected them to heinous acts. Jazzie unexpectedly gives him a vigorous kiss without giving him a chance to breathe. He reacts by making an effort to take off her shorts until she intervenes. Forcing him to lie on the bed, she undresses him, then herself. Jazzie planned to lash out at him with her unresolved rage.

She ascends onto him, pinning him with her hands, and kissing him until he is unable to bear it any longer. Jackson calls her name loudly. She put her hands around his neck and squeezed, pushing her universe harder and faster into his. She bounces up and down, as if on a trampoline, before flooding him. He held onto his favorite spot on her hips and plunges into her ocean. His desire to swim deeper overcame him. Giving him more, she slammed her hips onto him while screaming. Jackson's toes curled and he let go of his troops to signify victory.

"I love you so much," she murmurs with one of his hands that she placed over her heart, then collapses on top of him. Jackson observed they appeared closer to the balcony entrance. "Babe, I think our bed has wheels," he says, almost gasping for air. The bed was now on the other half of the room as they looked around. Jackson quips, "I need to make you angry more often, damn!" and they burst out laughing. He kisses her forehead while she is lying on his chest, he places one of her hands over his heart and says, "I love you more Babe." They doze off. The next day they hung out with their friends, riding ATVs on the safari, horseback riding on the beach, and speeding on Sea-doos in the ocean. Later that night as the majority of the guests were tucked in bed, Jackson made a fantasy she had come true. Jackson took her to where he had blacked out the night before. She could see why he drifted into such peaceful slumber. They viewed several cabanas along the shoreline from the blanket of stars that extends into the distance and is joined by the moonlight.

To get ready for the next day, the staff changes the bedding and closes the curtains in every cabana each night. Jackson locates the prior night's familiar cabana, and they go inside. After a long day of excursions, they collapsed onto the bed with their beverages on the nightstand. The grumbling of the waves crashing into the rocks was hypnotic. The breeze is enough to toss her hair as roughly as the ocean engulfs the shoreline. Jazzie is the focus of his attention as he lights a cigar they share. Jackson is in love with her and not just because she is beautiful. Her thongs are exposed thanks to her dress dancing with the breeze. Jackson passes her the cigar to smoke, then slips her dress up before taking off her underwear.

He commands her to continue smoking the cigar while he turns her over onto her knees, taking her from behind. Although Jazzie makes an effort to puff, her attention quickly shifts to Jackson and puts the cigar aside. Switching positions, he flips her onto her back, spreads her thighs apart, and then leads himself to her gateway. Jazzie never imagined this dream would ever come true in a million years, but they made love on the beach by the ocean. After that, they reclined there and fell asleep—together, just as he had the previous night.

On the shore at dusk the next day, their friends' intimate wedding took place. Jackson, the sole groomsman, posed next to the best man while wearing white linen pants set. Following the ceremony, the bridal party and guests made their way to the reception hall, which was located in a sizable, air-conditioned structure on the resort. As a member of the bridal party, Jackson sat at a large table with them.

Before the dinner plates came, Jazzie sat down with the other guests and placed her drink order. Sitting next to her, an elderly woman strikes up a conversation to get to know one another. Jazzie notices Jackson's gleaming eyes as he shines them in her direction frequently. "I think you have an admirer," the older lady says.

"I do? Who are you referring to?"

"Look at the handsome groomsman at the bridal party table. He's been looking at you ever since we arrived; too bad you're married." The elderly woman sees her wedding band, which, unbeknownst to her, is the ring Jackson placed on Jazzie's finger.

Blushing Jazzie responds, "Yes I am, to the groomsman."

"My, my, my, that's a blessing. His smile and the sparkle in his eyes tell me how much he loves you. My husband had that same sparkle even after fifty-two years of marriage. God rest his soul."

"I'm sorry he has departed. Fifty-two years is fantastic! What's your key to having a long-lasting marriage?"

"Sweetie, when you put God in whatever you do first, everything else will follow. My husband was my best friend, and I haven't seen a sparkle like that since he passed until now. He loves you wholeheartedly."

"He does love me, and I love him. I can't imagine life without him."

On their tenth anniversary of dating, a few years later, Jackson, Jazzie, Haley, and Elijah all returned to the same resort. They did not need any official documents to declare that Jackson was her husband and Jazzie was his wife; their connection said it all. They were each other's blessings and addicted to one another. Although no one could possibly comprehend their relationship, Jackson and Jazzie are content with it and enjoy every second.

CHAPTER 20

Journey through Uncertainty

⊰⊰⊰❤︎⊱⊱⊱

2020 arrived with more ferocity and destruction than Hurricane Katrina! When the pandemic started, Jackson and Jazzie were at Bike Week in Daytona Beach. The coronavirus was killing people and it made no distinctions. Several events were canceled, and the city's vendors were forced to depart. As other motorcycle riders fled, Jackson thought they should leave and go home. Jazzie was not ready to go, the hotel accommodation had been paid for, and no refunds.

They were unaware that these unusual events were marking the start of a "New Norm." Businesses, including bars, restaurants, grocery shops, and schools, experienced sudden closures. Visitors wishing to see their hospitalized loved ones were turned away. Worldwide, a growing number of people were dying daily. They were supposed to attend a concert, but they decided against attending because of the pandemic. An airborne virus called COVID-19 was spreading rapidly. People were becoming fearful and some starting to wear masks when venturing into public places. Jazzie was able to cancel and received complete reimbursement from Ticketmaster. Things were rapidly changing leaving everyone wondering when their lives would revert to normal.

When your existence alters to become something new, you must alter to become something new as well. "Social Distancing" was the new phrase frequently used to indicate that people should stand six feet apart. It described a new way of life. The pandemic stopped them from seeing each other as frequently as they were accustomed to.

Amber, Jazzie's friend, traveled frequently for business. Jazzie stops by the home to water the plants and check the mail twice a week. Jackson would meet her there so they could spend time together. Amber hasn't left home since the outbreak and has been working from home. Hotels were not receiving many, if any, customers because they were afraid of dying, so Jackson and Jazzie stopped going.

Their preferred hangout sports bar was briefly closed, preventing them from enjoying a satisfying burger and beer. There can be no picnic because the parks have been shut down temporarily. They might have had breakfast or lunch together every day on the phone while at work, but he was currently too occupied. As business declined, Jackson was forced to lay off some employees because there was a sudden decline in driving for a huge number of people. Jackson performed several positions at once to remain in business.

Jackson drops by her workplace occasionally on his way to work. He delivers French vanilla coffee or cappuccino and sometimes includes a sausage roll or breakfast sandwich. Some days, she prepares their lunch or places an order for it so they can eat together at his workplace or a nearby park. Jazzie's supervisor has everyone work remotely for the time being until further notice.

Jackson thought, "I must feel her; otherwise, my world will be different. Those around me will not like who I am without her." Without her dose of him, Jazzie struggles to concentrate, sleeps, and becomes easily agitated. Jazzie is sad because they have a schedule and things are currently different. Seeing him daily is a special moment, but now that things have changed, she finds it upsetting. Jackson reassured her that nothing would alter their connection, that they would always be there for each other, and everything would turn out alright.

Students have been attending classes online from home since the COVID outbreak. Jackson and Tammy alternate days helping the twins because the parents have taken on the role of teachers. Jackson wanted to surprise Jazzie with a quick escape, he missed her. He texted, "Will I see you today?"

"I'm not positive, maybe."

"I would like to see you today after work if you're free."

"Nope, no plans," she responds with a smile.

"Bring the grill and meet me at the Brookhaven Publix."

"Grill? Everything is closed, where are we going?"

"You always have questions. Trust me, it will be worth coming."

Jazzie purchased a propane grill for him to teach her to use last year, but they never got around to it. She appreciates Jackson's grilling skills, particularly the andouille link sausage. Working from home has been convenient. While still on the clock, Jazzie unpacks the grill, gathers some cookware, and gets dressed. She logs off her work computer at four o'clock and grabs the things as she dashes out the door. Jackson enters Publix to shop for a few things while he waits for her to show up: sausages, bread, chips, beer, wine coolers, and mustard. He notices Jazzie parked next to him as he makes his way back to the truck.

Jazzie was beaming from ear to ear as they hugged. When the truck was loaded, they climbed inside Jackson's truck and he drove away. Up until they reached Gwinnett College, the path they were taking was familiar. Jazzie was once more perplexed but held back on her inquiries. Approaching a security guard stationed at the gate entrance, Jackson waves as if they knew each other, and then they enter. He circled the campus in his car until he arrived at a remote lake with a park, swings, and a picnic spot.

"We're here!"

Jazzie's eyes were soaked in the scenery. The lake was surrounded by all kinds of trees: sugar maple tree, camphor tree, etc. At the center of the lake, there was a small island with a few huge trunks lying down and large boulders. On the trunks, there were some ducks as if they were having a sunbath party at the beach. Hovering above the lake were a few birds in the blue sky with fluffy clouds. The sound of chirping spread and penetrated quickly through the air, leaving the impression of both tranquility and delightfulness. It was serene, lovely, and quiet—all the qualities Jackson was looking for in a private getaway.

"I don't understand. Why are we at a college?"

"The majority of everything is temporarily shut down, including the schools. The security guard is a long-time customer, and he is letting us use this area. We are the only ones here, so we are free to do as we want. I realize it has been over a year since I promised to give you a lesson on how to use a propane grill, but today I keep my promise." There were a few benches and picnic tables close by. They set up grilling under the shade of a big willow tree to escape the burning sun rays. Jazzie switches on the Bluetooth speakers to blast jazz music and sets the table as Jackson assembles the grill.

She makes a mental notation of how to use the grill's controls for later use once Jackson begins. Jackson lets her take over cooking to get her accustomed to the procedure. He shows her how to switch off the propane and clean the line leading to the grill after the food has been cooked. "The sausages are delicious!" Jazzie says while snapping a photo of the package so she can buy them again.

The refreshing summer breeze blew softly, braising their arms, face, and neck. They engaged in conversation, laughter, drinking, eating, playing Uno, and racing each other on an adjacent swing. Time together was the antidote they needed to feel normal again. Jackson ignores his cell phone despite its continual on-and-off ringing. "Apparently someone needs you since they keep calling," Jazzie expresses.

"I don't know the number so it must be about work. I'm off and this is our time."

"It could be important. If it's not, you can tell the caller you will call them back later. You need to answer it."

"Jackson speaking," he says answering the next ring. "Say what? Man, who the fuck is this? How did you get my number? Bro, you know where I am, I will be waiting on your bitch ass!" Jackson hangs up abruptly.

"Are you okay, is something wrong?"

Gathering up all of their things, he packs up the extra food he cooks so Jazzie will have something to eat for lunch for the rest of the week. Jackson quickly replies to her and scans around the park, "Yeah, I'm all good, nothing is wrong. It's getting late and we need to leave." Jazzie is aware that something is off, but he will not say what, and she does not want to press the issue.

"Thank you so much for doing this for us," she says and hugs him.

"I told you I was going to keep my promise. It took a year, but I did," they both chuckled and prepared to leave.

Later that night Jackson texts her, "You busy Babe?"

"Hey you! I was thinking about you, I'm not busy, what's up?"

"Do you know how to shoot a gun?"

Jazzie wonders does this has anything to do with that phone call he received at the park earlier, but she tells him, "No, I don't."

"Do you have something planned for tomorrow when you get off?"

"No Sir, nothing yet, why?"

"Tomorrow we are going to get you a gun and go to the gun range so I can give you a lesson."

"I don't need a gun."

"You need one, these clowns out here in this world are on some crazy shit."

"Okay, if you think I do," she responds.

"I do Babe, I just want you safe and to know how to protect yourself."

"You're spoiling me."

"I can stop if you want."

Jackson was being funny, but she told him to not stop. Feeling blessed to have him in her life, she falls asleep in a peaceful place that only he could take her to.

"Good Morning Everyone!" Jazzie says spritely when logging onto Zoom for an office meeting. Unable to wait for lunch, she heated a sausage for breakfast and was ready to start her workday. Jackson and she flirted all day, but she couldn't get rid of the impression that he was keeping something from her. They met at the gun store after she got off work. Jackson bought him a Smith & Wesson .40 and her a 9mm after testing out several firearms. She practiced using it during their time at the gun range.

Jazzie continued to feel uncomfortable and questioned Jackson about what was going on. He only said, "I want you to be safe." He asked her to give him time without offering her a clear response. Whatever it was, Jackson was shaken and paranoid. After leaving the range, she was hoping for a Happy Ending, but it is obvious that Jackson is thinking about something else.

CHAPTER 21

Threats and Turmoil

꧁ ♥ ꧂

Jackson receives a hysterical call from Tammy while he is at work. She discovered a dead rat and a message that read, "You are next Bro," in their mailbox. He calls Elijah to ask him to go to his house because he lives close by and has the day off. Jackson calls Jazzie while driving home. He makes small talk but secretly wants to know if Jazzie and her family are safe without alarming her. The kids were taking classes online in their rooms while she was doing fine and working from home.

Jackson sighs in relief. Elijah pulled him aside when he got home. "Man, what the hell is going on?" Jackson rubs his temples and informs him of the threatening phone messages he has been receiving that refer to him as a dead rat.

"Where are the girls?" Jackson questioned franticly. Elijah advises him to calm down because they were completing coursework online and did not know about the incident. Jackson made sure Tammy had a pistol because she was familiar with how to use them. Jackson composed himself before deciding how to proceed. Elijah made a few contacts and arranged for modern cameras to be placed all around Jackson's residence and all of his businesses.

Corey is behind the threats, Jackson speculates. He contacts a few people and learns that Corey is still behind bars. He has someone checking into who might be threatening him, but it will take a few weeks before they have any results. Once he and Elijah secure his home, Jackson asks him to not mention this to Haley until he can find out who is behind this, she will tell Jazzie. Elijah agreed since they had no answers yet. When Elijah left, Jackson had a glass of Crown Royal and ice to relax his mind. He wanted to see Jazzie, but he did not want to leave his family until he knew they all were safe. Until he could find out where the threats were coming from, Jackson needed extra protection.

Since Amber would be at her boyfriend's home, Jazzie wanted to see Jackson for a quickie there because she could not stop thinking about him at work. She confirmed that he would be available after work, and they made arrangements to meet at Amber's place to fulfill their craving for one another that evening. By the time she logged off her work computer, Aiden had already begun cleaning the carpet. The house requires thorough cleaning because they are hosting her grandfather's 90th birthday celebration at their house on July 4th. Jazzie helped clean the flooring after which she took a bath and dressed so she would be ready when Jackson texted. Brandon is eating pizza and watching a horror movie when she joins him on the sofa and grabs a slice.

Jackson ate dinner while working on a project in the mancave until the twins returned from school to prepare for the college admission exam. He reached for his cell phone to check when he heard the alarm system signaling that someone had entered the home. "Hey Daddy, I'm home!" Tia screams at him.

"Okay, your mom left you girls dinner in the oven. Where is Mia?" he screams back.

Tia sprints downstairs to the mancave to see him and says, "We were finished with the test prep at 5 p.m. When we left, I went by my job to pick up my paycheck and she was coming home. She was going to start on the practice workbook and apply ointment to the heat rash on her face from wearing her face mask for so long. She should have beat me home."

The clock struck 7 p.m., and Jackson glanced at his smart watch, only to find a haunting absence of any messages or missed calls. Concerned, he dialed her number, but his heart sank as the call went unanswered. While he drove Mia's car to his shop earlier to have one of his staff rotate her tires and perform an oil change, Mia was using Jackson's vehicle. Just as he was about to embark on tracing his vehicle, the phone rang. Mia's tearful voice echoed through the phone with a sorrowful tone.

"Daddy, someone ran me off the road into a ditch! He was driving a dark red Mustang and on the front license plate was written: I am my Brother's Keeper." She continued speaking with a trembling voice. "The police are here!" Jackson hurried to the accident site after learning that she was unharmed. When Jackson arrived the police were taking Mia's statement while she sat in the ambulance.

"I'm sorry about your car Daddy. The man driving the dark red Mustang kept pushing me into the ditch and blocked me from passing him." Mia said sniffling. She was frightened and eager to return home.

"I can replace that vehicle, but I can't replace you, sweetheart," Jackson says and hugs her.

Jackson had the tow truck driver, whom he knew, take his vehicle to his body shop. Mia was released back to him after the paramedics were done treating her cuts on the scene. He drives her home while holding her near to him.

Jazzie was baffled as to what was taking Jackson so long, but she has since learned that he had a mishap.

After putting Mia to bed he texts her a picture of his totaled car at about 10 p.m.

"Are you all right?"

"Mia drove my car to school today and someone ran her off the road,"

"Oh, my goodness, how is she doing?"

"She's fine but shaken up."

"Take care of your baby. I truly understand and we can talk tomorrow."

"Thanks, Babe, for understanding."

"Of course, I also have teen drivers, and I worry daily about them operating the vehicle or riding with friends. Try getting some rest yourself, good night."

"Good night, Jazzie; I'll hold you soon."

CHAPTER 22

Five Times is a Charm

J azzie awakes with concern for Mia and how she is knowing. From her own experience, she knew that the day after a car accident you typically feel sore. Jazzie texted Jackson saying, "Good morning baby, check Mia to see if she is sore."

"I will. Good morning, I'm just waking up." Jackson stayed up late on the phone with Miller, a childhood buddy who is back home in Dallas. They chatted and drank while catching up on recent events. Jackson intended to spend a week at his parent's house in Dallas working on carpentry projects, mowing their large yard, and organizing his father's shed of old items. Miller invites Jackson to accompany him on a guys' weekend getaway to Oklahoma for the birthday of one of their friends.

Since he is fully staffed at all of the Crown Performance Centers, this was the ideal moment. Businesses were reopening, and some school activities were taking place with everyone wearing masks. The growing number of Coronavirus cases in Texas and his separation from Pinky are what worries him. Pinky is what he refers to as Jazzie's hot receptacle. Being apart from her for so long was going to be difficult for him, and Jackson required his favorite toy. They had time to work that out, but Jazzie hoped he would feed her well before he left to go out of town. They still have an itch from yesterday that needs to be scratched right now. No matter what hour it was, she was going to him as soon as it was safe to do so.

"I want my Pinky!" he texts.

"I want my joystick baby. I'll take care of you when I get there, I promise."

"Should I release myself?" Jackson asked.

"Noooooooooo!" Earlier, she sent him a pornographic video, but he warned her against masturbating, and now she did the same.

"If I wait, I might release too quickly."

It would take the edge off, so go ahead." Jazzy relented.

"Then you have to make me release twice."

"Okay, I'm confident I can!" She likes to challenge him because he never backs down.

"Babe, what are you going to do to your joystick?"

"Take my time, make love to it, and whatever else I want."

"Shiiiiiii........... show me!"

"Which room are you taking me to?"

"I don't care, whichever you want!" he responds anxiously.

Putting him to the test she answers, "You already know where I want you to make love to me."

"Which room, you like doing it everywhere!" he exclaims with a smile.

This is particularly accurate because he sets her ablaze and she is powerless. Jazzie appreciates the flirtatious foreplay they are engaging in. This will make them both more passionate, and Jackson will dare her so he can have bragging rights when she taps out. Jackson will soon be having fun on her playground.

"I want to make love in your bedroom, in your bed. I want you to be naked and ready with a drink for me." Jazzie challenges him again.

Tammy departed to attend the twins' away game. Jackson was aware that from around 6 p.m. to around 1 a.m. everyone at his home would be gone. Although a location for their "Happy Ending" has not yet become accessible, today he can no longer bear the agony of being without Jazzie.

"Come over to my house," Jackson texted.

"Stop playing! What are you doing?"

"Thinking about Pinky. I'm serious, come over."

"Where is your family?"

"They all are gone attending the twins' game, in a three-hour-traveling county."

"Are you sure about this?"

"I'm certain, park in the garage, and I'll have a drink ready for you."

"I'm going to need a double, I'll be there soon." Jazzie hesitated but eventually gave in to the urge as she drove into his subdivision. She says, "Hi, I'm here," when phoning Jackson to announce her arrival.

"The garage door is open, come inside," he replies. Although they have been dating for eleven years, she still experiences butterflies before seeing him. She pulls her car into the garage where Tammy usually parks and walks inside. Jackson yells to her, "Babe I'm upstairs," when he spots her on the camera. She waits by the entrance, unsure of whether she should go upstairs or wait for him to come down. Since Jazzie has still not made it upstairs, Jackson shouts once more. After seeing his and other people's shoes there, she follows suit and leaves her own by the entrance in the hallway and heads upstairs.

Jackson was there, in the room she desired, when she looked for him at the top of the stairs. Jazzie wanted to make love to him in his bedroom tonight, leaving him to recall her essence, curves, and scent. It made no difference that this room should have been off-limits to them. But Jackson understands what she wants because he also desires it. She likes the freaky things they do in his office at the shop, but this night is different. Jazzie chose not to wear any lotion or perfume out of caution, but her scent still lingers deep within her spirit.

He was waiting for her standing stalk by the bedside when Jazzie strolled into his bedroom. Her go-to channel for making love on Pandora, the Tank channel, is playing. Jackson hands her a glass of vodka and cranberry juice to sip. He brushes her hair tenderly while still finding it hard to believe she is actually standing in his bedroom. After touching her face, Jackson ran his palm down the length of her back, ending at her butt. "Why do you still have your dress on?" he asks, caressing her butt.

Jackson held her glass while Jazzie removed her dress to reveal that she was wearing neither a bra nor underwear. Peering up at him, she can see the intense passion with which he is focusing on her. Jackson's manhood prodded her in the stomach, signally he was ready. With seductive moves, Jazzie led him to his bedroom's gray two-seater sofa and repositioned the miniature cocktail table. She crouches down between his legs and takes his rigid pleasure into her mouth, then rotates her tongue slowly over the tip of his hardness. Jazzie continues to the testes by only applying pressure with her jaw. On her road trip downtown on him, she observes him enjoying it. Jackson watches her go a little bit faster and grows more.

Tasting his eagerness to release, she stops and says, "Not yet!" Jazzie positions herself on top of him on the sofa in reverse cowgirl and guides his hardness into her world. Jackson penetrates her further and she gets moister. Jazzie slams her roundness onto his manhood and tummy as she bounces up and down. "Not yet! We can't climax yet, I don't want to stop, damn you feel so good! So hard!" Jazzie is trying to control herself and thinks and continues riding him while feeling like exploding. "Get up, not yet!" she tells herself. Jackson ejaculates with force, and she jumps up to compel herself to stop, but it is too late; she watches in awe as it rockets out.

Jackson forbids her from turning around after she guides him to his bed and climbs up knees first. He forces her face down into the bed, butt high in the air, and enters her. Jackson is extremely hard once more as if his release was not only just a minute ago. He strikes her behind while observing the ripples of her butt swaying to his movements. Jackson accelerates, goes deeper, and then erupts once more. When he moves over to the bed panting, he lays next to her gasping for oxygen.

Jazzie was unwilling to stop because her thirst for him was more than normal. Jazzie is aware of and desires his remaining sexual desire. Feeling like he has one more inside, she challenges him and stimulates him into another erection. Jackson takes his time tasting her fruit until she shivers. He then ascends her, sliding his rigidity back into her juicy world. He is aware that she is trying to contain her orgasm and not soak his bed.

"Stop holding it back, let it go. Give it to me baby!"

"Not yet, no."

"You are mines!" With each thrust of his hips, Jackson sees her breast jiggling and sucks them. Closing her eyes, he orders, "Look at me!" After Jazzie does, she experiences an intense rush of heavenly bliss as they lay there in the letter "V" position, catching their breath. Jazzie believes they are done, but he turns to gaze at her. Jackson desires a complete fix of her after days of craving. His manhood is standing tall again when she looks down. He had already cum three times, which caused her pupils to enlarge in surprise. "I've been waiting on my Pinky, I need it," he says. She knows what is going to happen when he flips her over. Jazzie goes wild because of the way he hits a particular area. It is difficult for her to receive it without leaving any marks on him.

"I can't take it like this yet!" Jazzie moans.

"Yes! You can take it baby!"

"I'm trying. You feel too good!" Her body heats up as he moves in and out of her, making her feel wonderful. To avoid scratching him, Jazzie held onto the bed, the heating pad that was nearby, and the sheets.

"Fuck me baby, it's too good!"

"This my pussy!" Jackson tells her while pinning her wrist down.

When Jazzie screams his name, he dives down even further, and she loses consciousness they are in his bed. His perspiration is dripping onto her legs, side, and breast. He thrashes more powerfully as she reaches up to wipe his face. "It's coming baby it's coming!" he murmurs to her as he reaches another peak. She exclaims, "I love you!"

He responds, "I love you too!" Instantaneously they release together as a single entity. Jackson stands up and walks the space because he needs to breathe. Once he finally gathers his breath, he stumbles to the wall to turn the ceiling fan on before collapsing to the floor. Jackson missed her just as much as she missed him, and she lay stunned on the bed for a while.

Jazzie informs him, "Goodness, that's three times for me; I am done; I have nothing else to offer," She stood up, sipped her beverage, and lay down next to him. Jazzie rubs his chest, kisses his temples, and asks if he is all right. Although she knew he was now satisfied, he still had that same thirsty expression for her. Jackson motions for her to sit on his manhood while holding it.

"Are you serious?" she queries, believing he is kidding. Jackson is serious and replies, "You tapping out?" Jazzie was unsure if she could but still intended to try. She has not been able to ride him on the floor for a while due to her recovered fractured left leg. Jackson was harnessed up by Jazzie, who then drew him back inside. Monitoring her leg, it felt fine and pain-free, therefore slowly accelerated. Jackson grips his favored spot on her hips as he listens to her say, "My goodness, I feel you," and observes her breasts bouncing up and down. Ten levels higher in paradise and more self-assured is Jazzie. Leaning back even more, Jackson can penetrate her more deeply. Colliding with him, she exclaims, "I have to skeet baby!" and surrenders to the deluge.

He tightens his hold as he feels her overflow trickle down his thighs and testicles. He shouts, "Awwwwwwww!" after giving up the fight. They both were lying there, not speaking but thinking the same thing: Jackson climaxed five times. Never before had they experienced that, and it all occurred within two hours. Finally, Jazzie questioned, "Is there something wrong with us?"

Jackson responds, "Not at all, we are addicted to each other, there's nothing wrong with that. On another note, I could use some McDonald's fries." She chuckles when his stomach grumbles. They decide to adventure to a 24-hour McDonald's and indulge in some fries. While savoring each bite of the fries, they flirt with each other. Before heading back home, Jackson gives her a passionate kiss, time seems to momentarily freeze. A tingle of excitement courses through their bodies. "Wow!" she exclaims, her heart racing with affection for this man who holds her heart. Though they are intoxicated by each other, it is late and tomorrow is a workday.

Jazzie returns home, feeling a deep sense of satisfaction, a tingling awareness of his DNA soaked inside of her. The thought brings a smile to her lips, knowing that they are irrevocably bound together. Lying in bed, she reflects on the powerful connection they share earlier. "He is mine, and I am his," she whispers to herself, feeling a sense of comfort. As exhaustion finally sets in, she drifts off to sleep, wrapped in the cocoon of their love.

As the daybreak quickly creeps into the bedroom, it gently bathed in sunlight. Just when Jazzie was having a dream, her alarm clock decided to audition for a singing competition, rudely interrupting the tranquility. With an Oscar-worthy groan, Jazzie lunges to shut it off, wishing she could charge it with disturbing the peace. "Darn it!" she mutters with the kind of language only sleep-deprived people can muster. Secretly Jazzie was hoping that if she stared at the clock hard enough, it might rewind time, giving her a few more hours of much-needed beauty sleep. But unfortunately, reality wins this round, and she resigns herself to face the day with the grace of a half-asleep sloth.

CHAPTER 23

Pursuit of Survival

❧❧❧❧ ♥ ❧❧❧❧

Jazzie's job has returned them to working in the office but with social distancing. Exhausted from last night's intense lovemaking, she was eager to leave to take a nap. Sitting in her office, her mind replays the things Jackson did to her. Her attempts to take control failed when Jackson demonstrated who was truly in control. After work, she hurries home and climbs into bed for a power nap. It is Thursday night, and she wakes up an hour later to get a head start setting up for her grandfather's birthday party.

This will allow her to see Jackson tomorrow with more leisure. After finishing decorating for that evening, at 10:56 pm, her phone chirps. "I'm hard again!" Jackson messages. Jazzie anticipated that he would be satisfied for at least a week giving her time to recover. Jackson was off today which allowed him some time to recuperate from last night and his appetite for her increased more than usual.

Jazzie retorted, "You can sneak over here if you like, Brandon just left, Genesis is at her boyfriend's house and Aiden is working late." Not wanting to concede to defeat, she felt relieved when he texted that the twins were getting off work late—after midnight. Jazzie proceeded to apply a bag of frozen peas to Pinky to ease soreness after Jackson wore her out. Still exhausted from their love-making activity the night before, they both fell asleep while texting one another.

A decent night's sleep is definitely good for the body. After replacing the lost bodily fluids, Jazzie was revived and prepared to start her Friday.

7:59 AM "Good morning," she texts Jackson.

8:00 AM "Good morning"

8:00 AM "There's my baby!"

8:03 AM "I'm here."

8:17 AM "I see you now, do me a favor."

9:41 AM "What is it Babe?" he questions.

10:26 AM "Can I see you today?" Jazzie asks.

11:55 AM "Of course."

12:52 PM "Okay!"

Jazzie was delighted when he replied, "Of course," because she adored him. She chooses to make a two-layer sheet Key Lime Strawberry Margarita Cake for her grandfather's birthday. The secret to outstanding baking is the person's mood, and at the moment, hers is fantastic! Kem Station blurs through the speakers, it is her favorite cake-baking music. It nurtures her artistic mood. While she bakes and listens to music, she reflects on Jackson and their relationship.

The last few weeks have been like a fairytale. Jackson always looks sexy with his diamond studs and a fresh haircut. After their motorcycle ride last weekend, she asked to wear his diamond studs, assuring him that she would return them the next time he saw her. Teasing Jazzie, but without hesitation, he removes them, puts them in her ears, and informs her it is not necessary to hold the studs hostage to see him. They took a few night city rides in his truck. Jackson urged her to open the truck on the highway as she was driving. Jazzie found it surprising that a truck could feel like a rocket, but she could now understand what a Hemi was. Jazzie twirls in her kitchen grinning while thinking about him.

Today at the main Crown Performance Center store was slow since it was a holiday weekend. Ordinarily, Jackson would not ride on a holiday time due to mindless drivers, but he took his cruiser with him to work so he could detail and change the oil. Jackson would have completed and be ready to meet her by the time Jazzie had finished baking. His cell phone verifies the temperature is 98 degrees for a July 3rd day as the sun shines brightly through the painted blue skies. Rap music fills the auto shop while Jackson downs a bottle of cold water. While tending to his bike, he thinks about how much fun they have been having lately. Jackson was accustomed to drowning in his work and family obligations, but recently, he was truly living.

Without leaving Georgia, Jackson took her on an international trip as a surprise at work. For lunch, they dined at a tasty Asian restaurant. Afterward, they strolled and discovered an international market to explore. Jackson mounted her on the back of his bike and they rode to Little River Falls in Fort Payne, Alabama, It is a magnificent unmanicured waterfall. The falls have a forty-five-foot drop and are encircled by tall trees and lush flora. This encounter was hilarious and well worth the journey.

"Come on, we getting in the water." Jazzie insisted.

"We don't have bathing suits Jazzie."

"Roll up your jeans. We are only walking to the other side and back. No swimsuits needed for that!"

After rolling their pants and wading into the water to reach the other side of the falls, they were surprised by how deep it was. Jazzie's jeans were soaked to the tops of her thighs and his jeans were wet up to his knees. Jackson chuckled and made jokes once they got crossed the water to the other side of the rocks. He grabbed Jazzie's hand to help her out of the water. After doing so, Jackson slipped and fell onto his back on the rocks. Jazzie helped him up and after making sure that he was not injured, she laughed hysterically! Now the jokes were on him. These recent weeks have been wonderful, impromptu, and enjoyable. They are going through each day as if it were their last.

As Jackson was finishing up his cruiser, he spotted a dark red Mustang sitting in the parking lot. Jazzie's text message alerts him with a unique tone he assigned only to her.

2:32 PM "Don't forget your containers for your food."

3:05 PM "Oh okay, I will bring them. I just finished changing my oil and cleaning my bike."

3:09 PM "You have been busy!"

Jackson read the front tag plate, "I am my Brother's Keeper," even though no one had yet exited the vehicle. He realizes this is the vehicle that drove Mia off the road and becomes enraged. Retrieving his gun from a desk drawer, Jackson sprints outside to face the driver. When Jackson yelled, "What's up bitch-ass mother-fucker, you ran my daughter off the road looking for me! Here I am!" The dark red Mustang had been parked but sped off. Jackson phones Elijah as he rushes back into the shop.

"Hey man, any updates on the attack against me?"

"Not yet, but soon Bro. I put someone on to locate the car because something about Mia's accident didn't sit well with me. The car hasn't been seen yet, but they will appear."

"That same car with the front tag plate was just parked in my shop's parking lot but sped off when I tried to confront him! Whoever placed a dead rat in my mailbox, forced my baby girl into a ditch, and called my phone to threaten me is connected to that car!"

"Stay put man, I'll hit you right back," Elijah exclaimed as he began to experience chills. Thirty minutes later, Elijah arrives at the shop. To find evidence, they looked through the security cameras, but they could not find anything—not even the tag number—only the direction the car was traveling. They reasoned that based on the car's route, nearby businesses' security cams could identify it. Elijah was requested to accompany Jackson to his home, to allow him to check on his family. This request came after Jackson informed the workers that they could leave early for the holiday.

In a high-octane display of adrenaline-fueled action, Jackson geared up with a helmet and fingerless gloves before straddling his trusty sport bike, Suzie. Leaving his cruiser resting on its stand, he revved the engine and zipped out of the parking lot with lightning speed. As he turned onto Sugarloaf Parkway, a menacing dark red Mustang tailed him, lurking in the side mirrors like a relentless shadow. The streets were relatively empty, offering a stroke of luck that Jackson seized as he accelerated to stay ahead. Elijah, too, noticed the pursuing vehicle and readied his weapon, determined to stay hot on its trail. Both Jackson and the Mustang's driver engaged in a high-stakes race, weaving through lanes with breathtaking velocity. The situation escalated when the Mustang's driver started firing shots at Jackson, who deftly maneuvered onto Grayson-New Hope Road, narrowly evading the bullets. In retaliation, Jackson drew his gun and fired back, shattering the Mustang's windshield.

As the tension escalated, Elijah joined the fray, aiming precisely at the Mustang's back tire, nearly causing it to lose control. Seizing the moment, Jackson executed a quick U-turn, seizing the opportunity to approach the Mustang from behind and take out the other tire. The unfolding drama caught the attention of a vigilant policeman stationed at the nearby Quick Trip gas station. Swiftly calling for backup, the officer gave chase, with three more police units joining the pursuit to quell the danger. With determination etched on his face, Jackson knew he couldn't let the Mustang escape; whoever sought to harm him and his family needed to be apprehended. The intense chase continued, with police officers navigating the traffic as if they were in a high-stakes dance.

Elijah closed in on the Mustang from the left lane, while Jackson found himself sandwiched between two officers on his right. One of them attempted to halt him by bumping the back tire of the motorcycle, but Jackson showed his mettle, maintaining control of his bike. As they approached a green light, Jackson's eyes fell upon a silver four-door sedan preparing to turn left. Instinctively, he knew this situation was far from ideal—life, much like a card game, offered unpredictable hands and choices. Yet, like a skilled player in a high-stakes poker game, Jackson pressed forward, refusing to fold. The cards were dealt, and he was determined to play them with all the skill and courage he possessed. Like a card game, life is a game of skills, your options are, "Hit me," "Fold," "Give in," or "Lose." skills.

CHAPTER 24

Twist of Fate

❧ ♥ ☙

Jazzie finished baking the cakes and making a few dishes for the party. The house and the backyard were set up and ready for her family to come to celebrate Grandpa tomorrow. This is a great stopping point to meet Jackson. Looking at her cell phone, no texts from him appear, which is odd. She thinks, "Jackson has usually texted me by now."

6:23 PM "I have the cakes cooling and I can take a break now, what are you doing?" She sends a check-in text. Over an hour later, she continues preparing for the next day's celebration while waiting to hear from Jackson, and still, no text so she sends him another.

7:38 PM "Babe I'm ready. Where are you? Can you meet me at Haley's?" Jazzie is wondering where he is because she has not received any texts from him, not even a simple "Hey" or an eye emoji. She speculates that perhaps he became preoccupied and was unable to text, but Jazzie knows better. Jackson always finds a method to reach her via text, phone, or other means. Jackson believes she sometimes overthinks, but this feels off, This was not his usual behavior and she was becoming worried. Jazzie waited and still no response, therefore she texted him again.

10:16 PM "Hey Babe."

10:40 PM "I guess you're still busy. I will check on you tomorrow."

Jazzie's head is spinning while thinking, "This is puzzling; his last text was at 3:05 PM and since then it has been total silence. Maybe he and Elijah got drunk again, but even then, Jackson managed to communicate with me." Jackson is aware she worries about him and frequently reassures her that he is safe. The longer his silence, the higher her anxiety rose. After spending the entire day preparing food and setting she was pondering what happened to Jackson. Jazzie felt exhausted and went to bed. She struggles to fall asleep and wakes up around 1:39 AM. Jazzie examines her phone but has not heard from him.

Jackson's name does not appear as an inmate when she searches the local jail arrest records online, which was good news. Her throat tightens sensing that something is terribly awry. Jazzie laid her phone on the nightstand and tried to fall asleep after convincing herself that he was inebriated and needed to sleep it off. She tossed and turned once more before awakening at 3:52 AM to check her phone—again, nothing. Jazzie slowly slides out of bed making sure not to wake Aiden. Not a cloud was in the sky: a fiery glow, mingled with crimson, lit her dark bedroom. Gazing outside the window, she felt uneasy and thought, "What is it God? I can feel him, something is wrong?"

Jazzie gives up trying to fall asleep a few hours later. She crept downstairs to the kitchen at 6:15 AM and began making icing and decorating cakes while everyone was sleeping. She has not seen Jackson since they made passionate love Wednesday. Jazzie sends him another text in hopes of seeing him today before things get hectic at her home.

6:31 AM "Gm baby, where are you?"

6:40 AM "I want to see you today. I can't stay long but I want my kiss," Jackson is still silent. Finally hearing a pleasant tone from her phone, Jazzie got excited. She grabs it with all the vigor of a schoolgirl, anxious to find out what happened to him. Steve, a friend with whom they ride motorcycles, was the culprit, which perplexed her.

"Why is he texting me so early?" she wondered. "Steve may be curious as to whether Jackson and I are riding today. He knows we avoid riding on holiday weekends when traffic is particularly chaotic."

7:28 AM "Hi."

7:29 AM "Good Morning."

7:29 AM "Call me NOW!"

Jazzie's pulse raced as if she were getting close to the finish line when she saw his response. "Something is wrong," she mutters aloud. Her fingertips tremble as she presses the icon to dial Steve. "Is something wrong?" Jazzie immediately inquires when he answers.

Although he was hesitant to speak, Steve eventually said, "Yes, then you must not have heard?" he spoke, his voice filled with sorrow.

"Is it Jackson!" she enquires with shallow breathing and heart beating faster than a cheetah running to survive in the wild.

"Yes, Jackson was in a serious motorcycle accident," Steve said releasing a deep sigh. Jazzie weakened with Steve's words echoing in her ears. She stumbles to the kitchen countertop to grab for support. But instead collapsed. Lying on the floor she struggled to breathe, but she could not. It felt like someone was clutching her throat, stopping her from taking full breaths, but no one was there. Jazzie was all alone with tears flooding her cheeks and onto her nightgown. Regaining her ability to breathe and speak, she mumbles, "I knew something was wrong! Jackson wouldn't just stop talking to me. We were supposed to meet, I was waiting for him." Jazzie refuses to let the words, "Is he dead?" leave her lips. Jackson promised that he would not leave her by way of a motorcycle. Jazzie knows he keeps his promises. Struggling to stand, she questions Steve, "Where is he?"

"Gwinnett Medical Hospital, in ICU," he whispered. Jazzie starts moving and words flood from her mouth, but she does not hear herself.

"I have to find out what is going on! I have to see him! I have to talk to him! He wouldn't leave me like this. He promised me that he wouldn't go that way! Thank you for telling me Steve but I have to go now." Jazzie sobs in the middle of her kitchen floor as she drops the phone by her side. The clock pauses, the sounds vanish, and Jazzie feels a pain in her chest—it's her heart. It is crumbling. "I'm broken without him," she cries frantically and then screams, "Why? Why? Why? Why?"

Aiden moves around upstairs; after hearing her sobbing. Jazzie attempts to gather herself but is powerless to regain her composure and decides to hide from Aiden. She crawls to the hallway bathroom and shuts the door because her body is still shaking and in shock, and she is unable to stand. Jazzie's symptoms were similar to a cardiac attack. Her hands were sweating and trembling violently, accompanied by labored breathing, and nausea. Jazzie manages to get on her knees and reaches into the sink to switch on the water. "Splash cold water on your face and body. You have to settle down! Take some slow, deep breaths," Jazzie mentally instructs herself while taking sips of water from her cupped hands.

The sensation of cold water rushing into her face proved therapeutic. Jazzie's breathing slowed as her ribcage began to relax until the shaking gradually subsided. Meanwhile, Aiden descends the steps pursuing the source of the whimpering. Since the television was on and running water could be heard in the bathroom, he presumed it was the television and returned upstairs. Jazzie lay on the bathroom floor reliving the memory of their last romantic encounter just two days prior. She sensed the vibration from her Fitbit as someone called. Retrieving the phone from her robe's pocket, Jackson's name is flashing when she glances down. Jazzie was not sure if Tammy had his phone, but at this point, she did not care and swiped to answer.

Jackson utters in a graveled voice, "Babbbyy," and she breaks into tears, not caring whether or not Aiden hears her. Jackson was in pain as his voice was barely audible.

"Where are you?" Jazzie asked. "Steve said you were in a motorcycle accident, and you were hurt." To prevent another panic episode, Jazzie takes a slow deep breath while attempting to remain calm.

"I was being pursued—by the Mustang that hit Mia—Elijah and the police followed. My arm—fingers—right leg—both hips—broken. A car pulled out—in front of me by the QT gas station—on Grayson Road. I may need surgery, but I'm fine." Despite her best efforts to keep it from him because she knows he would be concerned about her, Jazzie cannot help but cry. Jackson does not want her to worry and downplay his injuries and suffering. She hears others in the background, possibly nurses and physicians. Jackson says, "I have to go. I love you, baby."

Jazzie replies, "I love you more baby." With her chest aching and eyes streaming with tears, he ends the call.

The water continued running while Jazzie sat on the bathroom floor and continued to sob while thinking, "This is a dream, it must be a dream! God has this all wrong!" Everything can change in one second. It takes one second to risk the precious things that you hold close to your heart. One second to hit send on that email, one second to engage in that fight, one second to change your life.

CHAPTER 25

A Mother's Wisdom

In a few hours is Grandpa's birthday celebration. To continue pushing to get everything required all the strength Jazzie could muster, which was not much. Her heart hurt, her mind was blank, and her body was in shock. With swollen eyes, Jazzie would find it challenging to keep her emotions secret from Aiden and the guests. Despite her inner turmoil, Jazzie made an effort to make the celebration memorable. The tables were set, the food was prepared, and all of the tents were erected in the yard. The early arrival of guests was fantastic because she wanted this to be over quickly.

Before Jackson hung up, her thoughts kept going back to his remark, "I love you," She called the hospital to find out his condition and received more surprising news.

Jazzie is told by the nurse, "I apologize, but we are unable to provide updates regarding shooting victims." Visitors are not permitted at the hospital until further notice since the epidemic is out of control. Her mind is searching for information that Jackson has not yet provided. Guests began arriving for the party and shortly afterward Jazzie grabbed her car keys and drove away. She felt the need to visit the accident scene to confirm that it was true. Driving cautiously toward the crossroads Jackson had mentioned as the scene of the incident knots start to develop in her stomach. Debris scattered down the side of the road and she activated her warning lights to block the lane.

She steps out of the vehicle with caution and circles to the passenger side which is nearer the side of the road. While inspecting the debris she discovered bits and pieces of Suzie, disrespectfully scattered onto the street. Pieces of Suzie's tire and frame, which matched those on Jazzie's bike were lying in a ditch. She picked up the matching piece and brushed the dirt off of it onto her shorts. Images of Jackson lying on the ground bleeding, hurt, and in pain spun in her head. She imagined him in need of assistance, but she was not there to provide it.

Jazzie yells out in the street, "I didn't know; I was at home baking and you were here in need of help." Tears filled her eyes. She stood in that lane sobbing for what seemed like hours before climbing into her car and toting a piece of his bike. More guests have come by the time she returns home. She rushes inside, walks past Aiden and Vivian, and then sprints upstairs to her bedroom. Jazzie walks into the bathroom, throws her clothing on the floor, and locks the door. To suffocate her thoughts, she starts the shower and steps beneath the water. Sliding down the shower wall she begs God for assistance.

"Please God, I will do anything you want me to do He doesn't deserve this, so please help him through it. He is a great man with a heart of gold for others. We both sinned but let me bear the punishment rather than him."

The successful celebration left Grandpa feeling like he had achieved million-dollar status! Everyone enjoyed themselves and the food she prepared. "Jazzie, I fixed you a plate and put it in the refrigerator, you look tired," Vivian said. Jazzie tries to be sociable and responds, "thanks!" but walks off. Vivian noticed something was wrong but refrained from asking before telling her mother. Jazzie clutched her phone and watched while everyone had fun.

"I need him to call back!" she was thinking when her phone began vibrating. It was him! She rushes to her office, which is quiet and isolated, and speaks with him there. Jazzie was desperate to see him and the sound of his voice caused tears to stream her face. She fought to control them for him. Jazzie could not conceal the anguish in her voice. Jackson knew that they needed to see each other for them to both be fine.

"Babe, I think I can do video chat, let me try," he cries while struggling to initiate the call with his weakened hands. Jackson sends a video request, which Jazzie sees and accepts. She is relieved to see him but concerned about a police officer standing near protecting him and she notices that he has severe road rash. After receiving pain medications from the nurse, he seems to be more at ease.

The incident occurred on the street you enjoy riding your motorcycle on," Jackson explains to her. "If I had to do it over again, I still would rather this happened to me instead of you Jazzie." She sobs because, despite his agonizing pain, he prioritizes her well-being over his own.

"Don't cry, baby," Jackson begs her, "You're going to make me cry," while he watches her pain.

After wiping her flushed cheeks and eyes, Jazzie admitted, "I went to the accident site."

"Why did you go there?"

"I needed to see it for myself."

"What did you see?"

"You. Pain. Pieces of Suzie are still on the road, I got a piece for you." Jackson tells Jazzie every detail he can recall. Suzie's tires had just been replaced and she would have been sold the following week. Things started to change when he saw the dark red Mustang. Jackson took Suzie because the cruiser was still on the lift getting an oil change. The pursuit took place on a roadway that Jazzie frequently rides her bike on alone. A woman makes a split-second decision to turn left. She did, leading them to T-bone, sending him flying off the bike over the car hood.

Jackson skidded onto the scorching asphalt without wearing a motorcycle jacket—only a t-shirt. When he regained conscience early the following morning, he was in the hospital with a fractured arm, fingers, right leg, both hips, and stitched up like an old doll. The police continued to pursue the Mustang, and some of them stayed with Jackson to revive him with the assistance of a bystander who was a medical professional. While the driver of the dark red Mustang eluded capture, the passenger was apprehended. Because there was an attempt on his life, the police are protecting Jackson and his family.

Tammy was permitted to stay at the hospital for a short while, but she was informed to leave due to the pandemic spreading. Jazzie is happy that Jackson's phone worked, allowing them to stay in touch. They chuckled when he claimed that Tammy was attempting to take his phone even as he lay perishing. Jackson insisted on keeping it because he needed to contact Jazzie. She playfully suggested to him that perhaps we could purchase an Otter box for his body after the phone only sustained a few scratches. Although he was in agony, he smiled a little—they both did.

Jackson wanted police protection for her. After haggling with him, Jazzie consented to have an officer parked close to her house. If Aiden questioned why the police were sitting there, she intended to make use of the new neighborhood watch established by the Homeowners Association.

Jazzie offers air kisses before hanging up when she notices the nurses returning and realizes that he needs to rest. Once everyone has left after the party, Jazzie tells her mother and Vivian what happened to Jackson. She was careful to not mention the shooting. "Someone wants him dead, and the police will be stationed nearby," she shared. It was too much for them to hear, they were shocked that she was able to get through it. Vivian, the kids, and her parents view Jackson as family. Jazzie explains to her mother what ensued with her after learning about Jackson.

"It was a panic attack," Mrs. Williams clarified while expressing concern for them both. "You can't help him if there's a problem with you," she advises with motherly wisdom. "Jackson is facing a long battle; I know you love him. He needs you to be strong, so he can be too. Look after yourself first, you have to, before you can look after him. What are you two planning on doing with this relationship?"

"I don't know Mom. It's just too many people that can get hurt."

"God already knows your pain. You're hurting and Jackson too. You two are in love and you shouldn't feel ashamed. I want you to be free in God's eye to be happy and in love." Deep down Jazzie knows her mother is right, but she does not know how without breaking someone's heart. Jackson was her Knight and always came to her rescue, kissing Jazzie's boo-boos. Now he needs her to rescue him.

CHAPTER 26

Jazzie's Journal

❧⟡♥⟡❧

Jackson lies in the hospital floating in a cloud of morphine, but unable to move. He reflects on the recent events that caused him to be hospitalized. The police have no leads on the driver and the passenger is not talking at all. Someone wants him dead, and he does not know who, or why, but they almost succeeded. Trying to live right and leave the criminal activities behind has caused Jackson enemies. If you want to know who you can count on for support, stop spending your money on them. If you are left with a dollar, who will remain in your corner?

Jackson wants to keep his word to Jazzie and not be a part of that world, but something must be done. He is running out of time and needs to act fast before he misses another chance. As requested, Tammy called his "Clean Up" contact. Sleeping is challenging since he keeps replaying the accident in his thoughts and has nightmares. In his dream, while riding, he abruptly collides with a brick wall, jumps, and painfully awakens. Though a strong man, this catastrophe is too much.

Jackson appears to be in a pleasant mood when Jazzie speaks to him. Every time they talk, she finds out about a new injury. "Do you remember when people used to call me a thrill seeker?" Jackson says with a sigh. "Well, that thrill is gone now." You had asked me before what could make me stop riding motorcycles, and I think I've found my answer. I'm going to sell my cruiser. I'm just grateful you weren't on the back this time," Jackson adds.

Jazzie is perplexed as to why God permitted this to occur. Jackson rides and drives carefully; he does not deserve this. He is a kind, generous, and giving man. She places guilt on herself and says, "I should have baked sooner; if I had, he would have been with me and not on the bike. She tosses while thinking, "All I want is to lay in this bed by myself." Their mutual friends have called her to inquire about him. Jackson informs her that the ICU is taking excellent care of him and has planned the first two of three procedures for the following day, but she feels that this is not quick enough. To help relax her mind and avoid another panic episode, Jazzie decides to record her thoughts in a journal. Rather than talking to someone, she prefers to express her thoughts in writing.

July 6 – Monday, she writes ⟶ ⫸⫸⫸

Today, I don't want to go to work. I'm unproductive and mindless. I've been asked what happened by a couple of our close friends, and I'm tired of talking about it. All I've known for the past eleven years is him. He sounds okay but is in a lot of discomfort. He often drifts in and out of sleep. Sydney, his nurse, spoke with me and believes I'm Jackson's sister. She informed me that he will undergo two procedures on Wednesday beginning at 8:30 a.m. I'm ill with worry, my stomach hurts and I'm still unable to eat or rest. When I contacted the hospital following the accident, I learned the reason I couldn't locate him. Shooting victims are given trauma names rather than their own for security reasons.

Samuel is his name, which you must ask for. I was able to get the name from Sydney by using my savvy interpersonal abilities. I created Jackson a keepsake bottle out of beach sand and shells that we found on a trip. He keeps it on his desk at work to remind him of me. Elijah brought the bottle to me; he seemed upset and sleep-deprived after witnessing the accident. Before delivering the bottle to the hospital, I composed a little note to include with it. I hope he can smell my scent on the note and knows I'm close.

Sydney met me in the lobby and assured me she would put it in his room. I told her that I would get all the members of his Medical Team lunch for taking great care of my brother. I played my role, being careful not to leak information for Tammy to discover. After Sydney returned upstairs to her station, I sat in that lobby thinking, "I'm so close to him, yet not allowed to see him." The security guard sitting at the counter was blocking everyone. There was no prospect of me getting in.

I only needed five minutes to see and touch him. I simply cannot stand to leave him here alone. After Jackson woke up, he called. He thought I might have stopped by to see him, but he knows that's impossible because no one can. He smells my aroma and notices the small envelope as he turns to look at the bottle. "I love you more than any actions, any distances, and any words," it said when opened. Jackson asked how I managed to get the bottle into his room. I informed him that I had a few tricks under my sleeve.

July 7 – Tuesday, she writes ————⟩⟩⟩⟩

Still unable to sleep, so I'm worried about the surgery. He shouldn't be by himself, but Tammy is probably talking with his nurses. This morning I arrived early for work and sat in my car. Jackson typically parks to the left when he brings me breakfast, but it has been unoccupied for days. I cried and prayed to God in the darkness of my car, where no one could see me.

"Dear God, please let Jackson recover with no complications. I'll comply with whatever you ask of me, but I and his family need him." As of right now, I've decided to do a spiritual fast till his recovery from surgery tomorrow. I only drank water all day, no food. Jackson advised me to eat so I could maintain my energy, but this fast was for the two of us. We will both be carried by my prayer and faith. Jackson requested that I get the police report for insurance purposes. When the ambulance was on the way, Gwinnett County noted in the report that he was dead on arrival. It makes my heart race to think that he was even near to it. He'll overcome this, I'm confident of it. Today, Jackson brought up a conversation he had with his mother.

Over the long Fourth of July holiday, Jackson and I planned a bike trip to Beale Street in Memphis, a well-known tourist destination. R&B music, dining, and nightclubs are all within three blocks. Our next stop was Dallas, where we would spend the night and visit his parents. We don't typically ride on holiday weekends, however, we both had a week off work, so it was the perfect chance. After breaking my leg, we were going to cancel the trip. My ankle was still swollen, and I hadn't yet totally recovered.

I decided that I could still make the trip but on the cruiser with him. Jackson's mother told him that she had a bad feeling about us riding that weekend and to wait until the following one. We took his mother's advice and chose not to ride. Instead, we took a comfy car to St. Augustine and had a great time. Sadly, his mother passed away four months later. On the same holiday weekend, exactly two years later, Jackson suffered an accident that his mother had an uneasy feeling about. Jackson requested that I take pictures of Suzie.

Today after work, I stopped by the tow yard. They verified that I was Jackson's sister before having me sign some paperwork. Since no one was permitted on the grounds due to the coronavirus, the front desk employee snapped the photos for me. Goodness gracious, the entire front of the bike was gone, the exhaust bent, the gas tank where he must have smashed into was smashed, and the footpegs along with the back seat were gone. When I arrived home, I went into the garage and stared at my bike shocked at how shattered Suzie was. In my heart, I know that Jackson has a special angel, his mother.

Even from heaven, she was protecting her son. Like her, Jackson is a strong individual who provides for his family. Recalling a picture of Jackson's father, he looks just like him. In our video chat, I told Jackson I could see why his mother *fell in love. Whatever I ask for in prayer, I should believe it and receive it, according to a Bible verse I once read. He shouldn't fear anything since God and his mother are with him. God isn't done with Jackson yet; he still has a plan for him. Following our prayer, I told him to hurry up and return to me, and he said, "I promise." I used my Pandora natural sounds to unwind and imagined we were back on the beach, laughing and making love while playing in the sand. Finally, I can drift off to a safe place.*

July 8, Wednesday, she writes →>>>>>

Today has arrived, and my thoughts are all over the place. I feel weak, and nervous, with dark bags beneath my eyes. When I spoke to Jackson at 6:30 a.m., I overheard someone say, "It's time."

He tells me, "I have to go now, baby."

I reassured him, "I'll be right here waiting for you. I love you so much. You better come back to me."

He replies. "I love you too and I promise, I'm coming back to you," and hangs up. I continued to hold the phone when silence took over. I Google every aspect of his injuries, treatment, procedure, and length of time required for his surgery. Surgery should take two to three hours, but while I'm at work, I can't help but keep an eye on the time. Every hour on the hour, I pray. Our circle of friends is checking on me and some said I didn't look well. They advise me to eat something, but I've been fasting for days and I'm still working with God. My energy comes from my faith.

I called to see whether he was recovering around 12:30 p.m. "He's still in surgery," according to Sydney. "this process takes a while." I return to my job and begin filing documents to speed time up. At 1:30 p.m., my phone rang, and I noticed his number on the screen. Jackson responded when I answered, "Baby, I'm back." Although it was barely a whisper, his words gave me the breath I needed to exhale.

I laughed as I replied, "Yes baby, yes you are!" He says, "I love you; I will call you back."

"I love you more!" Jackson kept his word while being unconscious. He and I are both fine; Time to eat! I followed through on my promise and gave Jackson's medical staff lunch for fifteen people. Sandwiches, wings, fruit, potato salad, garden salad, chips, desserts, and beverages. Tammy undoubtedly spoke with them, but I wanted to express my gratitude and appreciation for looking after MY MAN. They were appreciative of the letter I included with their meal. Thank God! I can eat now too, this food is so good!

July 9, Thursday, she writes————————➤➤➤

Jackson is doing better today, although he is still in pain. At least the discomfort is not as awful as when he initially entered the hospital. He doesn't deserve this; no one does, and I feel horrible for him. Until he gets better, I can't get the motivation to accomplish anything. This is not right. Why did our reality need to change when we weren't bothering anyone? I'm enraged! He would be living rich and untouchable if he were a thug. The people who try to live moral lives and treat others kindly always suffer the consequences. Yes, I acknowledge that we have acted improperly, but that is between us, and it doesn't affect anyone.

This man is one of a kind. He inspires me and has an incredible will. Though I'm now fine, I was angry about why this happened. He even made a joke today and smiled a little, but I can see he must be hurting and will be for a while. Just to experience his warmth in person would be wonderful. I suppose I'll take a shower right now. Tonight, he and I will pretend to meet on the beach. Leviticus 5:17, If someone sins and does what is forbidden in any of the LORD'S commandments, even though they do not know it, they are guilty and will be held responsible.

Are we being punished?

CHAPTER 27

A Daring Plan to Reunite

Just one week ago, Jackson and Jazzie were enjoying life; today he had two major surgeries to restore his quality of life. He is still unable to comprehend what has occurred. To regain stability, he has prosthetics, screws, and pins in each hip. Although it occasionally hurts and is uncomfortable, a catheter was implanted to help with urination. Jackson's physician visits to see how he is doing. "Good morning Mr. Davenport, how are you feeling today?"

"I'm still dealing with a lot of pain all over."

"My friend, you're really lucky; the fact that you're experiencing discomfort is a very good indicator. Rest today and don't try to sit up; maybe tomorrow. To allow the metal stem to merge with your body, and heal, you're forbidden to walk for a few months. I'll have a hospital bed and a wheelchair sent to your home before you're discharged."

"A few months is two months, right?"

"Let's watch how quickly your body heals and accepts the prosthetic. Do you have any other questions?"

"Yes, when will I be able to go home?"

"Once you are sufficiently stable, we'll move you out of the intensive care unit and assess from there. Right now I'd say four weeks." Jackson's demander changed hearing this news. For the remainder of the day, he followed the doctor's instructions and slept which allowed him to escape the pain. Jackson continues having nightmares, but he hopes it will eventually get better. Meanwhile, it stalks him. One day after his operations, on Thursday, he sits up in the chair; Jackson is eager to recover and restore his life.

Excited, he calls Jazzie to share his accomplishment. "Babe, I'm sitting up in a chair!"

"I thought you were supposed to wait another day or so?"

"I felt like I was ready and Sydney assisted me."

"I'm so proud of you! Now, even a small amount of food would give you more energy." Jackson has not had much of an appetite, he is beginning to. He receives numerous calls from worried parties but avoids most of them as he does not feel like repeating the same story to everyone. Tammy drops off to the nurse some toiletries that Jackson prefers over the hospital brand and his phone charger.

After receiving permission to enter his room, the police detective arrived bearing news. The detective inquired, "How are you doing, Mr. Davenport?"

"Although I've had better days, at least I'm still around. How may I assist you?" Jackson asks.

"Do you recognize this man?" The detective displays a photo of a young man with shoulder-length dreads, a tattoo dated 8/14/1953 on his right forearm, small dark brown eyes, and prominent cheekbones.

"Yes, that's Matthew. He's like my godson. I lost contact with him when Corey, who is his father, and once my friend went to prison." Jackson ponders while gazing at the image of why the detective has Matthew's picture.

"He's also the Mustang's passenger. How about this person? Jackson sees the detective holding up another image. The man in the picture looks familiar and has the same tattoo as Matthew of that date but on the front of his neck. Jackson has seen this date, though he is not sure where.

"I don't know him, but he looks familiar. I think I saw that date somewhere else, but I don't remember where. Who is he?" Jackson questioned.

"He's the driver, Eric Miles, the brother of Corey Miles." The detective holds up Corey's mugshot. When Jackson tries and fails to get up, the heart monitor's alarm begins beeping and flashing. The detective advises Jackson to calm down.

"Relax, Mr. Davenport! Your heart is racing and your blood pressure is up!" The two nurses rush into the room explaining why the alarm is sounding while punching buttons. The doctor enters and begins to examine him, forcing the detective to leave.

"No!" shouts Jackson. "Let him stay!" They instruct the detective to step outside. Once they had Jackson calm and sedated, the detective was notified he only had a little while left and would need to leave.

"What's going on Detective, why are they trying to kill me?"

"Corey had intended to kill you before he was incarcerated. Eric was recently released from prison, he continued the plot. The passenger, Corey's fifteen-year-old son, Matthew is a brave young man. He admitted to knowing what his father and uncle had done and provided proof to back up his claims."

"His son? He's just a boy."

"Corey directed Eric to take you out but leave your family alone, anyone else in the way is a "Casualty of War." The attack on your daughter, Mia was meant for you, Mr. Davenport. When Eric realized it was her driving your car, it was too late. Eric is currently detained and facing several charges, including two counts of attempted murder, cruelty to children, endangering children, fleeing the scene of an accident, felony firearm possession, and more. Corey will have additional charges coming soon."

"The tattoo date, I remember now. Corey has it on his back. Do you know what it means?"

"It's their mother's birthday. While Matthew was under her care, she passed away a few years ago from breast cancer.

"Why do they want me dead?"

"Greed, jealousness, hatred Mr. Davenport. Believe me, in this line of work, I see it all the time."

"What's going to happen with Matthew?"

"No charges will be brought against him. He'll be placed in foster care if we're unable to locate family members. Don't be concerned about it; we need you to get better." Police guards were being removed from the hospital, Jackson's home, and Jazzie's street. Jackson finds it incomprehensible that someone he once considered a brother and who he trusted with his life secretly loathed him. Jackson would have sacrificed almost anything for Corey, but his vengeful wrath spilled over into the lives of Matthew and other innocent people. He phones Jazzie after the detective leaves to reveal the shocking news. Jazzie is delighted that the truth and danger are no longer a threat. She feels awful for Jackson because he genuinely believed that he and Corey formed a brotherhood. Jackson feels himself drifting back to sleep after telling Tammy.

Jazzie felt better and after work wanted to celebrate with a drink. At a favored nearby Mexican eatery, Haley, Mrs. Williams, Yvette, Vivian, and Jazzie get together. After taking their orders for meals and drinks, the waitress came back with chips, salsa, and a pitcher of peach margaritas. Since Corey and his brother were no longer a danger, her mind felt at ease. Jazzie says grace in place of Mrs. Williams as their burrito, beef dip, churro beans, and quesadillas are delivered. It was nice to laugh and smile; it was like an ice cream cone on a hot summer's day, refreshing. While they were eating, conversing, and drinking, Jazzie had a thought.

"Mom, where can I buy scrubs from?"

"Anywhere but Wal-Mart has better prices. Why?"

"I think I can sneak into the hospital to see Jackson."

"What! I know that drink hasn't gone to your head already," replies Haley.

"No way!" Vivian squeals, "They're only letting the employees in."

"I would blend in with the staff if I dressed like a nurse. I can sneak into Jackson's hospital room unnoticed."

"Have you lost your mind child?" Mrs. Williams asks with disbelief.

"You work for the hospital system, what do you think?"

"You won't be able to get in. Only employees are allowed into the hospital for now," confirms Yvette.

"At least I can try. I don't know what the color of scrubs means, which one should I buy?" Jazzie asks, determined.

"Social workers wear gray and nurses wear dark blue."

"I can wear dark blue, be a nurse."

"You could and it's best to go during shift change. They have twelve-hour shifts."

"Okay, I will go at 7 a.m. and blend in with the morning staff."

"You need to put your hair up," Yvette continues.

"I can put it into a ball, so it won't hang."

"I'll have bail money ready," Haley responds sarcastically.

"Mama, you're not going to stop her?" questioned Vivian.

"She's grown. God has a bigger plan. As parents, we pray and have faith. Now, can I have a refill of margarita?"

"We need another pitcher but make it a Texas margarita. Vivian exclaims, "We're all accomplices!" Everyone burst into laughter.

After leaving the restaurant, Jazzie stopped at Walmart near her home and selected a sassy navy blue scrub set. While Aiden was in the shower, she Googled all the hospital entrances but discovered there was only one, through the security desk. Quickly, Jazzie packs a lunch bag with snacks and toiletries for Jackson just in case she gets stopped and uses this as an excuse. Once Jazzie heard the shower shut off, she hid the bag. Everything was prepared and set to go the following morning.

Aiden awakened at 4:40 a.m. by the bedroom alarm, Jazzie was in bed pretending to be asleep because she had the day off from work. An hour later, he was dressed for work and kissed Jazzie on the forehead, taking care not to disturb her. Aiden goes downstairs to the kitchen to retrieve his lunch from the fridge. He leaves the foyer with his briefcase and car keys and heads to the garage. Jazzie sprang to life after hearing his Charger roaring as he backed out of the driveway. She dashed into the bathroom vigorously washing her face, brushing her teeth, and pulling her hair into a firm bun. After placing a pair of small earrings in her ears, next to Jackson's diamond studs, she cautiously applied makeup to her face.

After donning the scrubs and finishing with a spray of perfume Jazzie reviewed her disguise in the mirror. She appreciated the sensation of the fabric and the comfort it provided. She slips on the tennis shoes Jackson bought her and declares to the mirror "Let's give this a shot! All they can do is tell me to leave! The things you do in the name of love." And with that, she grabbed the lunch bag and scurried out the front door. Time to put her daring plan into motion.

By 6:45 a.m., she pulls into the hospital's visitor parking lot and observes workers arriving for the day. Purple, gray, light blue, dark blue, and green scrubs all headed toward the same entrance where she had first encountered Nurse Sydney. Due to Coronavirus, it appears that this was the only access. She collects the lunch bag and the required face mask. Jazzie strolls past the security desk and onto the elevator while blending in with the flurry of colors. "I'm so glad this is the end of my week," a woman in gray scrubs exclaims aloud.

"I hope no one calls out sick because I need to leave on time today," a woman in purple scrubs responds,

"I'm tired already and I haven't even gotten off the elevator," Jazzie joins in to blend.

"Which floor, ladies?" A man asks while wearing green scrubs. They were all moving up as they called out their floor numbers. Jazzie did not know which way to go once she exited the elevator when the light on the fifth level came on, so she pretended that her phone had rung. "Hey… your dad is picking you up, I'm working late…I already cooked dinner for you guys… Mommy has to go clock in. I'll call you on my break…I love you." Jazzie looked in the direction of Room 566 and saw it while she pretended to be on the phone.

There was no turning back now, she reasoned as she passed a nursing station where several of them were gathered in a cluster. Jackson's room would be close to the nurses' station of all places! Silently, she opens the door and enters the dark room. Jackson prefers it this way. Jazzie cautiously scrutinized the bandages, bruises, and injuries while lightly stroking his chest to wake him, without startling him. Jackson opens his eyes and stares, only her eyes and hair are visible due to the face mask. He blinks as if he were seeing a ghost but he knows those eyes. He remembered Jazzie's teasing about sneaking into his room but never imagined it would be a reality.

"Babe? Is that you?" Undoubtedly, Jackson asks.

"Yes, it's me!" Jazzie removes the mask, exposing her face. Jackson's deep, dark eyes glitter with a boyish gleam, warming and delighting Jazzie's heart. His happiness is infectious, and she cannot help but smile alongside him. When Jackson smiles at her, the world stops and all they can do is bask in their love. Words failed them, but she was overcome by intense emotions as her lips engulfed his in ferocious kisses. Jazzie lightly traced her fingers across his taut skin as she gently caressed his face.

Their embrace drew a curtain of electric passion that transcended the dull clinical surroundings. Jackson sank deep into the embrace, comforted by the warmth of her touch and scent, the kind of healing his soul needed. Even though he was engulfed in rapture, she could not hold back her tears. Jazzie felt her heart swell with love and longing, gratefulness for the opportunity to be in his presence, validating the sincere bond between them. "I can't believe you did it," he chuckles; "This is one for the memory books," he felt his soul energized.

"You know I wasn't going to let no one, or nothing keep me from you," Jazzie says while she continues kissing him.

"You are something!" Jackson exclaims with joy.

"Now that the shift is changing, a nurse will soon arrive to take your vital signs, so I'm going to stand by the window."

Once Jazzie stood by the window, two nurses entered the room to examine him. One of the nurses noticed Jazzie and inquired, "Are you a family member?" before they proceeded to check him out.

"No, I'm a friend who learned he was here. I work upstairs."

"Oh, okay. We're doing our assessment."

Jazzie looked at Jackson and said, "I'll try to return on my next break."

"We're almost finished," the nurse remarked.

Jazzie responded, "Okay, I'll wait." Jazzie thinks, "Please don't ask me to help with his IV because he'll be messed up, I have no clue how to do that!" Jackson and Jazzie laughed uncontrollably when the real nurses departed.

Jackson confessed, "It's not anymore floors above us on this side."

"Oh well, I never said I worked in this building upstairs," she replied with a grin.

Alongside the bed, Jazzie approaches him again and kisses him. She fumbles in her pocket and pulls out her phone to take a picture to show the doubters that she indeed made it in.

"May I examine your wounds?"

"I don't want you to see me like this," Jackson responds feeling humiliated.

"I love you, and all of your scars. You are and always will be my sexy man, my husband." Hearing her say this gives Jackson courage, even though it hurts for him to display his wounds. Jazzie kisses the injuries that were accessible and says with one hand over his heart, "I love you."

"I love you more," he replies after placing an injured hand over her heart.

"Sadly, I must leave before your nurse returns and asks me to sponge bathe the patient in room 571, or a code blue sound on the speaker."

Abruptly, his smile vanishes; he knows she must go to avoid being discovered, but he does not want her to.

"When I get in the car, I'll phone you," she said.

He replies, "Thank you, baby," appearing revitalized.

"I did this for us," she said, "because we needed to see and touch each other."

"Can I see that behind?" He made a flirtatious inquiry.

"Babe!!! "Stop that!"

"Come on, let me see it, baby."

He grinned broadly as she turned around so he could see her butt. "I'd better go before something else wakes up!" Once Jazzie was back in her car, she quickly called him while paying the parking fee. Jackson chuckled, still astounded that she had managed to get into the hospital, knowing he was likely dozing due to the pain medication.

Jazzie urged him to rest and let her know when he was up again. She texted a picture of herself with Jackson to Yvette, Ms. Williams, Haley, and Vivian, who were left in shock. Vivian replied, "Fortunately, you weren't a murderer because he would already be dead. Nobody confronted you about sneaking into the ICU, damn! They should be cautious since it's a pandemic." Nobody will truly understand the depth of their special bond, making that visit was like gold to them.

Later that day, Jackson was able to sit up longer and even brush his teeth and freshen up. Seeing Jazzie made him push harder. Seeing Jackson helped her heart to start mending. She returned later that night to the hospital and left with the security desk, a bag of his favorite chips, Classic Plain, strawberry soda, and a phone holder so he would not strain his hands as he watched movies. Jackson was doing better and regaining an appetite. He knows with her by his side, he can do this and be back to her soon. She is mine, all mine!

CHAPTER 28

The Road to Recovery

∽✦✦✦ ♥ ✦✦✦∼

After being in the hospital for over three weeks, Jackson is getting restless and he's ready to go home. At night he and Jazzie pretend to go on dates and meet in their dreams as they sleep. Although your body is in one place, your mind can be anywhere you want it to be. Once a day she sends him pictures of them two someplace and Jackson has to guess where they are. She tries different things to positively occupy his mind instead of his thoughts of the life-changing event. She can only imagine what else is going through his head but will not invade his space right now. His texting is limited because of his injured fingers, therefore his responses have been simple. No response is needed when looking at their pictures.

"Forward the pictures of Suzie to me?" Jackson asked.

"I think you should focus on getting better. Right now it's not a good time. What did they bring you for lunch today?" Jazzie attempts to elude his request.

"Send the pictures, I want to see them." Although she does not agree, Jazzie understands and sends them. Quietly, he scans the pictures of Suzie's scattered pieces all over the road. It is heartbreaking but he is grateful to be alive and surprised that he is! Flashes of the accident flood his head again and become overbearing. He asked for a picture of her to erase the images and she sent two. Jazzie stood in her office in a fitted white dress and red strips going along the sides. The gold buttons that snapped along her hips were unfastening, slightly revealing her thigh. She has red high-heel pumps with a gold ankle bracelet. Jazzie's red earrings accessorize her heart necklace perfectly. Her hair was pulled up with strings loosely and eloquently hanging on the side. He texted back "That's what I miss most," Jackson misses her. Jazzie is impressed, this is the most he has texted in weeks. He is doing better every day.

Jackson was relieved when the doctor released him to go home. He calls Tammy so she would be on her way and then calls Jazzie. She texted him a few questions to ask the doctors when they came to go over his release. Once ready to leave, he calls Jazzie back because he knows going home he would not be able to talk to her, just text. "Babe, I'm leaving here soon."

"That's great news, where is Tammy?"

"She's waiting outside. I'll let you know when I get home."

"Tell her to fill your pain prescription soon. Focus on getting well and call me whenever you can. Don't worry about texting, I know it's difficult."

"Okay, be careful."

"Always." Jazzie was feeling glum, she knew that they would not be able to talk as often now that Tammy was taking care of him. However, she still was delighted that he was doing well. She was pleasantly surprised when Jackson sent her a text later that evening saying, "I love you."

She replied thanking him and asking him to stop texting until his finger healed, "just focus on recovering," she urged before ending her text. Jackson's living room was converted into a bedroom. He was released with a hospital bed, wheelchair, and a portable toilet. Neighbors, friends, family, and his biker buddies all pitched in. They bought a ramp to his first level of the house so he could get around, cut grass, and do anything else that was needed. The twins were ecstatic to have him home and kept him entertained with chatter, laughter, and watching movies.

Tammy is dedicated to her caretaker duties and Jackson is well taken care of, surrounded by many people who are providing him with the support he needs. Jackson and Jazzie kept in touch throughout the day, with easy conversations that were not too wearisome for him. She would send him a couple of pictures each week for them to have a game of guesswork. Jackson loved to spot memories in the collages she sent. He spends part of the day sitting in his wheelchair or on the couch, but much of the time he sleeps, as his body is not strong yet. When Tammy and the twins are away on errands, he speaks to Jazzie on the phone. This always brought a smile to his face. Jackson was finally beginning to eat fruit - something Jazzie had encouraged him to do for a while.

Two weeks following his discharge home, his pain was subsiding some and his injuries were healing. His first medical appointment presented several challenges. They had to enlist the help of neighbors to get him out of the house and into Tammy's car and back inside his home afterward. The catheter remains in place since his hips have not completely healed. The sutures were removed, giving grounds for optimism that he will be able to start physical therapy soon,

A few days later, Genesis was involved in a car accident and her car was destroyed after flipping multiple times. Despite this, she was left with sore muscles and not a single mark. Even through this turmoil, Jazzie maintained a resilient attitude and managed to stay focused and determined.

The following morning, Jackson texted her early. "Good morning, Babe, I miss you so much."

"I miss you a lot too, good morning. I constantly think of you. Mr. Davenport, I would wait a lifetime for you."

"You had better. I deserve it!"

"Want to take a picture?"

"If it's you," Jackson answers.

She sends him amusing photos of activities they engaged in on several occasions, but he was hoping for a different type of picture. He says, "Babe?"

"Yes, sir?"

"What's my Pinky up to?"

"Honestly?"

"Yes!"

"Pinky misses you, but I'll try not to arouse you. I relived the moment you made love to me during our last encounter. You filled my nectar five times, by my count. Pinky dances whenever I hear your voice or catch a glimpse of your seductive eyes on me. We are yours."

"Ouch!" This word escapes his lips, his pain level rises as he starts to awaken. Jazzie felt awful because she could tell he was becoming aroused, therefore changed the subject and decided to not text him a conversation like this right now, even if he asked her.

"Are you okay? How are your fingers and thumb?" she asks.

"Still not easy, just okay," he replies but feels his manhood trying to rise and the pain it creates.

"Take it easy and pace yourself," Jazzie could tell by his text that today was harder than usual for him, he was struggling with something.

"I need to medicate, today is a so-so. I'll check on you later," he said.

"Okay, kisses, I'm thinking of you."

"Me too Babe," Jackson missed her and Jazzie could hear it in his voice. Jackson has difficulty recovering. The road rash on his body was gradually healing but left a trail of scaling skin shedding on his bedsheets. His phone rang constantly due to family and friends who wished to inquire about his status. They would stop by to visit unannounced to ask about specifics. Although Jackson tried to avoid talking about the incident, questions kept coming up. He yearned only for peace and quietness. As Jackson lay in the hospital bed, dozing, he wished for his mother to be with him. His thoughts were a sad mantra of "Why me, why now, it was all so perfect?" before drifting back to sleep.

Jazzie began her day with a prayer to God and thanked him for the small blessings in life. She agonized over being helpless when it came to aiding Jackson and blamed herself for the incident since she yielded to temptation. While driving back to work the song, "The Battle Is Not Yours." by Yolanda Adams was playing on the radio. The sadness in her heart was released by a flood of tears. She needed this reminder that the battle was God's and not hers. Jackson is feeling better today. After a night of sleep, he is more motivated to resume living. He texts Jazzie while Tammy makes him breakfast because he suddenly ended their chat yesterday.

"I'm missing you."

She says simply, "I miss you too Jackson," and makes an effort not to arouse or attract him in any way.

"What are you wearing today?"

"Just a dress," she replies. Her high heels exposed how lovely her toes were and were freshly painted to match her attire, and her purple dress accentuated every curve of her shapely figure. She had her hair pulled back into a ponytail today, exposing the diamond studs in her ears, and wore a light dusting of makeup.

"Let me see."

Jazzie respects his request to avoid flaunting a suggestive pose and takes a simple one instead. Today she left her job earlier to let a contractor, whom Jackson knows, come to her home and renovate her kitchen, including the addition of a bigger oven for making treats. Jackson reaches out while she's on her drive home and can tell that her nipples have hardened. He craves to see and touch her.

"When will I see you again?"

"Hopefully when you are allowed to move again. Elijah can bring you to meet me."

"Okay. When will the contractors be at your house?"

"They're already there. I appreciate you sending them."

"I have to go; Tammy is coming back."

"All right, I'll text you later."

Jazzie detected sadness in his voice and sent him a message when she arrived home. They would both be happier if they could meet up face-to-face. Tammy had him under her watchful eye, and the twins were usually nearby. Unfortunately, at present, they have to wait for an opportunity. Jazzie was flipping through her phone and came upon a video of them on a trip they took to a secluded island. She shared the clip with him.

"We look fantastic in this video," Jazzie declares.

He responds, "Come see me."

"Where is your family?"

"Tammy and the twins are attending a meeting at school to discuss the upcoming year. Could you please visit me?"

"I can, Genesis will remain with the contractors. How am I going to enter the house?"

"I'll unlock the door with the app on my phone and raise the garage door."

"Okay, I'm getting into a comfy dress and will be there soon." Jackson is a technology expert and has outfitted his home with all the latest gadgets; even his light bulbs were controlled by an app. When Jazzie was in front of his house, she called. Jackson instructed her to pull into the driveway and enter the garage that he opened using the phone app. She was familiar with entering his house this way, so she opened the door without any trouble. Approaching his makeshift bedroom by walking through the kitchen, she calls out to him, "Babe it's me."

Jackson's face lit with delight when he saw her and gestured for her to move the tray table and come closer. Jazzie was wearing a dress that zips up the front and after pushing the tray away, leaned into his hospital bed and planted a passionate kiss on him. Jackson noticed how full and shapely her breasts were against his body and could not resist the urge to massage her behind. He felt a tinge of desire that led him to reach for her dress's zipper. Jazzie quickly interjected, "No baby, it may hurt if you get aroused!"

Jackson pleaded with her and eventually, she relented, allowing him to unzip her dress and expose her nipples. Jackson began to suck her nipples and she began to moan as he explored between her legs with his partially healed fingers. When he grunts, "Ouch!" she quickly pulls away to change the vibe and zips her dress.

"Let me see how your injuries are now."

"No, I don't want you to see me like this," grudgingly he replies.

"You are the same sexy man I met eleven years ago, I swear."

"It's nothing sexy about this." Though Jazzie had seen his wounds when Jackson was in the hospital. He was still uncomfortable with exposing them to her. Through the bed sheets, Jazzie can see that the endeavor to get his manhood to calm down was successful. She tenderly lifts his shirt, understanding the experience he has been through, evidenced by the scars. Again, she kisses each one. He takes the blanket as Jazzie attempts to pull it down, and she looks at him. Jackson hesitated to show his shame, eventually his trust in her allowed his arms to move. Jazzie examines his other wounds, all the while being careful not to inflict any more pain.

She bent down to kiss his stomach and inner thighs, as well as the stitches on his knees. Looking him in the eye, she reassures him, "I will always love you, no matter what marks you have." Jackson is in awe, and despite his pain, pulls her close to him and kisses her passionately. Jazzie desires to move further with him, but as he starts to become aroused, he yells, "Shit!" Jazzie quickly gets up.

"I'm going to sit over here on the sofa." Jazzie spends some more time with him chatting.

"If the outcome was different, have you done everything you wanted to do in life?"

"You know I'm a simple guy and pretty much content with things."

"What about when your mother asked when will you plan on attending church?"

"You're right, my mom did ask me that, but I'm in a good place," Jackson responded. However, his involvement with Jazzie, and his love for her outside his marriage, had left him ill-prepared for church attendance. Memories surfaced of a conversation with his mother during a visit home before she passed away. "I'm glad to hear that you're doing good son, but you know, attending church used to be such an important part of our family's life. It's not just about spirituality; it's also about being a part of a community, finding support and guidance to be a good husband, and lead your children in the right direction" his mother's voice echoed in his recollections.

"I understand where you're coming from, Mom, but things are complicated right now. A lot is going on," he confessed, his voice tinged with uncertainty.

"Complicated how?" his mother probed gently; her concern evident.

Jackson hesitates, "Well, you see, I've... I've been spending time with someone else, someone I care about deeply. It's not something I'm proud of, but it's just how things have turned out."

"Jackson, are you talking about another woman?" His mother asked with concern.

"Yes, her name is Jazzie. We've connected in a way that I can't easily explain. It's like she understands me in ways that no one else does," Jackson admitted, his voice carrying a hint of vulnerability.

Sighing, his mother responded, "Jackson, while I want you to find happiness, I also want you to remember your commitments to your marriage and family. Infidelity can cause so much pain and damage."

"I know, Mom, and that's why I haven't made any hasty decisions. But the truth is it's difficult, I can't even imagine walking away from Jazzie! We've built this refuge together, a safe haven from all the chaos in our lives. I love her, Mom," he confided.

"You love this woman; therefore I can see you're in a tough spot. Son, going back to church, could provide you with some clarity and perspective. It might help you navigate these complications and make better choices."

"The last thing I want to do is appear hypocritical, Mom. Attending church while being involved with Jazzie feels wrong! I'm trying to honor my emotions and family, even though it's all so difficult," he expressed with a touch of remorse.

"Nobody is indeed perfect, son. We all make mistakes. But acknowledging those mistakes and seeking guidance to make amends is an important step. And remember, you're not alone in this. We're here to support you, no matter what."

"I appreciate that, Mom. It's just hard to see a clear way forward right now. I love you and appreciate your words of wisdom," Jackson says softly.

"Time waits for no one, son. Think about what truly matters to you in the long run and what's right in God's eyes. Our love for you will always remain faithful, regardless of the obstacles. I'll keep praying that God shows you the answer."

Immersed in his mother's words, he didn't notice Jazzie trying to get his attention. "Jackson!" she finally exclaimed, snapping him back to reality.

"I'm sorry; I was lost in thought," he admitted with a faint smile. Jazzie glanced at her watch, aware that she needed to leave before Tammy and the twins returned. Reluctantly, she prepared to part ways, sharing one last heartfelt kiss before departing.

"Thank you; seeing you always makes me feel better," Jackson says with a smile. She checks to see if he is securely fastened in the bed, shifts the tray back to his arm's length, and then walks away, leaving her scent on his finger. When she arrived home, she sent him a text.

"I'm home."

"I'm happy that you were able to come by. Feels like you are still here."

"I still feel your touches and lips on my nipples."

"You always know how to make me happy."

"We will have our time soon," Jazzie assures him.

"You're mines!" he reminds her.

"Yes baby, 100%."

"I'll be chasing you around in no time."

"You are doing that now!"

"I'm bad," he laughs, something that feels like a stranger these days.

"I'm trouble Babe; I wanted to climb on top of you in that bed."

"I'm not scared."

"Get some rest, I will be right here," She knows he tires easily and the conversation needs to change.

"I love you, Mrs. Davenport," Jackson utters her unique name.

"And I love you more than any action, any distances, and any words, Mr. Davenport."

"You used to tell me that all of the time!"

Surprised, she replies, "I didn't think you remembered."

"Yes, I do! I remember everything about us." While the twins watched a movie, Jackson was lying in bed thinking about Jazzie. He always gets delighted when he sees Jazzie's fictitious name on a text stamp or phone call, and so does his body. Even on the worst days, just seeing her brightens his day. He enjoys seeing her all dressed up and seductive. The nightmares are occurring less, which helps him to sleep better. Jackson knows he has to keep pushing to return to Jazzie and he drifts off into a tranquil dream.

Jazzie had a pleasant bubble bath before getting into her pajamas and climbing into bed. She contemplated Jackson's mother's inquiry to him and honestly, both of them needed to return to church. Had he asked if she had accomplished all the things she wanted to do, Jazzie's answer would be no. Although she loves Aiden and thinks he is amazing, she realizes that he would be better off with someone else.

It was customary when Jazzie was a child for young women to get married by the age of twenty-one, whether they were ready or not. Jazzie had always wished her partner shared similar interests and were in love. Jazzie desires to conduct all activities in a godly manner without having to conceal or fabricate their affection. Like other couples, she wants to enjoy entertaining their friends at their house. Instead of getting out of a hotel bed and returning home to lie to Aiden with a heart filled with guilt. She wants to be able to fall asleep with Jackson at night and wake up with him in the morning.

Jazzie counsels Genesis to enter a relationship with the person she is in love with and be free to tell the world. Jazzie and Jackson are opposed to hurting others. She has a bit of him and a taste of that experience, therefore, Jazzie is content with their relationship as it stands. Jazzie struggles with the notion that she is costing Jackson his moral integrity. But she loves him so much; how can she let him go?

CHAPTER 29

A Risky Encounter

Jackson was dreading his doctor's appointment. The next step to feeling more like himself is having the catheter, which he finds repulsive and uncomfortable, removed today. He arrives early to prepare for a cystogram test, MRI, and to check both leg lengths. Dr. Taylor outlined what was going to happen and then the nurse started an IV. Jackson received a sedative, but he was still aware. After there were no more questions, Jackson was moved to a procedure room. Two hours later, they were done and the catheter was removed. His hips were healing properly and bladder functions were normal. Jackson was concerned about his manhood but was relieved when he received confirmation it was fine, and he texted Jazzie right away.

"Ahhhhhhhh."

"Is it out?

"Yes!" Jackson exclaims.

"Outstanding, Happy Birthday!" His birthday is tomorrow, and she was praying they would remove the catheter so he could have a happier birthday.

Jackson has worried senselessly about the functionality of his reproductive organs since his accident and is keen to determine if it is working. While Tammy is driving, he is looking through his secret app on his phone all of Jazzie's pictures. He saw a photograph of her wearing a white dress with high slits which revealed her succulent thighs.

"Look at that leg!" He forwarded the photo to her.

"I remember that night, you were all over me!"

"You just don't know how badly I wanted you that night," Jackson replies.

"I was only being myself."

"You always have that effect on me," he flirts.

"You do the same to me! My nipples have been doing their own thing with a thought of you." Jazzie was too embarrassed to acknowledge that her nipples had been aroused the entire day. Her bosoms were so full that they were spilling out of the upper area of her undergarment.

"I'm getting harder now, and it feels good!" He is gladdened that his manhood is once again functioning normally.

"Yes, show me!" Jazzie says.

"Regardless of what you are wearing, you turn me on."

"Send me a picture when you can so I can see for myself," Jazzie requested.

"I just did." At the doctor's office, he had already taken a picture.

"That's him, Welcome back!"

"He wants to feel you sliding up and down."

"In due time, I will."

"That time is today!"

"How?"

"The twins are at work from 4 p.m. to 11:30 p.m. today and tomorrow. Mia's car is overheated, and Tia's car needs a rear tire, so Tammy is taking and picking them up."

"Can Pinky play with you if I promise to be careful when you're ready?"

"Yes, feel free to slide on me; I'd enjoy that. I'm ready now."

"Now? Are you sure?"

"Yes, when can you come to me?"

"When do you want me to?"

"Tammy leaves to pick up the twins at 10:15 p.m. Come after she leaves."

"Are you sure Babe, don't rush it. We can wait."

"Come tonight, I'm certain of it."

"Since it's your birthday tomorrow, you might have a lot of visitors tonight."

"I don't think so. I've been in pain with that catheter, so I haven't mentioned my birthday to anyone plus the pandemic is rising."

"You have so many reasons to celebrate your birthday. I've got a token for you."

"True. I'm upset that I missed hearing your voice today."

"I understand that you were busy."

"Are you going to cum for me, baby?" Jackson is tired of circling the issue.

"Most definitely!"

"Being in my Pinky will feel fantastic."

"I'll be gentle."

"I also had my staples removed today and almost completely healed. I'm ready for you."

"Let me know when she is getting dressed so I'll be in the neighborhood when she leaves."

"Okay, I'm looking at your picture so my manhood can rise. It feels so good."

"Which one?"

"All of them, I'm taking turns. It doesn't hurt anymore! I'm enjoying simple things in life!" Jackson laughs.

"I'm coming to see for myself. I'll take a shower and be ready when you text."

"Okay." Jazzie is excited about seeing him. She is aware that he tends to get a bit too frisky without his fill of her, however, ultimately making sure he is cautious is essential. She gets in the shower and washes her hair, shaves her underarms, and Pinky completely off. Once she is done, she places moisturizer on her skin and refrains from wearing any perfume that leads a trace of her path into Jackson's house. She wears easy-access shorts and a tank top that provides a good view of her breasts, no panties, and a bra. Finally, she applies mousse to her damp curls and awaits his message.

Around 9:40 p.m. she heard the ding of her phone. Jackson says, "Hey, we won't have long."

"It's enough for me to touch you but I need to be in your neighborhood when she leaves out."

"True."

Jazzie responds, "I can wait," though she is hesitant to leave.

"Wait, for what? I've been waiting for you long enough."

"Wait for a better time, but I can still come if you want." Jazzie did not think he was healed enough for this, but Jackson was not taking no for an answer.

"Now is good, she is getting ready."

"Are you sure about this?"

"I'm sure, come on."

"On the way."

Jazzie grabs her wallet, and before the clock strikes 10:32 p.m., she is out the door. Aiden is putting in extra hours this evening training new employees, she predicts she will be returning home before him. As she travels in complete darkness, Jazzie keeps an eye out for wandering deer on the side of the road. She gets into Jackson's area ten minutes later and is about to text him when he phones.

She answers, "Hey Babe, I'm in your neighborhood."

"Park in the driveway next to Mia's car, behind Tammy's SUV in the garage," he directs. "Should I stay in bed or sit on the chair?"

"Wherever you feel comfortable. I don't want you to move if it's not necessary and fall. What I need is Rodney and he moves just fine."

"Have you been doing squats to prepare for him?"

"I didn't expect you would be ready this quickly, but I did a few," she chuckles, "You are too fast."

"I told you I was coming back for my Pinky!" Jackson exclaimed with pride.

While Jazzie parks, she notices Jackson's truck is gone, indicating Tammy was driving it. She enters the house through the garage, passing Tammy's SUV on the way in. As usual, Jazzie removed her flip-flops and left them in the hallway by the door. She then walks into his temporary room and undresses. Jackson was already undressed due to his road rash and needing to get the air to heal. Jazzie finally reached him and grabbed his hands, pulling him up towards her.

Jazzie delicately raises his legs and places them on the floor. Once stable, Jackson shifts his body to the left towards the portable toilet. She stands beside him to shelter him from falling. He grasps the armrest of the toilet, dragging it closer and sliding onto it. Jackson looks thirsty for her. After setting himself into a comfortable position, Jazzie made sure he was all right before leaning in to kiss him. His lips were still soft.

Kneeling between his legs onto her knees, Jazzie looks at him with passion. Jackson is anticipating what she will do next. She guides his right hand to place over her heart, expressing, "I love you." Taking her hand and kissing it, he then puts it over his heart and replies, "I love you even more." She grasped his manhood with her right hand and started to massage him while rubbing his chest with her left. His body had an intense response to her tender caresses. Jazzie moves to slide her tongue up and down his length, and then she steps away. She kissed his chest and faced her backside to him, planting herself over his manhood with great care. As she moved up and down, they both began to sense a strong need for one another. Finally, when their climax is built to the point of no return, she screams, "I'm going to cum," as he cries out in delight, "Aaaaaawwwwww!" She shuddered and let out a deep sigh before she melted into him, dripping down his manhood, the sweetest pleasure.

Turning back around to face him, she observes his erection tinted white. Trying to avoid letting her flow wet the carpet, Jazzie is still in the throes of her orgasm. Jackson asks her to fetch paper towels from the kitchen. Acting quickly, she retrieves them and thoroughly wipes the traces of their lust off him. Glancing at the clock, Jazzie notes they still had some time remaining. She returned him to the bed before gathering the paper towels and depositing them on the couch for later disposal. Before leaving, she bends to deliver a fiery kiss, which he responds to by seizing her breasts and kissing her passionately while spreading her legs.

Jazzie attempts to get away, yet his hold stays firm. Suddenly, Jazzie positions herself on his bed, carefully straddling him. Lowering herself onto her knees, thrusting her breast in his face, she was ready to mount him in the hospital bed, when something interrupted them.

"Oh no!" she panics, as they both hear someone coming in through the garage.

His truck alarm blared and Jackson groans, "Fuck, it's Tammy!" Jazzie sprung off him nearly as fast as a superhero! Because of the location of her clothes and car keys, Jazzie only had time to choose one to snatch, which was her clothes. She quickly ran to the front staircase, opposite the kitchen, and tried to get her top on. If they were caught, Jackson would lose so much. Jazzie is undressed in their home, engaging in an intimate encounter with this woman's husband who is currently confined to bed! Not good! Should it come to that, Jazzie prefers to confront Tammy while clothed. After calming down and concentrating, she managed to put her shirt back on. Hiding by the stairs, Jazzie peeks to see which direction Tammy went.

While cleaning the kitchen countertops, Tammy said, "The girls didn't tell me they had a ride from work and called me when I got halfway there so I turned around." Tammy was not going back out and Jazzie had to conjure a quick plan before the twins returned home. Walking around to the other side of the stairs, she made eye contact with Jackson near the temporary bedroom and motioned at him that her keys and paper towels filled with their deception were on the sofa. Jackson made a gesture that suggested that she should go out the front door. When Jazzie notices him on the phone, she realizes he must be disabling the alarm. She moves stealthily in that direction, unlocks the front door, and sneaks out.

Jazzie was thankful that she had not locked her car doors or brought her phone inside, as normal. She climbed into her car and sent a text to Jackson. "My keys and shoes are in there. I'm inside my car parked in your driveway."

"Where are your shoes?" Jackson questioned.

"I left them in the hallway by the garage door," Jazzie replies. "Can you text Miller and ask him to come by and pretend I'm with him? I'll walk up the street so your wife won't see me sitting in my car."

"Okay, say you're Miller's friend and he dropped you back off to get his keys and to move his car. I'm about to call your phone."

"Where does Miller live?"

"Up the street towards the pool."

Jackson calls her and acts as if he is talking to Miller, "Yeah man, come back through the garage, I'm still awake. I see some keys sitting on the sofa." Then he whispers, "Hurry up before the twins get home." Mia and Tia know her and would blow their lie to pieces. Jazzie walks back to his house bare feet and enters the open garage. She was in disbelief but needed her keys and knocked on the garage door while going in and announced, "Hey Jackson, it's me."

As Jazzie enters the house, she retrieves her flip-flops and slides them on. When she sees Tammy, she asks, "How are you doing?"

Tammy replies, "Hey," as she looks up at Jazzie and continues cleaning the countertop. Jazzie ventures into Jackson's room and declares, "Miller said his keys are still here."

"Where is he?" Jackson asks playing along with this game of deceit.

Jazzie collected her keys and the paper towels and said, "Take care, Jackson, I'm sure you'll be feeling better soon." She wandered to the kitchen towards the doorway of the basement. intending to use the garage entrance.

"It's the other door," Tammie says. Recalling her time spent as Jackson's sex slave a few weeks before his accident, Jazzie knew that. Faking ignorance she asked,

"There are so many doorways. Did you want the garage door locked?"

"No, it's fine to remain unlocked," Tammie answered. Jazzie said her farewells and hopped into her automobile, starting it up and driving away in haste. As she drove off, her phone chirped.

Jackson texts, "Close!"

"Wow! No more of that Babe. That's the last thing you need right now, her finding out about me."

"Yeah, you're right."

"I'll stay away. I don't want to but it's best. Tammy is not stupid, and you need her right now. I'll figure out how to get your birthday token to you tomorrow."

Jazzie considered what had transpired once she was back at home. She was more worried about Jackson than she was about herself. Now more than ever before, he needs Tammy. They had a chance to visit each other while he was recovering, but that opportunity is now gone. While feeling remorseful, at this point, Jazzie realized their only option was to wait.

CHAPTER 30

Scent of Reflection

❧❧❧ ♥ ❧❧❧

Today is Jackson's birthday, and just being alive is a cause for celebration. Jazzie was determined to make it extra special. She has been going around Atlanta rounding up all of his friends and family -- including his Biker Family -- to sign a card, adding words of encouragement and funny phrases. At Party City, she snagged three balloons: one of which reads "Happy Birthday" and two of which read "Get Well."

At Publix, Jazzie put together a basket full of his favorite snacks such as chips, nuts, candy, and cookies. After last night's close call, she had the basket delivered to his home. A delivery confirmation showing receipt of the package is sent to Jazzie. When the package arrived, Tammy was blown away by the gesture. When she brought it to Jackson, he couldn't believe it – but knew who to thank and sent Jazzie a text saying, "I appreciate the card and goodies, thank you!"

I figured you would."

"I love it, Babe, thank you so much. It's very much like me!"

"I'm happy you love it. Happy Birthday! Want to do a quick virtual cake and candle celebration later?"

"Yes, that's great. Around 5:30 p.m., Tammy will be taking the twins to work, leaving me alone."

"I'll see you then."

Jackson was feeling quite well, combining laughter and the inspiration of wishes made on his get-well card. With the sweet words of love, jokes, reminiscences, and advice from close family and friends, he was elated. Although little actions are easily taken for granted, now, with Jackson's decreased mobility, a shower seemed to be a luxury. He dialed Jazzie's office number, longing to hear her voice and check how her day was unfolding. Reclined on his bed, nibbling on mixed nuts, he turned over ideas on how to get to the shower upstairs. Glancing down at the card from his well-wishers, a message stood out: *"It's not how long it takes to get there, but as long as you try, one step at a time."*

Recognizing this statement to be the answer, he asked his family for help. Together, they slowly made their way up the stairs with Jackson scooting upstairs, one step at a time, taking breaks as needed. After reaching the top of the staircase, they placed him back in the wheelchair. Tammy prepared the shower complete with a hospital chair — ready for him to comfortably maneuver over.

Jackson relished the relaxing flow of water washing over him and took a deep breath of relief.

With a few precise motions of his razor, he was once again himself — clean-shaven, his bald head glistening under the water, his beard and sideburns neatly trimmed. Jackson blissfully enjoyed the shower he had gone without for months, finding a rejuvenating sensation in the water cleansing his skin and the towel caressing it once again. Tammy and the twins helped him back downstairs to his bed. He sent Jazzie a picture and she noticed the contentment in his appearance and responded with a pleasant, "Yes, you are!" He close his eyes and drift off to sleep - dosed up on Percocet.

Jazzie stops at the store on the way home from work to get a small Carvel ice cream cake and a trick candle for the virtual birthday celebration with Jackson. Knowing Aiden would not be back from work around 7:00 p.m., she had enough time to whip up a meal and hop in the shower. Brannon wandered into the kitchen looking for signs that dinner would be ready shortly. Seeing his favorite cake tucked away in the freezer, he noticed it was a birthday cake. Just as Jazzie came downstairs, showered and in shorts and shirt, he yelled out, "Mom! Whose birthday is it?"

She removed the cake from the freezer so it would be easier to cut and said, "It's Mr. Jackson's; remember he isn't mobile so we're doing this virtually. Would you like to participate?" Brandon was quite fond of the idea and requested they divide the two-person ice cream cake in half for him. She had dinner ready but there was no word yet from Jackson at 6:15 p.m. Brandon was ready with the candle while Jazzie had the plates set up; all they needed was for Jackson to call. "Where are you?" Jazzie texts.

Thirty minutes later, he responds, "Home, Miller is here chillin'. What are you doing?"

"What I'm doing? I'm waiting for you to sing Happy Birthday with your cake. I see you are busy, it's cool."

"Hold on, wait for me. Give me ten minutes."

"I will try."

Before Aiden made it home, Jazzie had Brandon chow down on the ice cream cake after she took a photo of it. Curious, Brandon asks about the candle, so Jazzie dumps it in the trash. Unwinding for the evening, Jazzie's phone beeped while watching television with Aiden.

"Ready?"Jackson texts.

"We're already done; it's 8.27 p.m. I'll let you get back to your family, text me later."

"Thank you, Babe!"

"No problem," she responds dryly.

"I love you guys!"

"We love you too."

Jackson regrets having overlooked the virtual cake celebration. He spent the evening having dinner with Tammy, the twins, and a few buddies. Upon everyone's departure, he was getting tired. After getting him ready for bed, Tammy quickly nods off on the sofa next to the hospital bed. Mia and Tia followed, dozing down on the floor next to the hospital bed while inside their sleeping bags. Gazing at his family, sleeping soundly, Jackson's mind began to wander. To celebrate his birthday is a blessing. Despite Tammy being unremittingly supportive and having wonderful friends to help him, Jackson keeps replaying the previous night with Jazzie.

He recalls her curves, girlish smile, and hair behind one ear, inducing a growing arousal. Although Jackson still feels uneasy about what happened last night, he still craves Jazzie and his conscience is loud. Jackson murmurs inaudibly. "I know Tammy loves me, but I just can't help wanting Jazzie." He reflects upon the sorrowful expressions his twins had when they snuffed out his candle.

"Daddy, we never imagined we'd be able to see you again. We thought you were gone!" They tearfully uttered. He feels fortunate to have been granted a second opportunity to live and to do right. A familiar aroma dances in the room and he stirred with a peculiar expression. Scanning the room, nothing was there, all he could hear were the quiet rumblings of his own thoughts. The television was switched off so he could sleep, but the scent had grown stronger.

His mom's cigarettes. Jackson is curious why now he feels her presence. He knows what she wants in his heart but is reluctant to say it. The decision he had to make weighed heavy in his heart. In a resigned, yet weary voice he spoke, "I don't want to hurt her, Mom." Exhaustion took over and he fell asleep.

CHAPTER 31

A Rollercoaster of Emotions

With a bright new day ready to start, Jazzie felt re-energized. She chose a stylish dress that had been hanging in her closet for a while. Completing her look with cute eyelashes, a sleek ponytail, beautiful make-up, and fashionable heels, she was ready to head off to the office. Later she had plans with Yvette for an evening of drinks, but she still carried a heavy heart. To stay productive and focused on something positive, she decided to tackle a few projects at home that she had been putting off.

When Jackson calls, Jazzie lies about how lost she is without him, so he can concentrate solely on healing. Though they have been side by side for a long time, now her days and evenings are spent imagining the day they will be back together. Even if Jazzie acutely feels a tear in her heart, she is determined to patiently wait for the opportunity to see him in person again. Jazzie's life is a rollercoaster ride of highs and lows, but she knows that pushing her family and friends away is not the answer.

At long last, Jackson is steadily getting better. Soon, he will start physical therapy, which would need all of his attention. After savoring a cup of coffee and strolling through her phone, she fondly recalled a photo of them at the Monster Truck Event. It was a new experience for him, one he never did with his father. The delight on Jackson's face was etched in her memory forever. Jazzie texts the photo for their weekly picture-guessing game.

"Good morning!"

"Good morning, Babe, I love this picture of you!" Jackson answers.

"I wasn't looking at the camera correctly."

"I like how you were smiling and the Rhinestone head chain on your forehead," Jackson says.

"Thank you. That evening, we drank too much and couldn't find the car."

"Laughing hard…and it rained on us!"

"Certainly did! You could see my breasts when we eventually arrived at the car because I was wearing a white top. To help me dry off, you removed my blouse." When they discovered the car, her hair was wet and curly, as Jackson clearly recalls. He removed her blouse and jeans to dry her off in his truck with a towel, but he could not help himself. He unfastened his jeans, pulled her onto the seat, and pushed inside her as the parking lot echoed around them. Jackson is developing between his legs in bed as a result of that reminiscence.

"I need you Babe, I'm serious!"

"I need you too; we'll have our time when you're stronger."

"Elijah called and said to let him know if I needed to get out and take a ride."

"That's a wonderful idea; you should look at some other trees besides the ones in your front yard."

"I was hoping to see you."

"Wow, that would be great. I'll be here when you're ready."

"Mia will be at work, Tammy will get her brakes fixed at my shop, and Tia will be at her friend's house. Can I call you on video?"

"Sure, but text me in advance so I can go for lunch at that time and talk freely in my car and not at my desk."

"Okay, I'll talk to you later."

Jackson tussles with his emotions, determined to remain focused despite the relentless pull of his desire to be with Jazzie. Even though they have not seen each other for a while, he knows that they need to have a conversation soon, to discuss the weighty choices ahead. Jackson's mind is a battleground of conflicting thoughts. He realizes that no matter which path he chooses, someone will inevitably get hurt. The thought gnaws at him while tugging at his heart with each passing moment.

Memories of Jackson's conversation with his mother continually resurface and play like a filmstrip in his mind, as he wrestles with his internal conflict. He vividly recalls her compassionate face, her advice, and her concerns about his choices. The absence of her comforting presence weighs heavily, a presence he missed deeply, especially during challenging times like these.

Considering his next moves, Jackson is prompted to remember her guidance. He contemplates whether to seek solace through spirituality. Revisiting the church which once held importance for him could steer his uncertain path.

The happiness Jazzie brings into his life is undeniable. Their connection is unlike anything he has experienced before, a rare understanding that transcends words. It is as if the universe conspired to bring them together. But as Jackson mulls over his options, he cannot escape the reality that his actions will have repercussions, affecting not only his own life but would ripple through the lives of those around him. Jackson reflects on his twins, the innocent lives that depend on him for love and guidance. His love for them was undeniable. And then there is Tammy, his partner in the parenting journey, the one he made vows to. Her loyalty and commitment to his recovery were deeply appreciated. Despite the evolution of Jackson and Jazzie's relationship, their unbreakable bond could be shattered if he opts for God's will, morals, and his conscience.

The conflicting emotions surge within him like a tempestuous sea, threatening to engulf his sense of clarity. Jackson knows that he cannot remain in this limbo forever, it is time to make a decision.

Jazzie is starting to feel hungry at about 2 p.m. She is waiting for Jackson to call so she can eat and converse freely during her lunch break. Jazzie starts eating her lunch, assuming he is napping, when she hears her phone buzz. "Can you video chat now?" Jackson texts. When Jazzie replies yes, he phones her as she takes her lunch and walks to the outside employees' picnic area.

"I've been expecting you."

"Tammy had to fix my lunch before she left."

"Good for her," Jazzie says coldly.

"How are you feeling today?"

He looks sorrowful as he stares at her, and adds, "I had better days."

Jazzie notes how he appears, nearly in anguish. "Can you take your pain reliever if you're in pain?"

"It doesn't matter; it won't work on this pain."

Jazzie is perplexed and asks, "What kind of pain is that?" If your medicine isn't working, you should talk to your doctor about changing it. Consider using natural herbal therapy. It works well for Vivian!" Jazzie giggles but he does not laugh. She is aware that he does not use marijuana, but she merely suggested it to lighten the mood because Jackson was not smiling.

"Jazzie "I need you to listen to me," he says solemnly.

Jazzie puts her food down, and now she is overcome with worry.

"What is it, Jackson, do you have to go back to the doctor?"

"Baby I love you so much, but but but……this entire experience has been eye-opening. I don't want to hurt anyone, but seeing my daughters cry because they are afraid I won't return home broke my heart."

Jazzie cuts him off. "What exactly are you trying to say, Jackson?"

"I have to do the right thing for Tammy and our girls, so we can't continue like this anymore. Tammy is doing her best to support me through this ordeal. It's a chance for us to start fresh. I was hoping to discuss this with you face-to-face, but unfortunately, traveling is difficult for me at the moment. I apologize for doing this while you're at work, but this is the only time I have to myself." Jazzie feels like she swallows something huge and it is stuck in her throat. She coughs and clears her throat so she can speak.

"I'm happy that you, Tammy, the girls, and your dog can be a family. New house, new car, new truck, new friends...old me! I get it, it's cool. Understand this, she would never love you the way I do. Unlike her, it's not your wallet I want Jackson, it's you even if it means you being in a wheelchair. She is there because it's her role. I don't trust her so watch out for her. I'll work on closing our checking and saving accounts. The credit cards don't have any outstanding balances, so I will close them. They'll need your signature, but I'll sign for you."

"Baby, please..."

She firmly interrupts him. "Don't call me that! Let's keep it brief and to the point. Tammy is there for you, not me, because you won't let me. You can't see what she's up to, but you will. I overheard your neighbor, Miller, warning you to be cautious; you don't want to wind up like the man in the wheelchair in the movie "Diary of a Mad Black Woman" because of interacting with me. I never desired or requested your money, only your love, but you didn't tell him that! I'll support your decision because I want you to be happy, and if she makes you happy, so be it. I don't want you to shatter the twins' hearts, so it's all right with me. I'm glad this time allowed you and Tammy to rediscover each other and your mission. Keep getting better, and best of luck with your rehabilitation." Jackson sees her struggling not to cry, but the tears escape, running down her face. It hurts him to see her like this.

"Can I still text you and check on you?" He inquires.

"Are we supposed to be friends now? I'll be fine, you don't need to check on me. Concentrate on your family and recovery. I'm not the one that needs to be saved. I have to return to work." After ending the call, Jazzie and her entire body trembled as she wept. She allowed him to be her lifeline, lover, and best friend, now what? This is too much, there is no way she can go back to work. Jazzie returns to the office and informs her supervisor that she is ill and needs to leave. Exiting the office, Jazzie's phone rings. A close friend asks about how Jackson is doing. With annoyance, Jazzie replies, "Ask his wife! I'll call you later." She then gets in her car and drives away.

The pandemic had turned Atlanta's social scene into a dystopian nightmare. Jazzie was tired of the new normal of mask-wearing, sitting on every other chair, social distancing six feet apart, and the whole germ alert duty! She just wanted to have a drink and forget about today, 2020, and Jackson. Downtown was out of the question with the Black Lives Matter protest causing heavy traffic in the area. But then she stumbled upon a bar near

Vivian's house and called her to meet up. Vivian had been in quarantine and working from home which was getting tedious.

She eagerly agreed and dashed out the door after tossing on a jogging suit. When Jazzie walked into the laid-back bar, she saw everyone in masks and some bouncing in their chairs to the music playing. She only had her identification and credit card - no purse or cell phone. Jazzie signaled for the bartender to come over and dryly spat her drink order, "One Blue Mother Fucker!" As she settled into her seat, she noticed a guy across the counter staring at her. He signaled the bartender, and they talked as they looked in Jazzie's direction. The bartender approached her and said, "The gentleman in the red shirt wants to buy your next round." Jazzie looked over and saw a wedding ring on his finger and said sarcastically,

"Tell him to save it for his wife; I will buy my own drinks!" Jazzie was not in the mood for any bullshit today and it showed. She saw Vivian bouncing to the music when she entered the bar. "Oh, that's my shit playing!" "How are you, Sis?" Vivian embraces her.

"Shit," Jazzie remarked coldly.

"It must be some shit because you started off drinking hard!" She motions to the bartender. "Please give me a Coke and Hennessey, with light ice please."

"I needed something hard and strong today."

Vivian can tell something is bothering her. "I'm glad to see other humans besides myself in the mirror, girl! What's the matter with you?"

Jazzie confides in Vivian about her situation with Jackson, hoping for her support, but Vivian does not take her side. "Sis, you both knew that he was married and so are you. Jackson may be fine with you, but he's probably preoccupied with other things. His wife is there to take care of him and handle the things he can't do at the moment. Would it be appropriate for him to come to your house and for you to take time off work to care for him? No, Sis. He's doing what's best for himself and his family. Unfortunately, in war, there are casualties, and one of them is you. I could understand if he had said he was going to be with someone else, but it's his wife!"

"But what about me, what am I supposed to do?"

"I can sum up everything I've learned about life in five words: Life goes on without you. You're supposed to cry, cleanse your soul, and resume your life. Because of the type of man he is, you fell in love with him. He's still that man, doing what he feels compelled to do. You are being selfish and thinking about yourself right now. Jackson has a long road to recovery, and worrying about you will not assist him."

"It's no longer us; it's THEM. He doesn't want me."

"From a moral standpoint, he must do this. Jackson nearly died and has been granted a second chance to accomplish what is right in God's eyes. At the very least, he must try Jazzie."

"We committed major sins that were wrong, but it felt good because no one knew. We became so engrossed in each other that we forgot about our spouses, children, and duties. It aches because I love him so much but he is better off without me." She requests another drink from the bartender, making it her third.

"Find something for you to do that's positive and of good energy. What you two have is powerful. If it's meant to be, it will be but the right way."

"I can't see that right now," Jazzie groans, sickly.

"Did you eat anything today, Sis?"

"I started eating, lost my appetite, and then threw it away."

"You need to eat right now, and you need to put that drink down!" Jazzie jumps out of her chair and asks a waitress where the restroom is. Jazzie takes off running, covering her mouth with her hands as the waitress motions to the right.

The next morning, Jazzie awakes with a pounding headache and a dry mouth. She tried to sit up, but her body felt heavy and unresponsive. She looked around and realized she was not in her bed, yet the room was familiar. On a nearby dresser is displayed a picture of her and Vivian when they were little girls at church. This comforts her and she knows she is safe, at Vivian's house. She could not remember how she got there or what happened last night. She tried to remember the events of the previous night, but her mind was blank.

A wave of panic washed over her as Jazzie realized she had driven her car and didn't know where it was. She stumbled to her feet and made her way to the bedroom door, opening it slowly, she peered into the hallway. It was empty and silent. Sluggishly she walks to the kitchen for a glass of water and opens the refrigerator, of course, no food! She calls out to Vivian but does not get a response. Jazzie opens Vivian's bedroom door to check on her and walks in. "What the hell!" Jazzie sees the guy in the red shirt from the bar naked in bed with Vivian.

"Good morning Sis! This is..what did you say your name was?"

"It's Lamar."

"Lamar!" exclaims Vivian

"Get dressed and come out here, right now!" Jazzie commands Vivian. Jazzie knows he is married and does not want her sister to be in her shoes. Vivian came out with a robe, wondering why Jazzie's behavior was bizarre. "What's up with you, that was rude?"

"He's married, Vivian!"

"No, he isn't!"

"He is, just look at his finger! He tried to buy me a drink at the bar before you arrived yesterday." Jazzie was loud enough for Lamar to hear, and he walked out of the room with only a t-shirt and his jeans. He offers his hand and says, "Hi Jazzie, it's nice to meet you, but let me explain."

Jazzie refused to shake his hand and said flatly, "Do you have coronavirus?"

Vivian had enough and declared, "That's it! You will not be rude to my guest and for the record, he's not married like I said. His wife died three years ago in a car accident; he was driving. He's not Jackson, and while we're on the subject, text him. He's been worried sick about you!" Jazzie collapses onto the floor and sobs, feeling broken and lost. Her emotions are all over the place and out of control. This is not her; she is better than this. Lamar kneels to assist her and then retrieves a tissue from the bathroom. Lamar is sympathetic to the situation because he was once in her shoes.

"My wife and I were on our way to my mother-in-law's house to pick up the kids. She preferred to wait until the following day, but I insisted on going that evening. I didn't want to stop watching football the next day to pick them up. My wife was aware that I was tired, but I drove anyway. I dozed off, and when I awoke, it was seventeen weeks later. I was in a coma, and she had been laid to rest. I was unfaithful to her and never had the opportunity to make amends. The guilt was difficult to bear, and I didn't believe I deserved forgiveness. Your sister filled me in, and I can feel your friend's choice. He must do this; he has to try for his sake and his soul. He likely still needs you, but not in an unholy way. Do not grieve, for the joy of the Lord is your strength."

"Nehemiah 8:10," she confirms, looking at him.

Vivian blows the vibe, "Before ya'll have Bible study can we go hit Waffle House? I'm hungry and you know ain't nothing in my fridge."

"I'm Jazzie," she says extending her hand.

"Nice to meet you, and no, I don't have coronavirus," he laughs as he shakes her hand. "I offered you a drink yesterday because you appeared agitated, nothing more."

"I think I'll skip the drinks for the time being. I'm sorry for being such a…"

"Bitch!" Exclaims Vivian.

"I guess I was. I'm sorry Vivian."

"It's fine, Ms. Jazzie," Lamar says.

"Gi-rrrrl it's cool, we family. Are we done with the Kumbaya's now? May we go get some breakfast? My stomach is hitting my back?" Vivian adds her two cents.

CHAPTER 32

Navigating the Path of Healing

❧ ♥ ❧

Time stretched its invisible threads, weaving a web of silence that extended over two weeks. Jazzie and Jackson were left stranded in a void of unanswered calls and unacknowledged messages. Each interaction he made was ignored while she reconciled the shifts that had unfolded in her life, Jazzie was unsure of how to begin the process of healing while trapped in the clutches of uncertainty. She acknowledged the necessity of forging ahead on the path to healing though the starting point remained elusive.

The first step on this journey toward new horizons was to sever the ties that bound her to Jackson's world. A poignant reminder of their shared adventures was her matching motorcycle, it had to find a new home. It would be awkward to encounter his friends when they were no longer together, and they knew her as his girlfriend. The world that once embraced them as a united force now felt unfamiliar. Aiden, a beacon of support, rejoiced at the news of the motorcycle's sale, finding a buyer, his coworker. Before the final exchange of ownership, Jazzie took the beloved bike for one last spin, tracing familiar paths around the neighborhood.

With care, she shares knowledge with the new owner, detailing how to operate the LED lights, the precise oil required, and the rituals of maintaining the bike's gleaming chrome wheels and parts. All the accessories of their motorcycle adventures, including the riding gear, found a new home with the buyer. As the transaction culminated, Jazzie immortalized the bittersweet farewell with a picture, capturing herself alongside the new owner of her two-wheeled companion. A smile decorated her face, concealing the heaviness that settled within her soul. While the new owner rode off, reveling in the newfound joy of ownership, Jazzie's heart sank, drenched in a melancholic shade.

Returning to her bedroom, tears streamed down her cheeks, tracing a map of sorrow upon her skin. She sought solace in her bedroom and allowed herself to express her devastation. But during the waves of grief, a flicker of courage emerged. It was then that she made a decision, a vulnerable act of reaching out. She forwarded Jackson a photograph, revealing the buyer and the motorcycle, juxtaposed against her dresser is the customized tag "BABE." As Jackson's phone buzzed with the arrival of a text, excitement surged through his veins, only to be swiftly doused by confusion. In the palm of his hand, a picture came across of Jazzie standing beside a man, her bike, and the remnants of a connection he had believed to be unbreakable.

"Glad to hear from you, I was worried. Who's your friend?" Jackson eagerly questioned.

"He's not a friend, he's the buyer."

"Did you sell your bike?" Jackson probed further.

"Yes, I did."

"You loved that bike. Are you sad?"

"I'll be fine. He was really happy to buy it."

"What's next for you?"

"I have no idea. 2020 hasn't been very appealing to me."

"I know Babe, but it won't last forever. It was time to let the bike go anyway." It's difficult for her to let go of the feeling of missing him and the sweet sound of his voice calling her "Babe."

However, she understands the importance of moving forward. Lamar, Vivian's new friend reminds her. "Jackson, I understand and accept your decision to move on. I apologize for any unkindness I showed toward you when I was hurting. If you believe this is what you need to do, I won't stand in your way. I realize I'm a distraction in your life, and you need to focus on your goals. If it's alright with you, I'd like to check in on your progress from time to time."

"I apologize for upsetting you, Jazzie. It wasn't my intention. I appreciate your apology. Thank you."

Jackson loves Jazzie deeply, but he has to make a tough decision for the sake of his family. Jazzie is trying her best to remain strong, but she is feeling empty and alone. She recognizes that distancing herself from Jackson is the best course of action. For years, Jazzie has not been able to reciprocate Aiden's love because she always yearned to be with Jackson. Tonight, she needs Aiden's love to help her forget about Jackson, even if it is only for one night.

During the following weeks, Jazzie and Jackson messaged each other regarding his recovery. Despite her own emotions, Jazzie made it a priority to support his well-being. Although Jackson's physical treatment has become increasingly rigorous, he finds comfort in receiving messages from Jazzie, specifically her uplifting Bible verses. Today, Jackson has a physical therapy appointment and Jazzie sends him a text to wish him well, even though she is aware that Tammy is accompanying him.

"Good morning Jackson."

"Good morning, I was waiting on my thought for today, I'm going to need it."

"When trouble surrounds you and no one understands, try placing your cares in God's open hands. *Into your hands, I commend my spirit.... Psalm 31.5.* Today concentrate on being optimistic, not pessimistic."

"You always know how to get me motivated, thank you."

"You got this! You're most welcome and don't forget to take some over-the-counter pain meds and then your muscle relaxer afterward."

"Okay, thank you." Jackson is facing a challenge during his therapy, but he is motivated by Jazzie's words of encouragement. Her support helps him push through and complete his activity with even greater intensity. Afterward, he takes time to rest and uses muscle relaxants to manage any discomfort. His goals for therapy are to manage pain, improve hip movements, increase leg mobility, strength, and flexibility, and speed up healing. Jackson was eager to restore his ability to perform daily activities. He is happy to see progress in all of these areas today, and he remains focused on his ultimate aim of progressing from the wheelchair to the walker and, eventually, walking independently.

Later that night, while watching television with his family, Jackson's thoughts wander. He longs for Jazzie's infectious smile and the happiness she brings him. Jazzie has been a source of joy, laughter, hope, and life for him. Despite his struggle to stay focused on his family, a delightful sound from his phone indicates that a text message has arrived. Jackson smiles as he opens the texts and sees her name. "Hey champ, I know you killed it today; how do you feel after that?"

"I was just thinking about you, I feel pretty good. By next week, I should be able to stand for thirty minutes on my own and take a few steps. Right now, I'm using a walker."

"That's amazing news, I'm proud of you! The grill is waiting for you."

"LoL..it's been a long time, but I'm going to grill everything I can. I'll throw on a sausage for you."

"And don't forget the corn on the cob, apple, asparagus, baked beans, and margarita."

"Sure, I'll include all of that in my menu."

"Alright, I'll let you get back to your family. I just wanted to check in and see how you're doing."

"Thanks, Jazzie."

"No worries."

"Have a good night."

Jazzie opted to remain silent, but he knew she was still hurting. Nonetheless, he held onto the possibility that they could eventually reconcile a friendship. Her departure left him saddened. When Tammy noticed his aloofness tinkering with the phone, she inquired if he was alright. Jackson lied. When the twins leave for work, he tells Tammy that he will be fine if she offers him some special attention. He hoped it would keep Jazzie out of his head.

CHAPTER 33

Relapse

⚜ ♥ ⚜

Addiction refers to an intense desire to engage in activities that produce specific feelings, often accompanied by a flood of pleasurable chemicals called dopamine in the brain. When one falls in love, the brain's addiction-related region becomes active whenever thoughts of the beloved arise. Overcoming addiction is a challenging endeavor, and experiencing a relapse should be seen as an indication that adjustments need to be made in one's life or treatment. Within the depths of Jackson's being, he acknowledges the daunting path he would tread without the luminous presence of Jazzie by his side.

A companion in the form of a trusty walking cane adorns his side, a steadfast ally that empowers him to navigate his surroundings with newfound ease. Yet, his mind becomes a vessel overflowing with thoughts of Jazzie. This obsession clings to every crevice of his consciousness. Two months have slipped away since they last gazed upon each other and feels like an eternity. Battling nervousness, he summons the courage to reach out to Jazzie via text message after her workday, although he feels uncertain about the response he might receive.

"Hey, how was it at work today?" Jackson asked.

"It was a long day, but I finished a cake order for someone to pick up tomorrow." "How did your day go?"

"Hard, I've been missing you."

Jazzie pauses, unsure what to say, then responds, "I've been here."

"Can I see you?"

"Sure, I can go into the den and video call you."

"No, I want to see you in person."

"Why, is something going on?" she asks after a brief pause.

"I need to see you Babe, I miss you," Jackson confess, hoping she would agree.

"Hmmmmm."

"I can understand if you don't want to."

"That isn't it, Jackson. "I'm not sure you're in the right state of mind."

"Is that a yes or a no?"

"You aren't able to drive, and I refuse to come to your house again."

"Let's meet somewhere safe if I can work something out. And don't worry, I'll arrange for transportation."

"Yes, I'll come, but you better not try to drive!"

"Okay! "I'll see to it."

"Sure, okay."

"Get some rest, and I'll get to work on this right away. Have a pleasant evening."

"You do the same."

As the night drew on, Jackson's desire to see her only intensified. With the invaluable aid of Elijah, he meticulously crafted a plan to make it happen. He made sure to secure a reliable driver and a solid alibi to ensure everything went smoothly. The sheer anticipation of finally being in her presence consumed him, making it difficult to find solace in sleep. But eventually, he succumbed to slumber, temporarily escaping his longing for her.

Jazzie encountered a difficult time awakening this morning due to her sleepless night pondering over Jackson's intentions. En route to her workplace, she halted at Jackson's preferred coffee shop and procured a Friday's special that consisted of a double shot of caffeine and a delectable muffin. This will give her some energy to finish her workday and not think about the sleep she missed out on. As she settles into her office and prepares for a meeting with a client, she thinks about Jackson and how nice it would be to see him. Jazzie hears her phone chirping and fumbles through her purse searching for it.

"Good morning, beautiful," Jackson declares.

"How can you tell I'm beautiful when you can't see me?"

"I see you in everything I do, and you're beautiful."

"Why are you up at 8 a.m.?"

"I've got a doctor's appointment. Are you available tomorrow?"

"It all depends on why you're asking?"

"I have a way to see you tomorrow, but I will need your help."

"What exactly do you need me to do?"

"Right now, I don't want to be around a lot of people. Could you please book a hotel for us at our normal location? I'll pay you the money if you don't mind seeing me there. Elijah will bring me, but I will require your assistance getting out of the car and into the hotel."

"Are you sure about this? I can wait until you're better."

"I'm sure and I'm better. I need assistance with certain things for now."

"Fine, I can do that."

"Cool, I'm about to leave for the doctor and will text you later."

"Okay."

"I love you, Jazzie."

"Good luck with your appointment."

Jackson notices that she did not reciprocate his feelings, at least she agrees to meet him, which gives him hope. Briefly, they discuss his progress by the end of the day and finalize plans for tomorrow's meeting.

Sunbeams pounded on Jazzie's window Saturday morning, eager to be allowed in. She rose slowly, still clutching a pillow to her chest. Aiden emerges from the bathroom fully dressed. When he spotted her up, he flung the curtains aside. The bright beams of piercing light came dancing into their bedroom, ensuring Jazzie was awakened. She awoke with a smile on her face, unbeknownst to her. Aiden questions her as he continues to dress. "You must have had a nice dream last night?" He probes.

"Why, what happened?" She asks, terrified.

"You were mumbling something about jackstones and smiling."

"Oh yeah, jackstones, it's a Korean game that Vivian and I used to play as little girls. We used stones instead of jacks because we couldn't afford the genuine thing. Those were the good ole days." She had to think quickly of something to say other than her saying, Jackson.

"Yes, it was! Kids today have no idea what it's like to be unable to afford a three-dollar game. We had a lot of fun with sticks and rocks." Aiden chuckles.

"Where are you going?"

"Did you forget about the new mall project, which is being finalized today with some of the Commissioners?" He said while putting on his tie.

"Oh, absolutely, that's correct. Best wishes! When will you be back?"

"You can join us for dinner later this evening to celebrate."

"I'd love to, but I promised to take Daddy shopping for a new church suit."

"Have fun; I despise shopping. I need to be going so I'm not late setting up for my presentation."

Jazzie's heart was racing with relief, feeling grateful that Aiden had fallen for her deception and kissed her goodbye. Her mind was preoccupied with thoughts of seeing Jackson later that day, and she felt nervous while scurrying to her closet to pick out an outfit. Jazzie tried on several different options before finally settling on a stunning hunter-green bodycon dress that hugged her curves in all the right ways. She paired the dress with some chic wedge sandals, and as she studied herself in the mirror, Jazzie could not help but feel a sense of confidence wash over her.

Before leaving her house, Jazzie made sure to confirm with Jackson that their plans were still on for the day, and her heart raced waiting for his response. "Will he cancel on her or change his mind?" she wondered. To her relief, Jackson responded promptly, letting her know that he was ready and waiting for his ride. Jazzie stepped outside the warm sun on her skin, she could not help but feel a swarm of butterflies fluttering in her stomach. "Am I making the right decision by pursuing Jackson?" she questioned. Jazzie ultimately decided to trust her instincts and let the day unfold.

Before heading to the hotel, Jazzie had a few tasks, including grabbing food. Once she checked in, she let Jackson know she was there. When he arrived, he summoned her to the car for assistance. She requested the wheelchair from Elijah, but Jackson refused to let her see him again in it. He wanted Jazzie to see how far he'd come with the cane. Though initially apprehensive, Jazzie recognizes this gleam of pride in Jackson's expression and helps him to the room. Together, they carefully advanced towards the room, moving in sync step by step.

Once situated within the room, an undercurrent of nervous energy coursed through Jazzie's veins. Her desire to cater to Jackson's needs outweighed her insecurities, and she cautiously inquired if there was anything he required. Seeking to thaw the frost that seemed to encase their connection, Jackson ventured forth with a simple query to break the ice. "Have you been waiting long?" His words were a lifeline, an invitation for Jazzie to bare her soul.

Feeling the awkwardness that lingered in the air, she seized the moment, her words cascading forth like a waterfall of raw emotions. "Why?"

"I asked because I was trying to get here sooner but Elijah wanted to ride me around."

"I wasn't talking about that. Why did you want to see me?"

"I hurt you and can't move passed not having you in my life. I need you, Jazzie. I'm not me, without you."

"I had to process things in my way and in my own time. I get it, you can't do right by everyone, and someone has to get hurt, unfortunately, it's me."

When he sees the tears welling up in her eyes, he tries to stand, but she stops him. "Do you need to go to the bathroom?"

"No, I want to touch you," he responded with emphatic.

She carefully approaches the chair he is sitting in at the table and kneels in front of him, staring at him the whole way. As is customary, Jackson puts her wavery hair behind her right ear. He rubs her face as tears stream down it. He drew her close, with one hand over her heart, and says, "I love you so much Jazzie," and kissed her passionately. She fights the need to return his kiss but eventually falls in. She greets him warmly as he undoes her clothing. Jazzie gently helps him take off his clothes and kisses his healing wounds.

They now have each other, which is what they've been craving, yearning for, and needing all along. Softly saddling him in the chair, she rides him until he surrenders to her world. To make him more at ease, Jazzie transfers him to bed. Then she mounts his mouth like a steed, using his nose as a paintbrush and herself as a canvas to create a work of art—the art of love. Satisfying their addiction, they continued to gorge themselves on each other in a ravenous fashion for several hours until rest was needed. Jazzie reheats the meals she picks up for them and assists Jackson to the table. While eating, they reminisced about their world, laughing at shared memories. Returning to the bed, lying together like they use to, Jackson held her tight and she latched on like an ornament on a Christmas tree.

Reality sets in when Elijah calls to confirm he is on the way to pick up Jackson, putting an end to their wish for time to halt so they can continue spending time together. With a mix of tenderness and practicality, Jazzie took charge, assisting Jackson in restoring his disheveled appearance. Every touch, every adjustment of clothing, was an act of devotion and care as if they were mending the fragile fabric of their shared experience. There was an unspoken understanding that their time together was but a fleeting interlude, leaving them yearning for more.

In the depths of his being, Jackson harbored an ache that threatened to overpower him. Yet, he resolved to push through the pain, knowing that it was a small price to pay for the immeasurable joy he had just experienced. Thoughts of painkillers danced through his mind, a tempting refuge waiting for him at home, ready to dull his physical discomfort. But he knew deep down that this exhilarating risk, this brief but profound connection, was worth every ounce of his current and future pain. Jackson was gently loaded back into the car. As their gazes entwined, it felt as though time was slipping through their fingers, fleeting and delicate. She peered at him with eyes so profound, as if it were their final encounter in the realm of existence.

A bittersweet whisper escaped her lips, carrying the weight of farewell, "Goodbye, Jackson." Her words reached deep into his core, resonating with the raw emotions pulsating within his chest. A gentle touch upon her chest revealed a heart that beat for him, an unspoken declaration of affection. In that fleeting moment, with a breath that carried the weight of powerlessness.

"I love you," he expresses.

With a vulnerability, she mirrored his sentiments, with one hand over his heart, her voice trembling yet resolute, "I love you too." Their words hung in the air, a testament to the profound connection they shared. Jazzie turned towards Elijah, a figure standing on the periphery of their intimate sphere. With gratitude swelling in her heart, she offered him a wave of appreciation, "Thank you, Elijah. This time we spent together was truly invaluable."

In that transient moment of parting, Jackson and Jazzie held onto the fragile remnants of their stolen time, recognizing the preciousness of their connection and the sacrifices made for the taste of true intimacy. And as Jackson drove away, a symphony of emotions echoing in their hearts, they carried within them the imprint of a chapter that defied the boundaries of ordinary existence, forever etching their story upon the tapestry of their souls.

CHAPTER 34

Chioices and Conquesences

❦

Humanity possesses a remarkable characteristic known as conscience—a compass that distinguishes right from wrong. Ideally, armed with this knowledge, we are expected to choose what is right. To ensure good behavior, we establish laws and punishments, passing judgment and sometimes ostracizing those who deviate from the path of righteousness. We often deceive ourselves and others, convincing ourselves that we are doing what is right. However, the truth of our conscience cannot be evaded. Selecting the alternative to what is right carries a weight—a burden called guilt.

In the following month, Jackson finds himself increasingly burdened by stress, caught in a struggle between his conscience and desires as he grapples with the longing to reconnect with Jazzie. However, a significant juncture occurs on his 20th wedding anniversary, when Tammy proposes the idea of renewing their vows to start anew, effectively easing Jackson's guilt and reinforcing his devotion to their relationship. This choice is also influenced by a poignant memory of a conversation with his mother that often replays in his mind. She cautioned Jackson about the potential pain and harm of infidelity, urging him to uphold his commitments to his marriage and family. Guided by his mother's counsel and Tammy's suggestion, Jackson decides to renew their vows, marking a turning point on their 20th anniversary. Although he wishes to inform Jazzie about the vow renewal, he fears it would hurt her and cause further upset. Assisted by Elijah and Miller, he prepared for the ceremony while the cameraman readied the equipment to capture the special moments.

The cooks prepare the buffet and the exquisite three-tier wedding cake. Tammy meticulously decorates their home, creating an ambiance of beauty. Soft music fills the air as guests arrive and take their seats. Jackson and Tammy have invited a select group of close friends and family to partake in the celebration. During the ceremony, Mia and Tia deliver a heartfelt speech dedicated to Jackson, while he and Tammy exchange self-written vows. To Tammy's surprise, Jackson gives her an upgraded diamond ring. As a wedding gift, Tammy presents him with an all-expenses-paid carpenter to complete his mancave project.

Once Jackson fully recovers, he and Tammy plan to embark on a trip to Australia—an aspiration he once shared with Jazzie. From an outsider's perspective, Jackson seems to have attained the life he desired—a devoted wife, wonderful children, a loyal dog, and a supportive network of family and friends. Yet, there is one person who is not happy—Jazzie. Observing Jackson's lack of joy, Elijah follows him to the library when he sees Jackson slip away. "Here man, it's not alcohol but you can pretend until you are off all of that shit them docs got you on. You good man?" He gives Jackson a glass of Coca-Cola.

"Yeah, I'm ok." plainly he replies.

Elijah knows he is not and asks, "Need me to push you somewhere? I know it's loud as hell in here?"

"No, it's cool. I'm just tired." Secretly, he wanted to go on the patio alone, but Tammy wanted more pictures.

"Listen man, all good things come to an end. You have a great family, your life, better health, and your shops are number one in Atlanta. Anything else outside of that is irrelevant." Although Jazzie remains relevant to Jackson, he remains silent, averting Elijah's gaze. At that moment, Jazzie sends him a text, and a smile appears on his face.

"Hey, how's your physical therapy progressing?"

"It's quite painful, but I can now stand for at least forty-one minutes without the cane. Soon, I won't need any support at all. How's your day?"

"That's fantastic! Hard work truly pays off. Take it easy and keep up the good work. I had Taco Bell today, and it didn't agree with me. I've been in bed all day, sipping fluids and vomiting."

"Sounds like you might have food poisoning. I hope you start feeling better soon. I have to go now, but thank you for checking on me!"

"No problem. I'll check in on you tomorrow. Good night."

"Good night."

Jackson eagerly awaited a text from Jazzie. He was abruptly interrupted by Tammy calling for him to join the group photo. With Miller's assistance, Jackson's wheelchair was guided towards the den, where the joyful atmosphere embraced them. Gathering around the renewed couple, they prepared for the photo, chanting "Jackson and Tammy" for the camera. Jackson feels a momentary happiness.

Later that night, Jazzie lies in bed, her mind occupied with thoughts of Jackson. She searches for ways to assist him in his physical therapy, always seeking helpful information to share. A YouTube notification catches her attention, suggesting a new video titled "Twenty Years in 2020." Hoping to find some happiness amidst the pandemic's gloom, she clicks on it. What she sees leaves her in shock—Mia and Tia, wearing glittery masks, deliver a heartfelt speech dedicated to Jackson and Tammy. The video showcases Jackson in a wheelchair, Tammy kneeling beside him as they exchange kisses and renew their vows.

Laughter fills the room as Jackson playfully smears cake on Tammy's face. They share a dance, with Tammy sitting on his lap in the wheelchair. Jazzie notices familiar faces among the guests—Elijah and Haley, her friend, not Tammy's. The video's posting date reveals that this ceremony took place tonight, which she assumes is why he had to abruptly end their text conversation. Anger, sadness, disappointment, betrayal, and a sense of foolishness overwhelm Jazzie. Furious that Jackson didn't inform her and that her best friend attended, she realizes that he has moved on.

This video serves as confirmation, prompting Jazzie to acknowledge the need to move on as well. She sends Jackson the video link, wishing him a sarcastic "Happy 20th Wedding Anniversary, LIAR!" She refrains from sending him the workout information, realizing that he is in capable hands and no longer requires her assistance. At that moment, she comprehends the extent of her naivety and whispers to herself, "How could I have been so stupid?"

The next morning, Jackson and Tammy, exhausted from their wedding celebration and private celebrations afterward, find themselves up late. Tammy leaves to fetch breakfast while Jackson eagerly checks his phone for messages. Excitement washes over him as he sees Jazzie's name, anticipating the daily inspiration she typically sends. However, his excitement turned to devastation upon discovering the YouTube link titled "Twenty Years in 2020." He exclaims in disbelief, "Fuck!" He was feeling awful for failing to inform Jazzie about the ceremony.

He immediately sends her a text, "Call me please," but receives no response even after thirty minutes. Worried, he sends another text, "Can you talk?" hoping for a reply before Tammy returns home. Knowing that Jazzie is usually up by 9 a.m., he texts again, "Are you okay?" but the silence persists. Growing increasingly anxious, he wonders why she remains unresponsive.

Meanwhile, Jazzie, though still unwell, tends to her final obligations before leaving town. She notices Jackson's messages but quickly deletes them before reading. Before heading to the bank, she prints and signs a form with Jackson's name and proceeds to close their joint accounts, credit cards, and post office box. She redirects all final notices to Vivian's house, ensuring that everything is properly closed and settled.

Texting Elijah, she arranges to meet him in the parking lot of the Whole Foods Market at 2 p.m., seeking his help in delivering a package to Jackson. Although she arrives early at 1:15 p.m., she does not want to risk missing him. Elijah pulls up at 2:11 p.m., and Jazzie, wearing a mask, steps out of her car. Determined to complete this task swiftly, "Hi, I have a package that I need to get to Jackson. Can you give this to him when he is alone?" Sensing Elijah did not want to do it, she did not care or entertain it. "I'm sorry I have to go," she says while giving him the package.

He takes it and examines the small package and responds, "It's not a bomb is it?" Jokingly he laughs but he is serious. Ever since Elijah knew she sneaked into the hospital to see Jackson. Elijah thought Jazzie was too deep with a simple fling and was concerned for his bro/friend. Irritated by his insensitivity and his misjudgment of her relationship with Jackson, Jazzie retorts with a cutting remark, "Fuck you dickless bastard!" and gets into her car to drive off. Elijah, taken aback by her response, wonders what could be troubling Jazzie, as she is usually kinder.

Arriving at Jackson's home, Elijah hides the package he received in his shirt before going inside. Mia opens the door when she sees him on the security camera screen. "Hi Uncle Elijah, Daddy is in the den."

Greeting her with a hug, "Thanks, Mia. Can you bring me a glass of juice in there?" While Mia grabs him some juice, he makes himself comfortable on the sofa next to Jackson.

"What's up bro? You just chilling?"

"Yeah, wanna play a game of dominoes?"

"Sure, I enjoy beating your ass! I'll take it easy on you this time." Elijah's laughter echoes throughout the room.

"I'm a grown man. I issue out whoopings and I have one with your name on it!" Jackson teased.

"Yo Mia! Bring two glasses of juice and Kleenex for your dad, he's going to be in tears soon!"

"I can drink something strong now."

"Word? Where's the hard stuff, Crown Royal?" Elijah eagerly searches.

While Elijah makes them some drinks and grabs some potato chips, Jackson sets up the game on the game table. Engaging in friendly banter, they played a few games of dominoes, providing a welcomed distraction for Jackson during his emotional turmoil. Even after calling Vivian, he has not heard from Jazzie. As they play, teasing each other and enjoying the game, Jackson's worries momentarily fade away. Observing Tammy walking upstairs, Elijah seizes the opportunity to retrieve the small package he received from Jazzie and nonchalantly he tosses the package to Jackson.

"Here man, Jazzie asked me to give this to you, she was pissed man!"

Jackson's curiosity piqued, he sits up and asks, "When did you see her?"

"I met her at Whole Foods on my way over here today. She didn't look well and was cranky as hell. It must be her time of the month." Elijah explains. A relieved smile forms on Jackson's lips as he becomes aware of the loving and caring nature that Jazzie possesses, it must be inspirational. As he holds the package in his hands, he catches a whiff of her distinctive scent, a fragrance that instantly transports him back to memories shared. Lost in his thoughts, he contemplates the significance of this familiar aroma lingering on the package.

With a mixture of anticipation and trepidation, he tears open the package, revealing its contents. A look of unease settles upon his face, his eyes fixated on the sight before him. There, nestled within, are his diamond earrings he once delicately placed upon Jazzie's ears, alongside the ring he had chosen for her. Accompanying these sentimental treasures is a note that reads: *I gave you my heart, soul, trust, and spirit. In return, you gave me a lie that I will now turn into a lesson of strength. I love you more than any actions, any distances, and any words but I love myself more.*

The weight of Jackson's actions and the consequences of his choices become evident, and he must come to terms with the loss of Jazzie, his once-cherished love.

She's gone...

> *Love, a delicate dance of the heart,*
> *Release it, let it soar, let it depart,*
> *If it returns, it's yours, forevermore,*
> *If not, let go, and love shall restore.*

CHAPTER 35

Ferris Wheel of Fate

⊱⊱⊱ ♥ ⊰⊰⊰

Time, like a gentle healer, soothes the wounds of a broken heart with its patient touch. In the aftermath of heartache, the days may feel long and heavy, but as time passes, the pain begins to lose its sharpness. Memories that once caused tears to flow like rivers gradually soften, becoming bittersweet echoes of the past. Each passing moment allows space for healing, offering solace to the wounded soul. Slowly but surely, the heart finds the strength to mend itself, stitching together the fragments left behind by love's departure.

With the passing of days and seasons, the weight of sorrow begins to lift, replaced by newfound hope and resilience. Time, a faithful ally, unveils the beauty of moving forward, showing that healing is not forgetting, but a testament to the human spirit's capacity to mend and bloom once more. After six years, Jazzie navigated the treacherous path of healing, battling waves of pain, and learning to rebuild her shattered spirit. It was not an easy journey, but with time and unwavering determination, Jazzie slowly pieced herself back together.

Jazzie embraced every opportunity for growth and self-discovery. She threw herself into her career, excelling in her chosen field and becoming an influential voice in her industry. She poured her emotions into creating art through baking. Her artwork became a window to her soul. The world responded warmly to her creations, and Jazzie found a supportive community that appreciated her talent. Through her journey of healing, Jazzie also learned the importance of self-love and self-care. She embraced a healthy lifestyle, finding comfort in regular exercise, meditation, and taking care of her well-being. She discovered the power of forgiveness, not just for others but also for herself, as she let go of the burden of blame and guilt as her family format changed.

Among the vibrant lights of the downtown Ferris wheel in Atlanta, Jazzie held Brave's hand with youthful excitement, guiding him into their exclusive VIP pod. Her heart swelled with nostalgia as she remembered when this very structure was first erected, always yearning to experience it. She and Jackson, the man who had once captured her heart, had always intended to ride it together, but life had other plans, and the moment slipped away. As the Ferris wheel gently lifted them into the night sky, Jazzie's imagination soared.

She envisioned herself and Jackson sharing this enchanting ride on a warm summer evening, mesmerized by the sparkling skyline and the moonlit glow. Tonight, finally, she fulfilled her longing and brought Brave along, hoping to introduce him to the magic of downtown activities. As the wheel rotated, they encountered another family on a neighboring pod.

A little girl's fear echoed through the air as she protested against the height. "No Grandpa, it's too high; I don't wanna do it!" Jazzie could not see the man clearly, but she witnessed his compassionate response, comforting the little one until she felt at ease. The little girl says, with a sweet declaration to the man, "If you say so, but just this once!" they embarked on their ride.

The Ferris wheel continued its graceful dance through the sky, accompanied by joyful music. Jazzie, entranced by the twinkling stars and the moon above, could not help but reminisce about Jackson. She envisioned what it would have been like if they had experienced this together, the thrill, the intimacy, the love. They would have been members of the "Mile High Club" on this Ferris wheel. Brave says, "What's funny?" after hearing her chuckle.

Jazzie gives him a hug and a cheery one-word response, "Life," she said. She had faith that he would eventually get it when he was older. Little did she know that Jackson and his granddaughter, Shona, were also on the same ride, lost in his own precious memories. Jackson smiled to himself, reflecting on the nights he wished he could have brought Jazzie here. A chuckle escaped him as he imagined the playful moments with Pinky they could have shared on the Ferris wheel, hidden from prying eyes.

After Shona noticed her grandpa's grin, she asked, "Why are you smiling?" Jackson planted a kiss on her forehead and replied, "Life."

In her innocence, she asked, "Who is Life?"

With a sly grin, he retorted, "You'll figure it out one day." As they disembarked, Jazzie and Brave headed towards the exit. Suddenly, the evening took an unexpected turn when Brave noticed his missing motorcycle toy. The boy dashed back towards their previous pod, and Jazzie, not far behind, accidentally collided with a man holding a baby doll and a little girl's hand. To her astonishment, she found herself face to face with Jackson, looking more handsome than ever.

"Jazzie?" he uttered in disbelief, captivated by her beauty just like the day they met at the package store.

"Oh my goodness, excuse me, I'm so sorry!" Jazzie knocks the baby doll he was holding to the ground. She bent to pick it up and looked up at him, she dropped it again. Shona grabbed the baby doll and said defensively, "You pushed my grandpa!" Jazzie was speechless to see Jackson. He could not believe his eyes and blinked to ensure his eyes were not playing tricks on him.

"Hi, Jackson! Ummmmm how have you been?" She tried not to stare but he was a work of fine art, desirable complexion, smooth skin, fine, sexy lips, and mustache. Jazzie has not felt butterflies in years and now they were making up for lost time.

"I've been well and working hard," he says as he cannot help from staring at her.

Jazzie looked down at the little girl holding onto Jackson's leg and said, "I'm sorry, I didn't mean to run you guys over. Are you ok?"

Shona nods "Yes," but she stands close to Jackson.
He introduced her, "This is my granddaughter, Shona, she's three years old. She's Mia's daughter. She is a lot like her mother at that age." They both laughed remembering how Mia was about her daddy.

"How is she doing and Tia?" Jazzie inquires.

"Tia is in law school and has no kids. Mia got married and both she and her husband are in the Air Force. What about you, what have you been up to?"

"I pretty much stay busy. I'm a Professor of Business at Georgia State University. I'm also the Youth Coordinator at Church. I let them help me run my bakery to earn money; you know, to keep them out of trouble and learn."

He says smiling at her, "You finally opened a bakery? Congratulations! You sound busy these days, when do you sleep?"

She smiles back "I find the time, trust me, I do. I mainly rest on Sundays after church."

"You would be surprised to know I'm attending church. How are Genesis and Brandon doing?

"What? You are in church, that's amazing! Your mother would be happy, I'm sure."

"I think she would be, maybe even shocked but I'm still a work in process," and laughs.

"Genesis is a police officer and isn't looking to have kids any time soon. She is also boxing and has a match soon at Eastside Boxing Club. Brandon just started working for Delta as an engineer. Already he has a girlfriend there, a sweet young lady, a flight attendant." Brave joins them after the attendant helps recover his toy. "This little guy is Brave and he needs to be dropped off soon to Brandon."

"Hi Brave, cool name, nice to meet you. He looks like Brandon. What's the name of the bakery, I would love to stop by?" Shona tugs on Jackson's pants and says, "I'm hungry Grandpa, can we go eat?" Jazzie needed to get going as well, she wanted to drop Brave off before he got sleepy. Besides, she did not want to get into the name of her bakery.

"I'm glad to see you walking again. It's been great seeing you Jackson and it was nice meeting you, Shona."

"It's been magical seeing you again Jazzie. Tell ummm…, What's his name?… Henry? Thomas? Ben? Whatever his name is I said hello."

She laughed and said "Aiden! I see some things never change. I'll tell him next month when I see him."

"Next month? Is he still working out of town? Shouldn't he be getting a pension by now and fishing somewhere?"

"Ha Ha Ha, Not funny! I'll see him at Genesis's boxing match. We are divorced."

"Oh, I'm sorry to hear that." Truly he was glad to hear the news.

"Don't be, it was over with him the night I met you. I have to get going, tell your Sugar Baby I said hi." Jazzie sarcastically returns his smart remark.

"You're still feisty as ever. We aren't married anymore." Jazzie was surprised and did not comment on it.

"Goodnight, Choir Boy, again take care and it's great seeing you." As she turns and grabs Brave's hand, he says to her, "Can I call you sometime?" She thought for a moment and smiled; this felt familiar. Turning back around, Jazzie takes his cell phone out of his hand and puts her name and number in it. Jackson smiles and remembers when they first met and said jokingly "Is this your real number?"

Blushing she responds, "It's only one way to find out." Jazzie and Brave scatter away. Jackson watched her until he could not see her curves or bouncing hair anymore and it happened. His manhood starts reacting, "Dear God, this woman still has this effect on me!" admitting out loud.

After dropping Brave off for a weekend with Brandon, Jazzie drove home in deep thought. Recalling how sexy Jackson was looking made her twist in the driver's seat. When she reaches home, she enjoys the alone time so she can swim in her thoughts. After her shower, she slides on a nighty and retrieves a glass of wine from the bar. A soda would not relax her, something stronger is required. Later that night as Jazzie lay in bed, her phone rang with an unknown number. Answering it, she was met with Jackson's confident voice, bringing back memories of the passion they once shared.

"I'm checking to see if you gave me the right number," he announces. Jackson still touched her in places no man has ever been able to touch.

"I don't play games unless both parties consent to it." She was still the same—spicy, sexy, and curvy in all the right places. They spoke for hours, catching up on lost time, and reminiscing about their past.

Eventually, Tammy realizes that she could never win Jackson's heart the way the mystery woman he hides does. He had fully furnished her house, including the basement, and they agreed to split a significant portion of his motorcycle accident payout. They get along better as friends, and the twins only want what is best for both of them, even if that means separating. Mia enlisted in the Air Force after finishing high school and found love. Jackson respects her husband's ambitions and understands that like Tammy, any man she marries would need deep pockets.

Tia is studying Criminal Law and will be finishing up in another year. She was a lot like Jackson and very observant. He had just gotten back from Dallas visiting his family where they all are doing well. His father came back to Atlanta a year ago to live with him. Jackson found the most appropriate Assisted Living & Senior Care facility that provides excellent care for him and activities that he enjoys.

Jazzie tells him that she wants Aiden to have someone who loves him as much as Aiden loves her. She would never be able to love him in that way. "He deserves that, so I set him free to find it," she explained. "We do not talk much to each other unless I see him at one of our kids' gatherings." Jazzie also shared that her family is doing well, but she lost her grandfather a few years ago.

Vivian finally got married to a wonderful guy who lost his first wife in an accident. Haley is happily married as well to a wonderful man, and they have a four-year-old son. Jazzie looked over at the clock and needed to get some sleep for church tomorrow. She was enjoying catching up with him and did not want to hang up. "Oh my, I didn't realize it was 2 a.m. Jackson! I need to get some sleep so I can be at church early tomorrow to get the young adults together for a ceremony."

"You were always helping someone. What time do you get out of church?"

"Usually about 1 p.m."

"Do you have any plans after church?"

"No, I was coming home to cook dinner and watch the Lifetime channel."

"Would you join me for dinner?"

Jazzie thinks about it and remembers she never did get to grill for him long ago. "How about you come to my house, and I will cook dinner for us both?"

"That would be great. What would you like for me to bring?"

"Just you, let's say about 4 p.m. Is that ok?"

"That's a perfect time!"

"Great, I will text you my address tomorrow."

"It's a date!"

Jazzie blushed and said, "Yes, I guess it is." Jazzie felt a mixture of nerves and excitement, wondering what trick fate had on its agenda. Could this be the start of a love rekindled, a chance at the happiness they had missed out on before? The Ferris wheel's enchantment seemed to extend beyond the ride, weaving their lives together once more.

CHAPTER 36

Second Chances

Once the first rays of sunlight gently caressed the horizon, Jazzie's eyes fluttered open, and a spark of excitement ignited within her. The anticipation of the day ahead filled her heart, and she could not wait to embrace every moment. The moment she stepped into the familiar church doors, time seemed to playfully slow down, teasing her eager spirit. The solemn notes of the organ reverberated through the air as if urging her to savor each passing second. It was as if the clock itself conspired against her, knowing that if one attempted to hasten its course, it would only draw out further. But Jazzie was undeterred; she wanted to relish every verse, every prayer, and every word that would fill her soul with a sense of purpose and hope.

The church sermon titled "Second Chances" preached about the power of forgiveness, redemption, and the possibility of new beginnings. The pastor spoke passionately about how we all make mistakes, but with God's grace, we have the opportunity to start afresh. The message resonated deeply with Jazzie as she had been reflecting on her past lately. Little did she know that fate had a profound message for her that day. As she bumped into Jackson, she could not help but see it as a sign. The title of the sermon seemed like a direct message from God, affirming that this unexpected encounter might be the second chance they both had hoped for. As soon as the Pastor did the benediction, she flew out of the church like an eagle on a mission.

While driving home, Jazzie calls to check on Brave, who is currently on a spring trip with Brandon in Florida. Upon arriving at her cozy abode, Jazzie wasted no time, eager to make the evening with Jackson one to remember. With a sense of excitement dancing in her heart, she swiftly changed into something comfortable. Jazzie's fingers danced across her phone's screen as she texted Jackson her address. Butterflies fluttered in her stomach at the thought of him arriving soon. His response filled her with warmth, knowing he was equally excited.

Jazzie's preparations didn't end with mere anticipation. She was determined to return Jackson's kindness from that day in the park when he grilled for her. Still, a fan of jazz as she bakes, soft melodies hummed through the kitchen and the gazebo. She lovingly mixed up the dough for fresh garlic parmesan rolls, letting them rise to perfection. The aroma of a lemon pound cake filled the air as it baked in the oven, a sweet treat prepared especially for the two of them. With culinary finesse, she seasoned the steaks and prepared the sausage, all while whipping up a delectable broccoli salad that would provide a refreshing balance to the meal.

A spiced jasmine rice pilaf and crab-stuffed jalapeno poppers added a touch of adventure to the feast, ensuring a delightful culinary journey for both of them. Jazzie's attention to detail did not stop there. With a touch of nostalgia, she set the table inside the charming gazebo, where their dinner would be a feast for the senses as the sunset. The bar was thoughtfully stocked with some of Jackson's favorite drinks, a sweet reminder of their shared history. As the clock ticked closer to Jackson's arrival, she made her way to the shower, taking care to choose an outfit that showcased her natural beauty and sense of style. Jazzie wanted him to see her radiance, as she was finally able to let go of the past and embrace the possibility of a new beginning with the man she had always loved.

After meticulously curling her hair and artfully applying her makeup, Jazzie slips into a form-fitting crisscross dress, its hemline teasingly stopping midway along her thighs, revealing just enough to captivate. With a confident flourish, she pulls her hair behind one ear, accentuating her delicate features, and adorns herself with dangling earrings that catch the light with every graceful turn of her head. A gentle mist of a soft, alluring fragrance envelops her as she elegantly glides into a pair of matching comfortable low shoes.

With a graceful glide, Jazzie makes her way back to the kitchen. She spreads butter on the rolls and places them in the oven. Turning her attention to the pound cake, she whisks together a lemon glaze, a symphony of sweet and zesty notes that will elevate the cake to celestial heights. With every drop that falls like liquid sunshine, she knows she's transforming a simple dessert into an exquisite masterpiece. With an air of anticipation, she transfers her culinary creations to the gazebo, hoping this evening will be etched into the tapestry of her heart. Tending to the grill, the aroma of the two seasoned steaks intertwined with the heady fragrance of the evening air, weaving a rich tapestry of flavors and memories.

With every passing minute, her excitement grew, and she could not wait for their dinner date to unfold, a chance to rekindle the flame that had never truly extinguished. Then, a familiar sound echoes through the house—the unmistakable chime of the doorbell. Jazzie's heart leaps within her chest like a startled bird as the realization hits like a sudden gust of wind—it's him! Jazzie takes a deep breath. She was trying to steady herself as she whispered reassuringly, "This is ridiculous, why should I be nervous?" Her mind playfully scolds her for feeling this way, but the butterflies dancing in her stomach persist flapping with excitement.

Yet, deep down, she knows that the answer lies in the unspoken history between them, a connection that defies logic and reason, and she cannot help but wonder if fate has a hand in this moment. Finally, she reaches the door, her hand poised to open it and usher in the next chapter of their lives together. With a smile that radiates warmth and joy, she opens the door, and in the doorway stands Jackson, the man who has always held her heart captive.

"Hello, Jackson! Did you have any trouble finding it?" she asks, a warm smile spreading across her face as she welcomes him with a friendly hug.

As they embrace, she feels his breath gently caress her forehead, and a familiar scent envelopes her, sending a delightful tingle down her spine. Quickly pulling back, she invites him into the house. His eyes take in the beauty of her home, and he cannot help but admire her curves, the way she carries herself, and the intoxicating fragrance that lingers in the air. In his hands, he holds a banquet of flowers, knowing they are her favorite. "Not at all, this is a very nice house. These are for you."

"Thank you, these are my favorite flowers."

"I know." The joy in her eyes as she accepts them only adds to his delight.

"Come on in. I had this home built about five years ago. We're dining inside the gazebo, right this way." As they make their way through the house, he notices a large picture over the fireplace of Jazzie, surrounded by Genesis and Brannon while proudly holding Brave. The memories of their shared past flood his mind, and he cannot help but feel grateful for this second chance. A hallway enhanced with seashells leads them outside, where they step into a tropical paradise, complete with a beautifully designed fishpond connected to a cascading waterfall.

The sound of running water soothes their souls as they approach the charming gazebo. Inside, a tantalizing aroma envelops him, seducing his taste buds with its mouthwatering allure. The table is adorned with an array of tantalizing dishes and condiments, a testament to

Jazzie's culinary prowess. Her enthusiasm is infectious, and he cannot help but notice the familiar grill from their past adventures when she flips over some steaks.

"Hold up, is that the same grill we used when I took you to the park and cooked sausages for you?" he asks, a spark of nostalgia dancing in his eyes.

"The one and only! I figured I never returned the favor, and now I can," she replies, raising her glass playfully, causing him to chuckle at her teasing.

He chuckles "No fair, I don't have a glass!"

"Oh goodness, you sure don't. What are you drinking? I have strawberry soda, water, or Kool-Aid?"

"You are being funny now! I still enjoy my Crown Royal."

With a mischievous glint in her eyes, she unveils a fresh bottle of Crown Royal XO, playfully teasing him as she knows it is his preferred drink of choice.

"Will this do?" she quips, holding up the bottle like a playful treasure.

"Absolutely!" He beams while grabbing a glass with ice. The sound of ice clinking against the crystal echoes like a joyful melody.

"I wasn't sure if it was still your drink, if at all. Here is some hors d'oeuvre; they are crab stuffed jalapeno peppers."

"I'm starving, thank you. However, my drinking days have mellowed since my recovery. The medications I was on during that time didn't allow me to drink, so I've become more of an occasional sipper. I'm happy with this Crown Royal XO treat. And speaking of memories, it's hard to believe you still have that grill!"

"I like this grill and it's great for two people."

"Two people?"

"Or one. Or five. The steaks will be ready soon, you can wash your hands at the sink over there." Playful banter and shared memories create an atmosphere of comfort and ease as if the years apart had never existed. At this moment, they find themselves drawn back to each other, sharing laughter and toasting to the possibility of a new chapter in their lives. After Jazzie removes the steaks from the grill, she drizzles the savory sausage mushroom sauce over them. Jackson takes the opportunity to offer a heartfelt grace, expressing gratitude for the delicious meal and the cherished company they share.

"Thank you. I don't usually get the chance to cook lavish meals like this, because Brave is a fan of burgers and potato chips," she replied with pride in her culinary creations.

"He sure takes after you then, loving those burgers. I can imagine you spoil him," he remarked warmly.

"How's everything so far?"

"Your cooking has always been impressive, but this is on another level! You've outdone yourself, Jazzie. You should seriously consider opening a restaurant!" he exclaimed, thoroughly impressed by the feast before him. Savoring their meal, they effortlessly caught up on the years that had passed. Jackson shared the news that Elijah was now married and expecting their first child soon. Time seemed to blur as they continued to chat, the years apart fading away as they relived old memories.

Laughter filled the air as they reminisced about the adventures they embarked on and the places they explored together. Appreciating the breeze and mixing another drink, Jazzie could not help but notice Jackson's gaze fixed on the fishpond. She understood the significance behind it, realizing he never fulfilled the promise they once made together. "I finally had it done. There are six fish in there, one for each year with Brave."

"It looks great. I remember I was supposed to build that for me," he revealed, a hint of nostalgia in his voice.

"Yes, you were but I left the shoe case for you to do," Jazzie teased playfully, lightening the mood, and sharing a fond memory from their past. Jackson peers at her with intense passion in his eyes and they both feel it. As he always did, Jackson strokes her hair and tucks it behind one ear. The butterflies return so she rises to offer him dessert. "Are you ready for dessert? I baked a Lemon Pound Cake; is it still your favorite?"

In an emotionally charged moment, he stood, his outstretched arms gently pulling her closer, until they were face to face. "Jazzie, I have always loved you. In leaving, you ripped the breath from my lungs. I drove past your house several times but never saw you. I saw Bob? Billy? Thomas? Whatever that dude's name is? You changed your number and quit your job. Your parents said they couldn't tell me, only riddles from your mom. I eventually found out that you moved to Los Angeles through Vivian. I left messages for you everywhere I could think of. When I asked mutual friends, they said you had stopped talking to them. Your social media accounts were deactivated. Haley ended things with Elijah and refused to share any information with him. Why did you leave so abruptly? We should have talked about it?"

Jazzie stood before him; his heartfelt confessions echoed in her ears. Memories of the past flooded back, and she could sense the pain he had endured during her absence. "Jackson," she began, her voice carrying a blend of tenderness and resolve, "What could we have talked about? You wanted a life with your wife and kids, a life I couldn't witness as a mere bystander. My presence, as much as I cherished it, held you back from pursuing what truly mattered to you. I couldn't bear to be the cause of any disarray in your soul or the reason for any inner conflict." With a heavy sigh, she continued, "You were committed to your bound to honor your mother's wishes. In my heart, I knew you didn't need me in the way I needed you. The love I have for you is profound enough to set you free, to let you find the fulfillment you wanted."

Jackson, listening intently, revealed his own struggle in the situation. "Jazzie, I was trying to do right by everyone," he confessed, his voice tinged with remorse. "I couldn't find anyone willing to talk to me, except for your mother. She shared with me words of encouragement from the depths of her wisdom and said, "Let us not become weary in doing good, for at the proper time we will reap a harvest if we do not give up." Her hope and faith in our future kept me going, even in the absence of your presence. I never gave up."

A reddened Jazzie said, "I didn't know you came looking for me. It was just too difficult for me, but I learned to cope. I kept myself occupied until Brave came along and saved me; from that point on, I had a reason to keep going. During your time in the hospital, I followed up with my cousin Yvette, who works at the hospital, to find out how you were doing with your recovery. I stopped asking once you finished it and did extremely well. I was sorry I couldn't be there for you throughout your entire rehabilitation, but I had to take a step back. You and Haley were my best friends yet you both deceived me. I felt worthless. Since then, she and I have patched things up and are friends."

"You weren't baby. I needed to hear your voice, read your texts, see your face, and be inspired. I recently stopped by your parents' house to visit with them and they didn't mention you were divorced. Your mother told me to not give up, it is a purpose for us to find our paths back to each other."

In a tone of surprise, Jazzie inquired, "What brought you to my parent's house, and when did this happen?"

Jackson explained, "Sometimes I drop by to check on them and assist your dad with some tasks. That night when I saw you at the Ferris wheel, I had just left their place."

Jazzie shared, "Actually, I had visited earlier, and my mom wanted me to stay, but I had plans to go on the Ferris wheel with Brave before he left for his trip with Brandon."

"I had Shona with me. Your dad thought it'd be nice to take her for a ride on the Ferris wheel due to the pleasant weather. Since I never had the chance to do that with you, I figured I should take Shona before she grows up and has less time to spend with me." They shared a knowing laugh, figuring out two disciples.

Drawing her closer, Jackson spoke with sincerity, referencing Proverbs 15:13, "A glad heart makes a cheerful face, but by sorrow of the heart, the spirit is crushed. I wanted to do right by everyone, Jazzie. If only I had known the wisdom of the Bible back then, I might have understood what I needed to do. But now, I know it all too well—I know the scriptures, I know myself, I know you, and I know us. I want you, Jazzie. My wife, the one who has been right here in front of me all this time."

The intensity of their emotions reached a crescendo. Jazzie's heart fluttered as Jackson leaned in, gently caressing her face. Their eyes locked, rekindling the love that had never truly faded since the night they first met. As he kissed her, a wave of warmth swept over her, evoking a flood of sensations that made her knees weak. She had longed for this moment, yearned for him with every fiber of her being.

Regaining her composure, Jazzie pulled back, her love for Jackson evident in her eyes. "I never stopped loving you, Jackson," she confessed, "I did what I believed was best for you, following your wishes."

Jackson embraced her tenderly, assuring her with utmost certainty, "You are what's best for me, Jazzie. You always have been, and now, I want you by my side once more. Forever."

In a passionate and intimate encounter, Jackson and Jazzie's emotions ignited like wildfire. Jackson caresses the finger that once held a precious ring he had given her years ago. Abandoning everything in the gazebo, they rush inside the house to her bedroom, guided by the intense desire to reconnect. Inside the room, Jackson connects her Bluetooth sound system, knowing how Jazzie adores listening to music. With a mix of anticipation and reverence, he unties her dress, revealing her seductive, red-laced lingerie, which reignites the fire of his desire.

Jackson passionately kisses her and skillfully unclasps her bra. Entranced by the sight of her enticing, voluptuous breast, he missed her goodness. Undressing each other, they explore the familiar terrain of each other's bodies, cherishing the taste and touch that had been absent for far too long. Jackson's scars, remnants of his motorcycle accident, serve as reminders of his resilience and allure, making him even more attractive in Jazzie's eyes. Jazzie reciprocates her affection, by planting kisses on his chest down to his stomach. Then, to his extreme enjoyment, she unbuttoned his pants and pulled them and his underwear down to the floor. In approval, his manhood shows appreciation. Leading her towards the bed, he pulls back the sheets and removes her panties. Jackson places her on the bed and leisurely admires her figure.

Hunger surged inside him and demanded to feast on her jewels. Spreading her legs apart he tells her, "I missed you so much. I thought of you every day." Jazzie responds, "Show me," and he does just that. Caressing her body with his tongue, he comes to her jewels. With one finger, Jackson explored her inside and felt her thighs quiver. Removing his finger that displays her juices, he licks it and dives into her world with his tongue. She moans and grabs his head, he remembers how this drives her crazy. Jackson continues to grow just by hearing her receiving his gift. After a few minutes of indulging in her sweetness, Jackson needs to feel her intensity.

"I want you so badly baby," he whispers. Breathing heavily, she notices her wetness trickling from his mustache and eagerly exclaims, "I want you too, now!" Anxiously, he guides himself into her, becoming completely absorbed in a euphoric state. "You are mine, and you always will be. I missed you," he declares affectionately. It had been a considerable time since she had felt so incredible, surrendering to the overwhelming sensations. Jazzie climaxes intensely, and he experiences her flowing like a powerful river. In response, Jackson adds to the sensation, releasing himself inside her. The overwhelming pleasure causes his eyes to roll back, almost as if he enters a hypnotic state.

After Jackson composes himself, he positions himself on top of her. However, she deftly shifts from beneath him and settles between his legs, resting on his chest. Tenderly, Jazzie kisses his chest and then lets her tongue glide down to pleasure him. The gentle, wet motion of moving up and down arouses him once more, causing him to grow again. As Jackson gazes at her, he observes himself vanishing into her mouth, completely overwhelmed by pleasure. Just before reaching climax, Jazzie promptly straddles him, guiding herself onto him, and assuming control over his body. She initiates a slow and gradual rhythm, gradually increasing the pace.

Enthralled by the movement of her bouncing breasts, he cannot resist but to touch and suck on them, captivated by her every move. As Jackson sucks her breast, Jazzie intensifies her thrusts, moving faster and faster. Jackson expresses his affection with moans, saying, "I love you, Jazzie. I love you so much." In a whining tone, she replies, "I love you more, baby, I do," and begins trembling. Jackson anticipates her next action. Firmly gripping Jazzie's curvaceous buttocks, Jackson guides her body backward, causing him to penetrate Jazzie even deeper, eliciting a passionate outcry from her.

"Aaaaawwwww I feel that!"

"You suppose to feel it, baby. Don't hold back on me."

"You feel too good!"

"You'll always be mine," Jackson asserts, persistently pushing more of himself inside her.

"I can't take it, wait, wait!"

"I've waited six years for you, and I won't wait any longer. We are meant to be together," Jackson proclaims, gripping her hips firmly in his favorite position. Jackson admires the bouncing of her breasts with each thrust and continues with his passionate actions. Sensing her overwhelming arousal, he urges, "Give it to me, baby. It's mine!" Suddenly, Jazzie freezes and trembles, and he can feel the warmth of her climax, flowing down his manhood onto the bed. In response, Jackson releases a powerful climax, causing his toes to curl. Jazzie observes his euphoric state and allows the sensations to engulf his body. Eventually, she collapses to his right side, overwhelmed by the experience. Still catching her breath, Jazzie attempts to get out of bed, but Jackson grasps her hand, preventing her from leaving. "Where are you going?"

"I was going to get us something to drink."

"All I want is you, Jazzie. I'll never let you leave me again."

"You do have a lot to make up for, you can start with my shoe rack," she teased, smiling at him.

He expresses with one hand over her heart, "I love you more than any actions, any distances, and any words."

As she lays her hand on his chest, she whispers, "I love you even more." At that moment, any thoughts of getting something to drink were forgotten. They had a lot of lost time to make up for, and they did so... ALL NIGHT LONG! The night was a tapestry of passion, emotions, and rediscovered love. In each other's arms, they found solace and completeness, finally reunited after years of separation. Their love story continued, now rekindled with a fervor that nothing could extinguish. In each other, they had found the missing pieces of their souls, and they knew that from that moment on, they would be inseparable, forever intertwined in love's embrace.

CHAPTER 37

Heartbreaking Twist

In the morning's embrace, they both felt utterly drained and decided to take the day off from work. Jackson, still half-asleep, stumbled towards the bathroom and unknowingly opened a door leading to a magnificent balcony. The breathtaking view from the balcony displayed a lush garden and a cascading waterfall surrounded by picturesque landscapes. Two chaises and a small table sat on the balcony, while a unique flowery plant, reminiscent of their time in Barbados, graced the scene.

The music gently played from the Coastal Windmill ceiling fan, with twelve blades, that they had once discussed for their dream home. Jackson regretted the time he had lost with Jazzie and vowed never to let her go again. Stepping back into the bedroom, Jackson locates the correct door leading to the bathroom. When he returns to bed, Jazzie turns over and snuggles against his chest, murmuring, "I'm hungry." Jackson smiles affectionately and gently kisses her on the forehead, assuring her, "I'll cook us something, just lie back down and rest until I finish."

Jackson slides into his pants and t-shirt before quietly making his way down the hallway while admiring the pictures of the kids and their various achievements displayed throughout the house. His attention is drawn to a wall dedicated to baby pictures, featuring pictures of Genesis, Brandon, Jazzie, and a lot of Brave. It warms his heart to see the memories captured on those walls. Upon reaching the kitchen, Jackson turns on the television and the Keurig machine.

Lost in thought, he gathers the ingredients he needs, recalling how Jazzie prefers her grits. Jackson starts a pot of creamy grits, one of her favorite dishes. Being a fan of a hearty breakfast, Jackson fries up some bacon and sausage to accompany the meal. While the grits simmer and the meats sizzle, he prepares eggs, scrambling them softly to perfection. Once everything is ready, Jackson arranges a lovely tray with a flower picked from Jazzie's own garden. He includes a cup of coffee, a glass of apple juice, and a refreshing glass of water to complete the thoughtful breakfast.

With the tray in hand, Jackson returns to the bedroom, eager to surprise Jazzie with the breakfast made with love. "Knock-knock Babe."

Jazzie awakens to find Jackson at her bedside with a tray of breakfast, and she playfully exclaims, "You didn't have to do this. I could have come downstairs."

"I wanted to do it; besides, you look beat. Sorry, it took a while, but I had to navigate my way around your kitchen," Jackson replies with a smile.

"What? I should, you beat me up all night!" Jazzie teasingly throws a pillow at him, laughing.

"Don't waste this masterpiece of a meal. Is this how you treat your personal chef?" Jackson jests.

"It all depends on how it tastes," Jazzie playfully retorts. The breakfast turned out to be delicious and satisfying. However, Jazzie's left arm is still tingling, her back aches, and she has a headache. Jackson notices her rubbing her head, expressing concern for her well-being.

"You okay, Babe?"

"Yes, just a slight headache. Maybe I had a bit too much to drink last night and the emotions overwhelmed me." Jazzie reaches to caress his face, just like she used to, and kisses him gratefully. "Thank you for breakfast, baby."

"I'll check if you have something in the bathroom to ease your headache," Jackson responds, finding some Goody's Powder and instructing her to take one and rest. Jazzie drifts off to sleep again, lying peacefully on his chest. Satisfied that she is resting well, Jackson slides her off his chest onto the bed. He carries the breakfast tray back downstairs to the kitchen and starts cleaning up. As he moves outside to the gazebo to clean up, he replays last night's memories in his mind, feeling that Jazzie is still his irresistible addiction.

His emotions stir, and his desire reacts, growing at the mere thought of her. After an hour, he finishes tidying up and returns to the bedroom to check on her, where he hears Jazzie stirring, waking up. Kissing her on the forehead, he tenderly asks, "How are you feeling?"

"Much better now. I suppose I was just worn out from being so busy," Jazzie replies.

"I did notice you have your hands full with various things. Maybe you should consider slowing down a bit," Jackson suggests with concern.

"You might be right, but a shower will definitely help!" Jazzie responds with a playful grin.

"And a toothbrush would do wonders!" Jackson jokes, playfully holding his nose closed. In response, Jazzie throws another pillow at him, laughing.

They make their way to the shower and step in together, enjoying the intimate closeness. As they bathe each other, their passion reignites, and they make love in the shower. Afterward, they return to bed, continuing to share their love and affection in each other's arms. The rekindled fire between them burns brighter than ever before.

A few hours later they finally got up to dress. Jazzie needed to go by the bakery and do a bank drop and invites Jackson to go with her. Eager to see the bakery he agreed. Nestled in an upscale district with tree-lined streets and luxurious architecture, the bakery stands as a charming jewel in this high-class neighborhood. Its exterior exudes elegance, with a tasteful blend of modern design and classic elements. A pristine facade decorated with large, inviting windows showcases the delightful array of handmade baked goods inside.

Before stepping in, Jackson's eyes catch the name of the bakery, "Happy Ending," and a warm smile spreads across his face. He wraps his arm around Jazzie, pulling her close, and kisses her affectionately. "Great name for the bakery," he whispers into her ear, acknowledging the fitting and joyous sentiment behind it. Greeting them when the door opens the aroma of freshly baked pastries and loaves of bread fills the air, instantly captivating visitors with its tantalizing scents.

The interior is a tasteful combination of sophisticated aesthetics and cozy warmth. Rich, dark wood accents complemented by soft pastel hues create a welcoming ambiance, while soft lighting enhances the sense of comfort and relaxation. The bakery boasts an exquisite display of delectable treats, beautifully presented in glass cases, inviting customers to indulge in the decadent delights. The offerings include an assortment of handcrafted pastries, artisan bread, elegant cakes, and mouthwatering desserts, each carefully crafted to satisfy even the most refined tastes of the area's discerning residents.

In addition to the tempting baked goods, the bakery also offers a selection of specialty coffees and teas sourced from around the world, providing a perfect pairing for their delectable treats. To cater to its high-class clientele, the bakery extends impeccable service with attentive staff dressed in refined uniforms. They provide personalized recommendations, ensuring each visitor's desires are catered to with utmost care.

A sophisticated seating area allows patrons to savor their treats in comfort, surrounded by tasteful decor and plush furnishings. The subtle background music adds just the right touch of refinement without overwhelming conversations. Overall, this bakery in the high-class area is not just a place to satisfy one's sweet cravings but an exquisite experience, where the art of baking meets sophisticated taste, creating an unforgettable haven for those seeking culinary indulgence in an elegant setting.

Jazzie proudly introduces Jackson to her staff, and he is impressed by the warm and friendly atmosphere of her bakery when she gives him a tour. Jackson observes how she knows many customers by their first names, a testament to her genuine connection with them. Jackson fondly recalls how Jazzie has always been approachable and kind to everyone, even strangers when he would be ready to go. After leaving the bakery, they spend the day relishing each other's company and the newfound freedom to enjoy life openly.

They explore exciting places like the Georgia Aquarium and the Atlanta Zoo, immersing themselves in the wonders of the world around them. For lunch, they share a delightful picnic at the park, enjoying each other's presence as they play dominos. This sense of authenticity and openness between them brings immense joy. There are no more secrets or lies, and they no longer have to hide their love from anyone.

The feeling of being free to express their affection and be together brings them both immense happiness. Spending the night together without any restrictions or worries about leaving the hotel room feels like a dream come true. They both know deep in their hearts that this is how their relationship should be—open, honest, and filled with love and freedom.

On their way back to Jazzie's house, she sweetly invites Jackson to stay for dinner and spend the night, a request he had secretly hoped for. However, he needs clean clothes, so they make a quick stop at his house before returning to hers. Once back at Jazzie's place, she heads to the shower first, and Jackson follows suit afterward. Jazzie, feeling tired, decides to order food for their dinner.

They then snuggle up on the sofa, watching a movie and enjoying each other's company. Suddenly, Jazzie's phone rings and Jackson overhears her side of the conversation. "I'm so happy you and Brandon are having fun…You sound stuffed up, use your nose spray… Make sure you wear the helmet we just bought, not the old one... No, I'm just tired but I'm fine and my left arm isn't bothering me much now… Don't worry about me here alone… Okay, I will Brave… I won't forget to feed the fish… Tell Brandon to not forget all of your clothes... I love you too and see you in a few days."

When Jazzie hangs up, she notices Jackson's concerned gaze and asks if something is on her face, unaware of what he overheard. The love and responsibility she shows for her family leaves him even more captivated by her caring nature. "You haven't changed, always taking care of others. Let me take care of you. Have you been having problems with your arm?"

"It's not a big deal. I began working out with weights about two weeks ago, and I suppose I'm experiencing some soreness. I'm determined to keep this body snatched!" she said, playfully showing off in front of him.

"You're truly beautiful! I had this dream of constructing a house for us, based on our floor plan. You turned that dream into a reality."

"It's not fully complete yet. I still need my shoe case!" she mentioned with a hint of excitement.

Eager to begin working on it, he asked, "Show me where you want it."

"Okay, let's head to the bedroom, and I'll race you!" Jazzie playfully challenged, cheating, she leaps over the sofa to gain a head start. After spending time in her closet, they finalized the location for the shoe case. Jackson was determined to start building it tomorrow after work. Later that night, they made love, feeling the bliss of being truly free and blessed. Jazzie's life was nearly whole again; she had Jackson back in her life, a great job, a thriving bakery, renewed faith in God, a loving family, rewarding friends, and a proud mother.

With excitement bubbling inside her, Jazzie eagerly anticipated the morning to share the wonderful news with her mother and Vivian about her and Jackson rekindling their relationship. The thought of their reactions brought a smile to her face. Yet, there was still one more important task lingering on her mind, and she was determined to accomplish it tomorrow.

Jazzie calls out his name, "Jackson."
Looking down at her as she lies on his chest, he affectionately responds, "What's up Babe?"

"Did you take her to Australia?" Curiosity tugged at Jazzie's mind.

Meeting her gaze with passion in his eyes, Jackson reassures her, "No, that trip is reserved for just us, our special journey together."

"We can finally go?" A radiant smile lights up her face, and she exclaims like a giddy schoolgirl.

"Absolutely," he confirms, "tomorrow morning, let's call that travel agent and book our trip."

With an air of mystery, Jazzie hints at something she wants to discuss with him the next day, but for now, she expresses her love by placing her hand over his heart and saying, "I love you more than any actions, any distances, and any words."

Happily responding to her heartfelt gesture, Jackson kisses her gently on the forehead and places his hand over her heart, earnestly declaring, "I love you more, baby, so much more." In the embrace of Jackson's arms, she snuggles closer, resting her head on his chest, feeling the rhythmic beat of his heart and the gentle warmth of his breath brushing against her forehead. A sense of peace washes over her, and she exhales as if releasing any remaining tension or worries that may have lingered.

Jackson carefully tucked the diamond ring, the symbol of their love into his clothes when he picked them up from home. Sneaking into her room, he placed the ring gently into the nightstand by her bed, as if planting a seed of their future together. A few years ago, he had the stones from the diamond stud earrings she wore and returned to him.

With the help of a skilled jeweler, he had a unique ring designed specifically for her— an *Ever Us* Two-stone diamond ring that perfectly represented their connection and commitment to each other. Throughout all the ups and downs, Jackson never gave up hope on them. He always held onto the belief that one day, they would find their way back to each other. Now, with a plan in mind, he felt a newfound sense of purpose.

When Jackson finished work tomorrow, he would go to Home Depot to gather wood and materials for the shoe case he wanted to build for her. But before that, Jackson knew he needed to take an important step: asking for her parents' blessing to marry Jazzie. Feeling a mix of excitement and nerves, Jackson envisioned the future he hoped to create with Jazzie. He imagined the joy in her eyes when they called the travel agent tomorrow to book their trip to Australia, announcing it as their long-awaited honeymoon. Recognizing that they had delayed enough, he decided to propose at this moment.

Jackson turned slightly since Jazzie was lying on him, and retrieved the ring from the nightstand. Her hand rested on his heart, gently, he slid the ring onto her finger, and it fit perfectly as if it was always meant to be there. Taking a deep breath, Jackson found the courage to ask the question that had been on his mind for so long, "Jazzie, I want to ask you something. I've waited too long to ask you this, and I don't want to wait any longer."

She did not respond, and a peaceful smile remained on her face, reminding him of the many nights they spent sleeping together, she always smiled. Jackson, gently nudged her, saying, "Babe," hoping she was simply asleep. Yet, she didn't move or reply. A sense of concern swept over him, but he could not help but think she was playing a sweet prank on him.

However, as moments passed, worry turned to panic. He frantically shook her and called out her name, "Jazzie! Jazzie!" But she still did not respond. In an instant, everything shattered as she slumped over. Fear and anguish consumed him as he screamed out in pain, "Noooooo!" Jackson could not believe what was happening; it felt like a terrible nightmare he could not wake up from.

Epilogue

❧❧❧ ♥ ❧❧❧

For the past three days, Jazzie's family and friends have anxiously gathered in the Family Waiting room, their hearts heavy with worry and hope. Jazzie lies in the Intensive Care Unit, in critical condition and fighting for her life. The doctors can only allow one family member at a time to be with her, given the severity of her condition. In this tense atmosphere, the treating cardiologist praised Jackson's quick actions, acknowledging that his timely response had saved Jazzie's life.

Without his presence and immediate response, the outcome could have been much more doubtful, and Jazzie might not have survived. The medical staff diligently monitors Jazzie's vitals, watching over her with utmost care. Then, a miraculous moment occurs. Jazzie twitches and slowly opens her eyes, awakening from her coma. Her surroundings are unfamiliar, and she feels disoriented, attempting to make sense of where she is and what has happened.

The nurse by her side immediately comes to her aid, calming her down while seeking additional assistance. Gradually, Jazzie's agitation subsides, and the nurse gently explains the situation. Jazzie learns that she has suffered a massive heart attack and has been in the hospital for three days, a fact that comes as a shock to her fragile state. Despite her weakened condition, Jazzie manages to utter the names, Brave and Jackson.

The nurse reassures Jazzie that her family has been with her since her admission, their unwavering support and love evident throughout her ordeal. Relieved that Jazzie has awakened, the nurse promises to notify her waiting family in the Family Waiting room. The news will undoubtedly bring a wave of joy, hope, and gratitude to those who have been praying and hoping for Jazzie's recovery.

Jackson has not slept in days and paces the floor. He wonders what Jazzie had to tell him, everything was jumbled up in his head. Jackson recalls when the paramedics left to transport Jazzie to Gwinnett Medical Hospital. Jackson goes into the room that was mistaken for Jazzie's room and flips on the light switch. It is Brave's bedroom.

The walls are painted in a cheerful hue, sky blue and vibrant green. To add a touch of excitement, playful wall decals of his favorite things, motorcycles, cars, trucks, and trains. The bed is a comfortable and inviting centerpiece, a race car, with the popular Disney movie, cars-themed sheets. A Lightning McQueen ceiling fan hovers above the bed. To encourage organization and creativity, the room boasts plenty of storage solutions.

Brightly colored toy boxes, shelves, and cubbies help keep his toys, books, and belongings neatly organized. A desk with a child-sized chair is thoughtfully placed in a corner to inspire learning and creativity. It serves as his personal space for drawing, writing, and crafting, fostering a love for learning and exploration. Pictures of

Brave plaster the wall, but one picture left Jackson puzzled.

In this picture, a proud and radiant pregnant Jazzie stands at the edge of the vast ocean in Savannah, Georgia. The golden rays of the setting sun cast a warm glow over the scene, enveloping her in a halo of light that accentuates her beauty and grace. She stands with one hand on her baby bump, her smile reflecting the immense joy she feels in carrying new life within her. Surrounding her are Genesis and Brandon in the sand.

A motorcycle collection case that has colorful lights gleaming inside with several trophies, stands proudly for dirt bike competitions. Jackson examines a trophy display; a small inscription caught his eye. Viewing a suspicious date of birth and a familiar name. "It could not be, was his first reaction as reality spread through his mind.

Breaking his trance, a nurse enters the waiting room, she carries news that brings a glimmer of hope to Jazzie's anxious family and friends. "Ms. Collins is awake now. Her doctor will be out to talk to you all soon." She announces with a voice filled with relief and joy. The room fills with a mixture of emotions, anticipation, gratitude, and eagerness to see their beloved Jazzie once again.

"She has asked for someone named "Brave Jackson," the nurse adds. Jackson, standing tall and composed with little Brave by his side, steps forward, introducing himself, "I'm Jackson, and this little guy is Brave."

The nurse explains, "I'm sorry but Brave is too young to enter the Intensive Care Unit, but I'll see what I can do.

Meanwhile, another family member will be able to visit with Ms. Collins." Vivian and Haley start drawing straws when Jazzie's mother suggests that Jackson should go in first, knowing the significance of his presence in Jazzie's life.

With the nurse escorting him, Jackson enters the unit, his heart racing with a mix of anticipation and nervousness. Jackson's heart sinks as he sees Jazzie lying there, vulnerable, and weak, surrounded by a maze of tubes and machinery. The sight overwhelms him and tears well in his eyes. The realization that he almost lost her forever strikes him deeply, and the fear of losing her for good grips his soul.

The paramedic had removed the ring from Jazzie's finger before taking her to the hospital. Jackson holds it in his hand, a symbol of their love and the second chance they have been given. Overwhelmed with emotions, he kneels by her bedside. He was unable to contain the love and gratitude he felt for having her back in his life. "Marry me Jazzie, be my wife," he pleas.

With a trembling hand, she removes her oxygen mask and weakly signals for him to come closer. Her voice is barely loud, but her words carry a profound revelation. "Brave—I call him that— because he's like his father... strong...brave. His... real... name... is... Jackson... your son." Jazzie confides in him. Jackson presents a familiar ring, the one she had returned to him years ago, symbolizing their past.

But now, it has been upgraded with two diamonds, signifying the present and the future they can build together as a family. Since she has been in the hospital, he had it engraved with Elijah's assistance. Jackson reads the inscription inside the ring aloud to her: "My family, forever— I will love: Jazzie, Genesis, Brandon, Mia, Tia, Jackson Jr." This heartfelt message represents the eternal love and commitment of their beloved family. It is a declaration of their unbroken bond. Jazzie's tear-stained face lights up with emotion. She knows that this is where she belongs, with the man she loves and the family and friends they share.

Jackson slides the ring onto her finger and asks again with his hand over her scarred heart, "I love you, baby. Marry me, Mrs. Davenport?" With tears streaming down her face, her weakened arm reaches to place a hand over his heart and responds, "Yes... I... love... you... to..." There, in that hospital room, amidst the beeping of machines and the fragility of life, they make a promise to each other - to love, cherish, and support one another as husband and wife.

Jackson and Jazzie have a special, unique love, an unbroken bond. They both loved each other enough to sacrifice their own happiness. Life is precious and every moment in it.

If it's your time to leave this world, have you done all the things you wanted to do? If you have, Congratulations! And if you haven't, get going, tomorrow is not promised to us.

About the Author

Day Hardeman is a renowned romance author from Atlanta, Georgia. She is the eldest of three siblings, happily married for 30 years, a mother of three sons, and a grandmother to a lovely grandson.

After graduating from Clayton State University, she pursued her passion for writing while working as a Human Resources Professional, Notary Public, and Legal Administrative for over 25 years. During her career, she also served as a life coach and mentor for young adults.

In October 2021, Ms. Hardeman retired to launch her own company and focus on writing her first novel and other literary projects. Her writing process involves scented candles, jazz music, and a glass of red wine.

When not writing, she enjoys riding her motorcycle and ATV, DIY projects. Day enjoys spending time with family and friends, especially making memories with her grandson.

Her inspiring words of wisdom include, "Be hungry for success, but never let it consume you."

"Remember that you have choices," and "Don't just make a bucket list, live it."

Contact Information

Day Hardeman - Author, Speaker, Life Coach, Mentor

Thank you for your interest in contacting Day Hardeman! Whether you're interested in booking her for a speaking event, seeking life coaching, or looking for a mentor, you can find the necessary information below: Feel free to reach out with any questions or requests you may have. Day Hardeman looks forward to connecting with you and is excited to bring her expertise and knowledge to your event or coaching journey!

Website: www.DayHardeman.com

Social Media:
Facebook: Day Hardeman
Instagram: Daytwanna Hardeman
Tiktok: Day Hardeman

Media and Booking Inquiries:
Please direct all media and booking inquiries to the following:

Address: 255 N Main Street #462, Jonesboro, GA 30237

Email: dayhardemanllc@gmail.com

Phone: 470-713-4577

Thank You for Reading
"The Unbroken Bond"
By
Day Hardeman

Watch for new titles
By this author!

Your FB/Amazon Reviews
Are
Appreciated!

www.ingramcontent.com/pod-product-compliance
Lightning Source LLC
Chambersburg PA
CBHW060948030726
47503CB00003B/780